FOREVER

KINCAID BROTHERS BOOK TWO

NEW YORK TIMES BESTSELLING AUTHOR
KAYLEE RYAN

Cover Design: Book Cover Boutique
Photographer: Wander Aguiar
Editing: Hot Tree Editing
Proofreading: Deaton Author Services
Paperback Formatting: Integrity Formatting

Stay
FOREVER
KINCAID BROTHERS BOOK TWO

NEW YORK TIMES BESTSELLING AUTHOR
KAYLEE RYAN

Twelve Hours Ago

KENNEDY

WHY IS IT THAT WHEN one bad thing happens in your life, it seems as if a shit show parade of unpleasant events follows? Mine started with my failed marriage. Lyle and I met in college. We were friends first, and he eventually swept me off my feet. We dated for two years and married right after graduation. Somewhere over the past four years, we grew apart. A lot of that had to do with wanting a family. As in, I wanted one, and he didn't. I was told when I was sixteen that I might not ever be able to conceive, but there were other ways for me to be a mother. It's something I've always wanted. My husband agreed that when the time came, we could discuss it. We married, but over the next four years, the time never came that he was willing. There was never a good time to talk about adoption, or fostering, or any of the other options available to us. He just didn't want that life.

About six months ago, I sat him down one night and told him it was time to talk about it. He refused and said he needed some space. He packed a bag and left. He's stopped by a few times, and we'd talk on the phone a few times a week, but he wasn't budging, and neither was I.

He hasn't slept here since.

Honestly, something changed between us. If I felt as though

he loved me, truly loved me, I could handle giving up my dream of being a mother. The truth of the matter is that he was gone more than was here. He had late client dinners, golf outings, and a million other reasons he wasn't at home with me. His wife. He works in finance and hangs out with the guys from his work, who can only be described as a group of douchebags. I'm not dinging the entire finance workforce, but these guys are assholes to the highest power. I can't tell you how many times I've felt unnerved by their beady eyes roaming over my body, even with Lyle standing right next to me.

I don't want that life.

So six weeks after he moved out, we decided it was time to call it quits. I'm twenty-five, soon-to-be-divorced, and the second half of the shit show parade just called me. My grandma fell and broke her leg. She's out of commission for a while and needs me to come help her run her business. She owns Willow Manor. It's a small venue used for weddings, anniversary parties, and a host of other different things in her small town of Willow River, Georgia.

After talking to the doctors, and her neighbor Carol, I've been assured that she will be taken care of until I can get there. Luckily for me, I can work from anywhere. As a book editor for a host of indie authors, my job travels with me, which is why I'm frantically packing up my life to make the three-and-a-half-hour drive to Willow River tonight.

I take stock of my two open suitcases, and I think I have everything I'll need. I'm going through my mental list when there's a knock on the door. Glancing at the alarm clock on the nightstand, I see it's just after nine, and I'm not expecting anyone. Grabbing my cell phone just in case—you can never be too careful, especially living alone—I make my way to the door. On my way, I pull up the camera on my phone and see Lyle standing there. He has a key, but I'm glad he respects my boundaries and the reality of our current situation not to just barge in on me.

Pulling open the door, I step back, letting him enter. "What's wrong?" He tilts his head to the side to study me.

"Nothing."

"Come on, Kennedy. I know you better than that. What's going on?" He reaches out and takes my hand in his, giving it a gentle squeeze, and hot tears well behind my eyes.

"Grandma Hoffman fell. She broke her leg. I'm going to Willow River to stay with her for a while."

"Come here." He pulls me into his arms, and it's been so long, so damn long since I've felt his arms around me. I go easily, needing the comfort. I hate that I need it, but I'm taking it anyway. It's not him that I need, but the security of his arms. Regardless of the state of our marriage, he's familiar. "How is she?" he asks.

"Okay. Her neighbor and good friend, Carol, is at the hospital with her. I don't know how long she will be in the hospital, but I know I need to get there. They had to do surgery to fix the break. I'm packing now and driving there tonight." My grandma retired to Willow River five years ago. She bought Willow Manor and never looked back. Most grandmothers retire to our home state of Florida, but not my grandma. Nothing slows her down. She talks about her small town like it's the best thing since sliced bread. I've been there a few times during the holidays, but this year, I opted to stay home with my parents. Grandma and I had plans to take a cruise in January, which we'll have to reschedule. Thank goodness for vacation insurance.

"Why don't you wait and leave in the morning when the sun's out?"

I step out of his arms. "I need to get there." That's when I notice he's holding an envelope. "What's that?" I ask, but I already know.

The tears are back as he tells me, "Divorce decree."

I nod, waiting for the tears to fall, but they never come. I've accepted that our marriage is over. "When did you get it?" I manage to croak out.

"Today. My attorney called and asked if I wanted it mailed or if I wanted to pick it up."

"I told mine to mail it whenever it was official."

"I wasn't sure, so I thought I would stop by and let you know." He looks down at the envelope he's holding.

"It's official," I say. Even I can hear the sadness in my voice. I never thought I'd be divorced at the age of twenty-five, but here we are.

Before I know what's happening, Lyle pulls me into his arms and holds me close. "I love you too much to let you give up your dream of a family for me." He pulls back so he can see my face. "You understand that, right?"

I don't reply because even though he looks sincere, I know that our marriage hasn't been happy for a while now, and I'm not willing to brush that under the rug. It's more than him not wanting a family. We just drifted apart. Neither one of us fought to keep it from happening.

"I hate to see this hurt in your eyes." He leans in and presses his lips to mine, and I let him.

I don't know if it's because it's been so damn long since I've had this level of intimacy in my life or if it's the fact that I'm worried about my grandma, or hell, maybe it's the closure that we both need, but I don't stop him.

I let him kiss me.

I let him carry me to the couch, and one thing leads to another, and we're ripping at each other's clothes. Once we're both naked, lying on the couch that we chose together when we bought this house, he stares down at me. There is a silent question in his eyes.

"This doesn't change things, Kennedy."

"I know."

"Are you sure?"

I nod, and he dips his head to kiss me as he makes love to me for the last time. I know he's been faithful. That's not the kind of man Lyle is. He's truthful to a fault, but I'm glad. I wouldn't want either one of us in a marriage that we're not happy in. He doesn't want a family. That's a deal-breaker for both of us, so this is our reality and, with sudden clarity, the closure we both need.

Chapter 1

KENNEDY

T HE CLOCK ON THE DASH tells me it's just before nine in the morning when I hit the city limits of Willow River. I heave a sigh of relief. I've been worried about Grandma, and if I'm being honest, it's going to be nice to be out of town for a while.

Last night was... unexpected, but it was also closure. We got lost in the moment, but as soon as it was over, I righted myself, slid back into my clothes, and finished packing. Lyle left with a small smile and a wave, and that was that. I was mentally and emotionally exhausted and decided to go through my list one more time to make sure I had what I needed before grabbing a few hours of sleep. I managed a few hours but finally gave up at four. I showered, cleaned out the fridge, and hit the road by five.

My phone rings from its place in the cupholder, and I smile when I see the face of my best friend, Morgan, smiling back at me. "Good morning, sunshine," I greet her.

"Don't try to sweet-talk me, Kennedy Edwards. You were supposed to call me last night when you got in."

"Sorry, I didn't leave until this morning. Lyle stopped by last night."

"No. You are not taking him back. He took the light from your eyes. I don't think he did it on purpose, but no. Just no, Kennedy."

"He brought his copy of the divorce decree."

"Oh."

"I was up late packing." I pause, then drop the bomb on her. "After we had sex on the couch."

"What?" she screeches.

"I know. It just happened. I was upset about Grandma, and he hugged me, and then we were kissing, and then, well, you can figure out the rest."

"Did he stay the night?"

"No." I'm shaking my head even though she can't see me. "It's over. We both know it's over. It's been over for a long time. It was closure, I guess. At least that's what I'm calling it."

"Damn," Morgan mutters. "How are you?"

"Fine. Honestly. I mean, I had sex with my husband, well, I guess ex-husband as of yesterday. It was purely physical."

"I'm here if you need me."

"I know. I love you for it." I hear her baby girl, Iris, coo in the background, and I smile. I'm going to miss the little bugger while I'm away. "I hear my girl." I smile into the phone.

"I see how it is. I have a daughter, and I move to second place."

"Come on, Morgan, you know Iris is the best of you and Mitch, and those squishy little cheeks."

"They're so squishy," she agrees. "Fine, I forgive you," she adds. "Where are you now?"

"In Willow River. Just crossed over into the city limits."

"Are you heading straight to the hospital?"

"I am. Carol said they were keeping Grandma overnight, so I'm hoping they'll release her today."

"Give her a hug from me. Call if you need me, and remember to check in with me. I know how you let yourself get buried in your work, and without me there to drag you out of the house, I fear you'll be cooped up all the time."

"I'm helping Grandma run the manor," I remind her.

"I thought you said it was a well-oiled machine?"

"It is. Grandma doesn't know any other way but to get shit done." I chuckle. "But I'm sure there will be things I'll need to do, events I'll need to make sure go off without a hitch."

"Good." I can picture my best friend nodding and smiling. "You need to get out more."

"I love you, Morgan."

"I love you too. Be safe."

"Will do. Kiss Iris for me and tell Mitch I said hello."

"You know it," she agrees before ending the call.

Placing my phone back in the cupholder, I follow the GPS directions on the dash that lead me to Willow River General. Easily finding a parking spot, I park my SUV, grab my purse and phone, and make my way inside. A quick stop at the welcome center tells me that my grandmother is on the second floor.

Once off the elevator on the right floor, I easily follow the signage, finding her room. I knock softly, not wanting to wake her if she's sleeping. I don't hear anything, so I quietly push open the door and step into the room. My eyes scan toward the bed where my grandma is sitting up, glaring at the tray of food in front of her.

"What did those eggs do to you?" I ask.

She gasps and looks up, a genuine smile lighting up her face. "Kennedy."

"Hey, Grandma." I move to the chair next to the bed and pull it as close as I can get, sitting on the edge and dropping my purse behind me on the seat. "How are you feeling?"

"Good. Pain is controlled, and my appetite is ravenous, but this"—she points at her plate of scrambled eggs, sausage links, and toast—"is not appetizing in the least."

"What's wrong with it?"

"It's bland, and the toast is soggy." She leers at the plate and reaches for her cup of coffee.

"When do you get to go home?"

"Today. You know how it is. We have to wait for the dog and pony show of shuffling doctors in and out of the room, so they can charge me another two grand before sending me off."

I don't bother to stifle my laughter. "You mean the doctors who took you to surgery and used their very capable hands to repair your broken bones?" I challenge.

"The least they could do was feed me a decent breakfast."

"How about I run down to the cafeteria and grab you something else?"

"No. It's fine." She waves me off. "You just got here, and I've missed you."

"It's been what? Three months since you've seen me?" I don't mention the fact that I drove to see her a few days after Lyle left. I needed to get away, and spending time with Grandma in Willow River was exactly what I needed. I only stayed one night, and yes, it was a lot of driving for that short of a visit, but it was worth it.

"How are things?"

"They're done. Lyle stopped by last night with the divorce decree," I confess.

"And?"

"And what? I'm divorced." I don't know what she's looking for, but she's studying me intently. I squirm under her gaze, just as I did when I was a kid and stole cookies before dinner.

"What aren't you telling me?" She furrows her brow.

I cave under pressure. "We got our closure."

"Relations." She nods.

My face heats. "It was a mistake." I make sure to look her in the eye, so she knows that I'm telling her the truth. "Things have been over between us long before he moved out," I remind her.

"And you're okay?"

"I am." I bob my head. "In fact, I almost feel as though a weight has been lifted from my shoulders. I'm sad it's over. No one goes into a marriage expecting a divorce, but we are different people, and we want different things. Foolishly I thought when he said we could talk about it that he meant it. That's the first and only thing he's ever not been honest with me about."

Grandma nods. "He loves you."

"Yeah, but he's not in love with me, and I'm not in love with him. It just wasn't meant to be."

"Well, you're young and beautiful. You're going to find the man who will walk through fire for you."

"Can we let the ink dry before you start your matchmaking?" I tease.

"Oh, the ink is dry, baby girl. It's been dry for far too long. Last night doesn't count." She wags her eyebrows, and I can't help it; I laugh.

"We are not having *that* conversation."

"We don't need to." She takes her index finger and taps her temple. "I know these things."

"So," I say, dragging out the word, "how was your Christmas? I haven't talked to you since before you left for Aunt Aggie's." My parents and I had lunch, and exchanged gifts and they left for a cruise, while I spent the rest of the day at my best friend Morgan's with her husband and baby girl Iris.

"Oh, it was good. You know there is never a dull moment when your great-aunt Aggie and I get together."

"Trust me. I know all too well." I give her a pointed look, and she grins. We're both thinking the same thing.

"What? I was bringing you and your roommate holiday cheer." She holds her hands up in defense, but there is a twinkle in her eye.

"Grandma! You brought strippers to my dorm."

She shrugs. "They were wearing Santa hats, and everyone enjoyed themselves. I have the pictures to prove it."

"No." I give her a warning look. "You said you were going to delete those."

"What I said was that I wouldn't print them." She picks up her phone that's lying next to her. "I've got it all right here."

I open my mouth to scold her, but there's a knock on the door. "Oh, I'm sorry," Carol Kincaid says as she enters the room.

"Come on in." Grandma motions for her to take the seat on the other side of the bed. "I was just getting ready to torture my granddaughter."

Carol chuckles. "Sounds like I made it just in time." She turns her eyes to me. "Good to see you again, Kennedy."

"You too. Thank you for taking care of her for me."

Carol waves me off. "That's what neighbors are for."

"Not all neighbors. I used to live beside this old geezer who would just as soon spit on me than help me do anything when I lived in Florida."

"Grandma." I laugh. "That old geezer graduated with you, and you used to complain about his mowing his grass where it would blow over into your yard. You never gave that poor man a minute of peace." I shake my head when her smile grows.

"He didn't know how to mow the lawn."

My eyes find Carol's. "He gave her a going away party. He even had it catered," I explain, barely containing my laughter to tell the story.

"Maureen"—Carol places her hand over her mouth to cover her laughter—"tell me he didn't."

"Oh, he did. He even sent me home with all the leftovers."

"Kennedy, I think you and I need to spend more time together. I need more of these stories."

Grandma points at her friend. "I like you." Her grin is infectious.

"Looks like I missed the invite to the party," a gorgeous guy in dark blue scrubs says as he enters the room.

"Hey, sweetheart," Carol says. She stands and hugs him, and he kisses her cheek. "I thought you were off today?"

"I'm supposed to be, but they were short. I told them I would come in until they could find someone else. I started at five. I just clocked out and wanted to come to check on Maureen."

"That bride of yours let you out of the house?" Grandma asks.

His eyes light up, and damn, that makes him even sexier. "I left her sleeping in bed. She's been wearing herself out with the wedding planning and the pregnancy."

He turns to look at me. "Hi." He walks around the bed and offers me his hand. "I'm Brooks Kincaid, Carol's son."

I take his offered hand. "Kennedy Edwards, Maureen's granddaughter. Nice to meet you."

"You as well."

"So a wedding and a baby?" I ask.

He nods, and a smile lights up his face. "Yes, to both. We're actually getting married at the Willow Manor on New Year's Eve," he explains.

"You'll be working with Kennedy," Grandma tells him. "I've got a bum leg."

Brooks chuckles. "Can I get you anything?"

"Discharge papers?" Grandma asks hopefully.

"I'll see what I can do." He tosses her a wink, and I swear I can see her melt a little into her hospital bed. Not that I blame her. "Kennedy, it was good to meet you." He waves before turning back to his mom. "Palmer is stressing about the flowers. Can you stop by the house on your way home and talk her off the ledge? I've tried, but I don't know a damn thing about planning a wedding. I don't care about any of that stuff. I just want her to be my wife."

Now I'm the one who's melting into my chair. Lyle loved me, but I know now that he never loved me like Brooks loves his fiancée. I never saw the look in his eyes like the one that Brooks currently has just by talking about his fiancée either.

"Sure. I need to swing by Declan's and pick up Blakely first. She's hanging out there for a while so I could stop and visit Maureen. And I already had plans to go visit with Palmer. She called me earlier and asked if I could meet her and her mother at your place to go over some final details." Carol's face is the epitome of happiness.

Brooks laughs. "She loves being there."

"She does, but Declan always complains he never gets anything done during the day when she's there."

"I'll stop and grab some donuts for us."

"She's going to love that, and Declan is going to yell at you for spoiling her."

Brooks shrugs. "That's my job as her uncle. I'm sure he's been taking notes and is going to repay me when our baby is born." There's a sparkle in his eye when he talks about his unborn child.

Sadness washes over me. I don't know if I'll ever have that. If I'll ever find a man who's willing to adopt with me or foster, or even hire a surrogate, and potentially endure not only the emotional but financial burden to try IVF. My heart aches for the dream I've held on to. Even when the doctors told me it would never be possible, I knew there were other ways to be a mother. I can only hope that there's a man out there who will love all the broken pieces of me and want to build a life and a family with me, no matter how unconventional that might be.

"Kennedy?"

I shake out of my thoughts and turn toward Grandma. "Sorry, I spaced out."

"I was just telling you that Carol has nine boys."

"Well, they're men. Even my babies are now adults at nineteen."

"You have nine sons?" I ask, a little wide-eyed. I've met Carol a few times, and I knew she had kids, but *nine* boys?

Carol chuckles. "Nine rowdy boys who I wouldn't trade for anything."

"Brooks is engaged. What about the rest of them?" Grandma asks.

"Grandma," I warn. She, of course, ignores me and keeps her attention on Carol.

"Orrin and Brooks are the only two who are spoken for."

Grandma claps, and I laugh at her antics. "Stop. Whatever you're thinking, just stop." I hold my hands up in defense.

"What? You got rid of the man who never loved you the way you deserve to be loved. Carol's boys are all good men."

"I'm sure they are." My eyes flash to Carol, and I give her an apologetic smile. "But I'm here to help you take care of the manor, and I'll still be working my job as well."

"What is it that you do again?" Carol asks.

"I'm a book editor. Mostly for independent authors who self-publish. I love it. It gives me my reading fix, and I get to be a part of an incredible community who get to write their stories the way they want them told without a huge publishing house dictating the story."

"Oh, give me a romance novel and a few hours, and I'm a happy woman," Carol replies.

"Right?"

"My husband started a tradition when our boys were small. He takes them on a weekend of camping and fishing. No girls allowed. It gave me a weekend of no men in the house. Most of the time, I spend it reading all the books."

"Sounds like a great weekend to me."

"Most definitely. I do go get my nails done, and sometimes a massage, and meet up with friends for dinner, but the majority of my time, it's enjoying the quiet and spending time with my favorite authors."

"Carol, I think you and I are going to be great friends."

"Of course you will be. She's going to be your mother-in-law," Grandma adds.

Carol smiles widely while I roll my eyes. "Too much pain medication."

"I know these things," Grandma assures me.

If that were true, she would have warned me not to marry Lyle. As if she can read my mind, she speaks up. "I knew he wasn't for you, but you loved him. It wasn't my place to tell you otherwise. I won't tell you which of the Kincaid boys you're going to marry either, but mark my words, it's going to happen."

Before I can rebut her claim, the door pushes open, and an older man in a white coat enters. "I hear you're anxious to get out of here," he says to Grandma.

She looks at Carol. "Tell Brooks as soon as I'm able, he's getting an apple pie."

Carol stands, her smile lighting up her face. "I'll do that. You take care. Kennedy, I'm right next door if you need help with anything. In fact, I'll bring dinner over this evening."

"You don't have to do that."

"I want to. That's what friends and neighbors are for. I'll see you both later."

We wave, and then the doctor goes through his exam. To my surprise, Grandma is on her best behavior. He hands me a prescription with instructions for Grandma to follow up in two weeks. "Maureen, you behave." The doctor points at her. She tries and fails to look like she's innocent. My grandma lives her best life, and I love her for it. She has life goals for sure.

Chapter 2

DECLAN

MOST DAYS, I LOVE BEING a business owner. Most days, my customers aren't assholes. Today was not that day. Everything that could go wrong has gone wrong. It started out with me bringing Blakely with me. It's usually fine, but I'm always watching her like a hawk, so I don't normally get much done while she's here. Spending time with my daughter was not the shit part of my day, just so we're clear.

The shit started when one of my employees called in sick. Tanner is a young kid who is enrolled at the vocational school in Harris. As a part of his work program, he was placed here his senior year to work a few hours each afternoon. He's a good kid, and when he asked about staying on after graduation, I agreed. He's a good worker when he's here, but he's been calling in a lot lately. I need to sit down and have a talk with him, but that's something for another day.

The second part of this shit-filled day started when the parts that were supposed to be delivered were not. When I called to track them, they were in Ohio. They were on the truck for delivery this morning. At least that's what the tracking info says. However, when I called the company, my parts were now in Ohio. So that leads to the third shit part of the day. Calling the customer and letting them know that there will be a delay. I don't know where the damn parts are headed or when they'll get here.

The customer, an older gentleman who lives in Harris, was not impressed. Apparently, I'm an incompetent fool, and my business is going to tank if I keep treating my customers this way. It took every ounce of control I had in me to keep from telling him to go fuck himself. However, at the end of the day, this is my business. This is how I keep a roof over my daughter's head, food in her belly, and spoil her rotten with everything her little heart desires. Well, maybe not everything. My brothers are to blame for that, but I'm not completely innocent either.

And finally, although this isn't a bad thing except for the fact that it takes all my time, my phone rang off the hook. All. Damn. Day. I get that this is a business, and it's good that I've made a name for myself, but damn. I couldn't get anything done, so here it is, well after six when the shop closes at five, and I'm still catching up on things I didn't get done today. I'm going to have to break down and hire some help. Maybe a high schooler who can work a few hours every day after school to just answer the damn phone and take a message. Sure, I could let it go to voice mail, but I hate that shit. I'd rather talk to a person and leave a message than talk to a mailbox. So I'm adding hire a receptionist to my ever-growing to-do list.

Luckily for me, my mom watches my daughter, and when I called her to ask if it was okay to stay a little later, she, of course, agreed. Not that I thought that she wouldn't, but I didn't want to just assume and take advantage of the fact that she's my mom and Blakely's grandma. Apparently, according to my daughter, she helped my mom make dinner to take to their neighbor Maureen who fell and broke her leg. Mom said they were going to stay and visit and that she thought Blakely would cheer Maureen up. There isn't a single doubt in my mind about that. My daughter is something special and could charm a snake even with all of her four-year-old sass. I smile just thinking about the best thing that ever happened to me.

It's pushing seven, and I've had my fill. The work will be here tomorrow. Right now, I need a hug and a smile from my little girl. I want to take her home, make some dinner, and snuggle on the couch before bed. She's exactly what I need after this cluster fuck of a day. Grabbing my keys, I turn off the lights, rush to my Tahoe, and head toward my parents' place.

As I'm turning on their road, I get a text from my mom. I hit Accept on the screen so the computer voice reads it to me.

Mom: We're at Maureen's. Take your time.

I don't bother to reply. Instead, I turn my Tahoe into Maureen's driveway. I leave the engine running so that I can run in and grab Blakely and head home. My feet carry me to the front door, and I rap my knuckles three times before the door swings open, taking my breath with it.

"Hi," the beauty standing in front of me greets. "Can I help you?" She smiles politely.

Her long brown hair cascades over her shoulders, and those big brown eyes study me. "Hi. I'm Declan Kincaid. My mom and my daughter are here."

"Daddy!" Blakely comes running to the door and launches herself into my arms.

I catch her with ease. "Hey, squirt. Sorry I'm late." I kiss her forehead and hug her tightly. My body instantly relaxes. There is nothing like a hug from my little girl.

"Are you late?" she asks, furrowing her brow. "We've been having so much fun. Kennedy braided my hair." She turns her head so that I can see.

"Did you say thank you?" I prompt her.

"I did."

"Come in out of the cold." Kennedy steps back so we can enter the house.

I'm immediately hit with something that smells incredible. My stomach growls, reminding me I've not eaten since breakfast, and Blakely laughs.

"Daddy has a lion in his belly." She giggles.

"Hey, sweetheart," Mom greets. "How was your day?"

"Long." I sigh. "Blake, get your stuff together. We need to get home before the lion in my belly gets angrier." I kiss her cheek and place her back on her feet. She grabs my hand and pulls me farther into the room.

"Grandma cooked us gasagna."

"Lasagna," my mom corrects with a soft laugh.

"There's plenty," Maureen speaks up. "Why don't you stay and eat? That will save you from cooking later."

"No. You save that for yourself. How are you feeling?" I ask her, remembering my manners.

"I'm doing just fine. My granddaughter"—she points at the beauty who answered the door—"is here to stay with me while I recover. She's single," Maureen adds.

I turn my gaze to the beauty who stole my breath. I hold out my hand to her. "I'm Declan." I ignore the information that she's single that has my cock stirring. I'm a single dad. I don't have time to indulge, no matter how my body reacts to her.

She smiles, her face flushed, and she places her hand in mine. Her skin is soft against my rough, calloused hands. "Kennedy. Nice to meet you. I'm sorry my grandmother doesn't have a filter." She playfully rolls her eyes.

I chuckle. "I have eight brothers. I understand no filter." She chuckles, and the sound goes straight to my cock. I shift my stance to hide what she does to me. "Blake." I pull my gaze from Kennedy. "Get your things."

"But, Daddy, the lion is roaring really loud, and Miss Maureen told you you could eat, and Grandma made it, and you always eat lots when Grandma cooks."

"I insist," Maureen tells me. "Kennedy. Will you take Declan to the kitchen to make him a plate?"

"That's not necessary," I tell her.

"You might as well give in." Kennedy smiles. "She's not going to let you walk out of here without feeding you."

"I know someone like that," I say, glancing at my mom.

"Hey." She holds her hands up in surrender. "I raised nine rowdy boys who were always hungry and who had friends who were always hungry. I learned to cook for an army."

"Follow me," Kennedy says, nodding toward the kitchen.

I point at my daughter. "Behave." I really should be going, I left my engine running, but I'm a man, one who can't seem to say no to the beautiful woman leading me to the kitchen.

"Who me?" She points at her chest, and I have to bite my lip to keep from laughing. I swear my brothers, the twins, Maverick and Merrick, who are the babies of the family at nineteen, teach my daughter attitude. They are the reason she's four going on fourteen.

When I walk past Mom, I stop to kiss her cheek. "Thanks for keeping her later today."

"Oh, hush." She waves me off. "You know I love having her with me. We're best friends, right, Blake?" Mom asks.

"Oh, the bestest, but Miss Maureen and Kennedy too." Blakely is quick to make sure she's not leaving anyone out. She might be an only child and spoiled, but she's not a brat. Most of the time.

"Of course," Mom assures her with a smile.

I follow Kennedy to the kitchen, trying not to gaze at her ass as she walks in front of me. I'm failing miserably. "Have a seat," she says, pointing at the small table.

"What can I do to help?"

"I've got it. Besides, you are helping. Your mom really does cook enough for an army. Grandma and I would be eating this for a week," she says, referring to the large pan of lasagna sitting on top of the stove.

"I don't know if she knows any other way. Our family is growing, so it's only going to get worse."

"Growing?"

"Yeah, my brother Brooks and his fiancée are expecting a baby, our little cousin, Ramsey, who is like a sister to us, is getting married, and my older brother Orrin, he's practically engaged himself, so yeah, we're growing."

"I always wanted a big family," she says, scooping up a huge helping of lasagna, covering it with a paper towel, and popping it in the microwave.

"I joke that it's not all that great, but it's a lie. I loved every minute of growing up with my brothers. There was never a dull moment in our house, that's for sure."

"I'm an only child," she confesses. "I begged for a sibling growing up." She smiles. "I met your brother Brooks earlier today. He stopped in to check on Grandma."

"She seems to be in good spirits."

"She is, but nothing seems to get her down. My grandma is definitely one of a kind."

"I don't know her well. I was already moved out and living on my own when she moved into this place. I have seen her at barbecues, and I know my younger brothers, the twins, mow for her, and she pays them in cookies."

She laughs. "If you only knew the stories that I hear about the handsome young men who mow her lawn."

"Please don't tell them that. They're cocky enough as it is. They'll make sure we all hear about it over and over and over again." I shake my head in amusement.

The microwave beeps, and she removes the plate, placing it in front of me on the table. "Sweet tea, milk, or water? I could make some coffee," she adds.

"Sweet tea is fine. Thank you for this."

"You're welcome."

I don't take my eyes off her as she pours me a glass of sweet tea and brings it to the table. "Thank you." I accept the glass and take a sip. "Sit with me?" I don't know why I'm asking. My Tahoe is running, and I need to get Blakely home and give her a bath, but the words are out there, and I find that I don't want to take them back. I'm here, so I might as well soak up her company while I eat.

"Sure." She pulls out a chair opposite me and lowers onto the seat.

I take a bite, and the familiar taste of my mom's homemade sauce hits my tongue. I shovel the forkful into my mouth and barely even chew. I force myself to slow down and mind my manners, as my mom always used to remind us. Hell, who am I kidding? As an adult, she still reminds us.

"So what kind of work caused a lion in your belly?" she asks, a grin tilting her full, sexy lips.

"I'm a mechanic. I own my own shop in town. What about you?"

"I'm a freelance editor. I work mostly with independent authors in the romance genre."

"So you're able to work anywhere?" I ask, shoveling another bite. I love my mom's lasagna.

"Yes. Which makes it nice at times like this. It also helps that I was ready to get out of town for a few days."

"Sounds like there's a story there." I point my fork at her.

"Do nightmares count as stories?" she asks.

Slowly, I nod, reaching for my tea. I take a long drink before placing it back on the table. "Are you okay?" My eyes scan over her, and she doesn't look to be injured, but I know all too well that some pains aren't visible from the outside.

"I'm fine." She waves me off. "I don't want to bore you."

I look down at my plate. "I'm still eating, so how about the condensed version?"

"Let's see. The condensed version is I received my divorce decree yesterday. My now ex-husband, Lyle, moved out about six months ago. Our marriage had been on the rocks for a while."

"I'm sorry to hear that."

"It's fine." She offers me a soft smile. "I mean, it's sad, but it was time. We loved each other, but we weren't in love with each other. I don't know when that changed, but somehow over the last four years, it did, and well, we had some differences of opinion that helped to widen that gap."

"I'm sorry to hear that."

"It sucks. No one gets married thinking they're going to be divorced." She stares off into the distance for a few heartbeats before her eyes focus once again on me. "What about you? Married?"

I never talk about Blakely's mom, Cassie. It's painful, and I have so many regrets. "Never married," I confess.

"And Blakely's mom?" she asks, but then she's quickly waving her hand in the air. "I'm sorry, don't answer that. I didn't mean to pry."

"I think you've earned that." I smile, letting her know I'm not the least bit upset with her over her question. "I don't really talk about it much, even though my brothers and my parents tell me that I should."

"You don't have to tell me."

"It's only fair, right?" I ask, my eyes boring into hers.

Before she can answer, my daughter rushes into the room. "Daddy, did you feed the lion?" she asks, smiling up at me.

I chuckle. "I'm working on it."

"Can we stay longer, please?"

"Blake, it's getting late. As soon as I finish eating, we need to head home. You need a bath and then it's story time."

"Three stories."

At four, my daughter is a master negotiator when it comes to her bedtime stories.

"One story."

"Two." She bats those long eyelashes, and we both know I'm going to cave.

"Fine. Two stories."

"Yay! Love you, Daddy."

"I love you too, baby girl." I give her a one-armed hug before she steps out of my hold and skips around the table to hug Kennedy. "Thanks for my braids," she says, pointing at her head and her two French braids as if Kennedy needs the reminder.

"You're very welcome, Miss Blakely."

And just like that, she's racing back into the living room. "Don't run in the house," I call after her.

"I'm skipping," she calls back, making Kennedy and me both laugh.

"She's a handful at four. What am I going to do when she's a teenager?" I shake my head, a smile pulling at my lips. I take another bite of my lasagna and swallow before answering her earlier question. "Her mother passed away. Blakely was just a few weeks old."

"I'm so sorry."

I nod, feeling the familiar ball of emotion well in my throat when I think about Cassie. "Thanks. It's a long-twisted story."

"Well, if you ever feel like telling it or just talking, you know where to find me. I'll be here for at least eight weeks. Depending on how Grandma's leg heals but the doctors said a minimum of eight weeks. So I'll be around."

I take another bite before my gaze finds hers. There is something there. Something that speaks to me on a level I've never experienced before. I can't name it, but I feel in my gut that Kennedy is someone I can trust. "I might take you up on that," I finally say.

Even though I say the words, I don't think I will. I never talk about Cassie, something I know I should do. Blakely knows her mom lives with the angels and watches over her, but outside of that, we don't talk about it. She's too young to understand, and the pain of what I lost, what my little girl lost, and what Cassie lost is still too raw.

I quickly finish off my lasagna and stand. Taking my plate to the sink, I wash it along with my fork and glass, placing them on the rack to dry.

"Wow, a man who cleans up after himself." I hear from behind me.

I dry my hands on a hand towel and turn to face her. "I'm a single father. There isn't anything that I don't do." My voice is low and huskier than normal.

"Not something I'm used to."

"Real men get their hands dirty." I watch her throat as she swallows. "Thank you for dinner." With that, I head back to the living room to wrangle my daughter. If I stay with Kennedy a minute longer, I might show her exactly what I can do with my hands. This woman is too damn tempting.

By the time we're home and make it through bath time, I'm barely through the first story before Blakely is sound asleep. Kissing her softly, I make sure her night-light is on and the door is cracked. I'd love nothing more than to fall into bed, but there is a load of laundry in the washer that I need to swap over, and I need to pack my lunch for work tomorrow. I didn't last night and thought I'd run out to grab something today. That didn't happen, and hell if I don't hate those hungry lions in my belly. I chuckle softly, thinking about Blakely. That little girl has turned my entire world upside down, and I wouldn't have it any other way.

Chapter 3

KENNEDY

"Y OU DO NOT HAVE TO go with me." I close my eyes and pull in a deep breath. I love my grandmother, but damn, she can be exhausting and hard-headed. "I can figure out how to unlock the venue, Grandma."

"That's my blood, sweat, and tears, and I need to be there," she counters.

"Then why am I here?"

"To drive me." She gives me a cheeky grin, and I roll my eyes.

"Listen, today is just the rehearsal, right? It's going to be a small group of people. I can handle this."

"Small?" she asks incredulously. "This is the Kincaid family. There is nothing small about them. Not in numbers or the size of those men. You wouldn't make a lonely old woman miss out on all that eye candy, would you?" She bats her eyelashes for good measure, and I can't help but laugh at how ridiculous she's being. "And tonight is the bachelor and bachelorette parties."

"At the same place?" I ask her.

"Yes. They didn't want anything big, so I suggested the manor. We have a divider for the big ballroom. Men on one side and women on the other. The bride and groom loved the idea."

"So what needs to be done?"

"Nothing." She shrugs. "I had my staff raise the divider after all the holiday parties, and the caterers will bring a variety of finger foods."

"And you need to be there because?" I ask again.

"Because it's my baby. I've put all my time and love into that manor since buying it over five years ago. I want to be there."

"Grandma," I say gently, "I understand your need to be there, but you have to take care of yourself. I'm here. Let me handle this. I'll send you updates throughout the night. I'm taking my computer so I can work because it sounds as though there's not going to be much for me to do."

"What if something comes up that you don't know the answer to?"

I hold up my cell phone. "There are these really cool devices they call cell phones. Turns out you can reach anyone anytime and anywhere by just dialing their number." I reach over and grab hers from the coffee table. "Oh, look, you have one too." I smirk, and she rolls her eyes.

"Fine. But I want you to call me when you get there and call me with updates. None of that texting nonsense. I want verbal communication on how everything is going."

"Deal. I'll even send you a few pictures."

"That would be great."

"Now, is there a particular dress code I need to follow for tonight?"

"No."

"Good. I'm going to pack up my computer, and then I'll head over there."

"And what am I supposed to do while you're gone?"

"You're going to sit your rear end on the couch, with your leg propped up, and watch that series you keep telling me you want to watch but don't have the time." I point at her knee walker. "Use that. Don't be a hero and injure yourself further."

"I look like an old fool with that thing."

"No, you look like a woman who broke her leg and needs to stay off it. Use it." I point at the walker as I give her a stern look, and she reluctantly gives me a nod of acceptance.

"I want updates."

"I promise." With that, I rush to my room to grab my laptop and everything I'll need to settle into work while the dual parties are in progress.

Thirty minutes later, I'm unlocking the doors to Willow Manor and stepping inside. Feeling around on the wall, I find the light switch and flip it up. The entire foyer illuminates with a soft white glow. My grandmother's office is directly to the right. I step inside, turn on the light, and place my bag that contains my laptop and my purse on her desk. My cell phone rings, and I can't help but laugh. I know it's her calling me already. I don't even bother to glance at the screen. "Hello."

"You said you would call with updates."

"Crazy woman, I just walked through the door."

"Well, is anyone there?" she asks.

"Grandma, I literally just walked through the door. I had time to turn on the foyer lights, the lights in your office, and to place my bags on your desk before my phone rang. No one was in the parking lot. Just my car. Besides, you told me the parties start at seven. It's only a few minutes after five. I'm really early." I came early just to double-check everything and to get a break from her arguing about coming with me. I love the woman to pieces, but she's a handful.

"Fine," she grumbles. "The caterers are going to be there at six thirty, and the tables and dividers should be set up."

"Got it." I got it the first and the tenth times she reminded me, but hey, maybe the eleventh time is a charm.

"And they are bringing their own alcohol. They have assured me that they will have designated drivers."

"That's good. I'll keep an eye out," I tell her.

"What are you going to do until they arrive?"

This time I don't hide my laughter. "I'm going to work." In peace and quiet.

"Oh, well, all right, dear. Don't work too hard." With that, she ends the call. It's as if she turned into a different person in the last few seconds of our call. In all of my twenty-five years, I've never been able to understand her crazy ways, but I love her all the same.

Placing my phone on the desk, I start unpacking my laptop. I'm in the middle of edits about a broody fireman and am anxious to get back to it. It's a perk of the job to get to enjoy the first look at each story and help the authors make them the best that they can be. It's really the best job in the world.

Once my laptop is booted up and I have the file open in front of me, I allow myself to get lost in my work. That's why I jump out of my skin, well, really just the chair, but I jolt forty minutes later when the door to the manor opens. It's not time for either party to arrive, and it's too early for the caterers. I stand to greet whoever it might be, but before I can make it to the foyer, a tall, dark-haired figure appears in my doorway.

"Hey," a deep husky voice greets me. "I'm Archer Kincaid. My mom said that Miss Maureen could use some help setting up," he explains.

I smile and offer the gorgeous man my hand. I don't know what Carol fed these boys growing up, but damn. "Hi, I'm Kennedy Edwards. Maureen is my grandmother and a snake." I laugh.

"I'm not following," he says, but he's still smiling and holding on to my hand.

"She set you up. Well, I guess technically, she set us both up. Everything is done here. The caterers will be here at six thirty. The rooms are already good to go. Nothing needs to be done."

"Why are you here this early?" he asks, finally releasing my hand.

"She was driving me crazy," I confess, which causes him to laugh. "I work from home, and when she got hurt, I came to stay with her until she's back on her feet. Literally. Anyway, I was just getting caught up on some work."

"Well, I'm already here. Is there anything I can do?"

"Not that I'm aware of. I guess we can walk around and see if you think we need to add anything else or move anything around."

"Let's do it." He peels off his jacket and holy arm porn. He's wearing a tight-fitting long-sleeve T-shirt that tells me exactly what he's hiding beneath the thin layer of cotton. Muscles, lots and lots of muscles. I roam my gaze over every inch of him before meeting his eyes, and he smirks.

"Come on," I say, face red with embarrassment. I'm twenty-five, not fifteen. I need to stop acting like I've never seen a gorgeous man before. Besides, out of the three brothers I've met so far, if I had my choice, I'd choose Declan. He's sexy, and I want to run my fingers through his hair. Archer has longer hair too, but it's cut differently than Declan's. Archer's is shorter on the sides, whereas Declan's is more like Brooks's. Long all over, just not as messy as his brother's.

"So how is this set up?" Archer asks from his spot next to me as I lead him toward the ballroom.

"The one large ballroom where the wedding will take place has an automatic wall divider. It's already been expanded, or so my grandma tells me. Honestly, I didn't look when I got here, and I should have. I guess she was right to send someone to check on me."

"It wasn't like that at all." He comes to my grandma's defense. "I was at my parents' place, dropping Blakely off for Declan because he had to run into the shop for a customer of his who needed a tire changed. Anyway, Maureen called and said there was a lot of work to do, and she felt guilty for leaving it all up to you. I heard her talking to Mom since the call was on speaker, so I spoke up that I would stop by and help. I was just planning on lounging around with Blake until it was time to be here anyway."

"Well, thank you." I step into the ballroom and feel my way around the wall until I find the lights. Just as Grandma had said, the divider is in the room. With it stretched all the way across, going floor to ceiling, it turns the double entryway into a single for each area.

"Nice," Archer says, standing behind me.

"Let's check out this side first, but I'm certain they're the same." I step through the left door and survey the room. There are tables set up with table covers and centerpieces, and then along the far wall is where I assume the finger foods from the caterer will be. There is even a large refrigerator with clear glass doors on wheels that was brought out to place next to the food tables.

"How is that she's laid up but still managed to pull this off? She doesn't need me here," I tell Archer.

"She might not need you here, but something tells me that she wants you here."

"Are you the philosopher of the family?" I tease.

"Nope. That title goes to our dad. He's definitely a man of wisdom, or at least he likes for us to think that he is. He's always coming off with these snippets of life advice that he dishes out to my brothers and me."

"You can't just drop something like that on me and not give me a sample," I tell him.

He starts to reply but his phone rings. He reaches into his pocket and glances at the screen. "Let me take this one sec." He holds up his index finger with one hand while the other accepts the call and places the phone to his ear. "Hey, Dec."

"Yeah, I dropped her off with Mom and Dad. I ended up coming over to the manor early. Maureen said that her granddaughter needed help." He pauses. "Yeah, Kennedy. I'm with her now." He listens again. "Nah, we got it covered." He chuckles and then says, "See you soon." He ends the call, sliding his phone back into his pocket. His eyes are sparkling with mischief.

"What?" I ask when he just grins at me.

"Which of my brothers have you met?" he questions.

I don't know why he's asking, but I answer him anyway. "I met Brooks at the hospital. He stopped in to check on my grandma, and then I met Declan and Blakely later that day."

He nods. "Damn, we're dropping like flies," he mutters.

"What are you talking about?" I chuckle.

"Nothing. Don't mind me." He waves me off. "Is there anything we need to move or adjust on this side?"

"I don't think so. Looks good to me. Let's go check on the other side and make sure it's good as well."

Together we make our way to the other side, and it's set up the same way. "Looks good." Archer nods.

"Agreed. Now, what should we do?" I ask.

"This is your show, Kennedy," he reminds me.

"Actually, I'm just my grandma's puppet. She had this handled. Other than being here to unlock the door, I don't think I'm needed."

"How long are you staying in town?" he asks, pulling out a chair and motioning for me to sit.

Knowing we have a lot of time to kill, I do, and he takes the one right next to me. "She's going to be in a cast for at least eight weeks. I plan to stay until she's completely back on her feet again."

"It's nice that your job gives you that flexibility."

"I am lucky. What is it that you do?"

"I'm a mason. Which is basically a fancy way of saying I lay brick and block all day long. It's good money and hard work, but I enjoy it. You?"

"I'm a fiction editor."

"Nice. Beauty and brains."

I don't get the chance to tell him that he doesn't need to blow smoke up my ass when we hear the front door open. It's still a little early for the caterers, but they might just like to be early. Archer and I turn toward the doors when he comes into view.

Declan.

He peers into the room next to ours and then peeks his head into ours. "Brother," Archer calls out. "That might be a new record," he jokes.

Declan glares at his brother before his eyes land on me. In long strides, his legs carry him to us. He stops beside my chair, smiling down at me. "Kennedy."

Damn, his voice is sexy. "Declan."

"I told you we had it covered," Archer tells his brother. I have to turn my head to look at him because I can hear the humor in his voice.

"Didn't want to just sit at home and wait," Declan tells him.

"Uh-huh," Archer replies. "I was just getting ready to tell Kennedy here a few of our dad's words of wisdom."

"Don't bore her to death, Arch." I can hear the affection in his voice for his father and his words of wisdom.

"What?" Archer feigns offense, placing his hand over his chest. "Don't let Dad hear you say that."

"Come on." I look between the two brothers. "You can't hold out on me like that."

"There are too many to repeat." Declan chuckles.

"Except there is one that he has repeated over and over again. It's almost as if it's our family mantra."

I rub my hands together in anticipation. "Let's hear it."

"Work hard. Love harder," Declan tells me before his brother has the chance.

I nod as the words begin to take root in my mind. "You know, those are good words to live by. However, sometimes no matter how hard you love, it's just not enough. Eventually, that love disappears."

"You talking from experience?" Archer asks.

"You don't have to answer that," Declan tells me.

He seems agitated, so I place my hand on his arm to soothe his ruffled feathers. "It's fine." I drop my hand and turn to address Archer. "I was married, recently divorced." I don't bother telling them we got the official notice this week.

"Damn, Kennedy. I'm sorry. He's an idiot, though," Archer replies.

I smile. "Thank you. Our marriage was over a long time ago. To be honest, I'm no longer sure we should have even gotten married in the first place. We were good friends, and then we were more, and now we're divorced."

"Well, that clears things up. You're drinking with us tonight." I turn at the sound of the new voice and see a woman about my age walking toward us. She stops when she reaches me and offers me her hand. "I'm Ramsey, best friend to the bride and cousin to these lugs." She points at Declan and Archer.

"Nice to meet you. I'm Kennedy. My grandma Maureen is neighbors with their mom."

"Aunt Carol told me you might be here tonight. And from that end of that story, I just heard you could use a night out."

"I'm actually just here to unlock the building and lock up when you leave."

"Nope. You're officially invited to join us."

"Hey," Archer speaks up. "What if I was going to invite her to hang out with us?"

"Archer." Declan's voice is a low warning that does nothing but elicit a laugh from his brother.

"I'm not taking no for an answer. Besides, Palmer is preggers, so she can't drink. We need someone to help us consume all the alcohol that's currently in the back seat of my car."

"Babe, I think you went overboard," another delicious-looking man calls from the open doorway.

What in the hell are they feeding these men in Willow River?

I watch as he walks toward Ramsey. His arms are loaded down with reusable shopping bags, but when he bends his head, she meets him in a soft kiss.

"Thank you."

The way he looks at her... no man has ever looked at me that way. Lyle and I dated for a year, were friends before that, and married for four, and not once at any time during our history together did he ever look at me like I was his entire world.

I want that.

I want to be someone's world.

I want to be someone's number one.

I don't know what my future holds, but I do know that I'll never settle for less ever again.

Chapter 4

DECLAN

I CAN'T TAKE MY EYES off her. She's watching Deacon and Ramsey as if they are the greatest things she's ever seen. I feel an elbow in my side, and I silently grunt before turning my glare on my little brother. He smirks, and I fight the urge to roll my eyes.

"Where do you want this?" Deacon asks Ramsey.

"Kennedy?" Ramsey defers the question.

"The refrigerator is ready for drinks, and the caterer is going to set the food up there on the tables along the wall." She points to where she's talking about.

"This is all alcohol," Deacon tells her.

"Right." Kennedy stands, and Deacon follows her to the refrigerator.

"She's cute, huh?" Ramsey asks.

I look down at my little cousin, who, in the last few years, has been more of a sister to my brothers and me. "Yep." I know what she's trying to do, and it's not going to work. I keep my expression neutral.

"I think I'll ask her out," Archer says.

He takes a step forward, but my arm juts out, and I slap him in the chest, halting further movement. "No." So much for staying neutral. If anyone asks her out, it's going to be me.

"What do you mean no? She's single. I'm single, and we're both hot as fuck. I don't see the issue," Archer says. He takes another step, but my arm holds him back.

"Not happening."

"What's not happening?" Deacon asks.

My head whips around to see that he's not alone. Kennedy stands next to him. Her eyes volley between my arm holding my little brother back and my face. "Archer's just being an ass," I mutter.

"I'm going to run to the kitchen and grab a couple of freezer buckets and fill them with ice," Kennedy tells us. She holds up her phone. "Grandma said they're in the storage closet."

"I'll—" Archer starts, but I'm quick to talk over him.

"I'll help." I drop my arm, glare at my brother, and motion for Kennedy to lead the way. I hear Archer cackling with laughter behind me, but I ignore him. I have no doubt Ramsey is also sporting a wide grin. I love my family. We're all close, and at times like this, it's a curse. They know me, sometimes better than I think I know myself. I can't hide my interest in Kennedy from them no matter how hard I try.

"You okay?" Kennedy asks once we're out of earshot.

"Yep." My reply is clipped, and I take a deep breath. I don't want to be an ass to her.

"You sure?"

I exhale slowly. "Yeah, just been a long day." That has to be the reason I'm being so territorial over her. She's in town to help her grandmother, and she's recently divorced. She doesn't need Archer sniffing around.

"I think this is it." She stops in front of a door. I watch as she enters the code into the keyless lock. It beeps and the small light flashes green. Pushing open the door, she hesitantly takes a step. She feels around on the wall, taking a step farther, and yelps.

On instinct, my hands reach for her, pulling her back against my chest. "I've got you," I tell her. She's breathing hard. The sound of her heavy breaths fills the darkened room.

"I'm sorry. I was looking for the light and... I tripped and... I'm so embarrassed."

"Don't be." My arm is snaked around the front of her body, holding her to me. I can't help but notice that she's a perfect fit. Her body molds to mine as if she were made to be right where she is.

She releases a long shuddering breath, and her shoulders relax. "Thank you for saving me."

She moves as if she wants out of my arms, but no way am I letting her go, not knowing what's surrounding us. "Stay," I whisper, my lips next to her ear. I feel her body shudder, and my cock thickens. Knowing that I need to get myself together, I place my hands on her hips to steady her. I keep one there while the other searches the wall for the light switch.

"Found it," I tell her, flipping the switch. The room illuminates with a soft glow, and she turns to smile up at me. My heart stalls in my chest. She's the most beautiful woman I've ever laid eyes on. Her big brown eyes have this sparkle to them when she smiles, and I instantly want to know what they look like when she gets off. Do they sparkle, or are they filled with heat and desire? And her lips, are they as soft as they appear? I squeeze her hip, sliding an arm around her waist as I bite down on my cheek to keep myself from bending my head and finding out.

"Thank you." Her smile is bright, and her cheeks are flushed. I can't help but wonder if that's the embarrassment or if I have that effect on her. I hope like hell it's the latter. Does she flush like that everywhere? My eyes dart to her chest. She's completely covered, but my imagination is vivid when it comes to her, and I can see her in my mind. Her chest flushed, nipples tight.

"What are we looking for?" I ask, trying to control the urge to kiss her while pushing the images of her naked to the back of my mind. This is not the time. It's been years since a woman has had this effect on me. Hell, I don't know that I've ever had this reaction to anyone before her. Instant and blazing hot. I push it down and try to pretend I don't want her.

"Grandma said there would be freezer buckets to store ice for drinks." She steps over the box that almost tripped her and scans the room. "There." She points at the top shelf, where two black buckets with lids sit.

Stretching her arms above her head, she attempts to reach them. Moving quickly, I step behind her, once again aligning her back to my front. "Let me," I say, my voice husky. Kennedy falls back to her feet, which places her body even closer to mine. She's trapped in front of me while I work on bringing the first bucket down from the shelf.

Snaking my arm around her waist, I hold her close. I can feel a slight tremble in her body, and it causes my cock to twitch behind my zipper. It's been a long damn time since I've let myself be this close to a woman.

I place the first bucket on the floor next to my feet and reach for the other one, all while she's trapped in front of me. "Now what?" I ask once I have the second bucket off the shelf.

Instead of releasing her, I wrap both arms around her waist. She leans into my touch, and fuck that does something to me. My heart begins to thunder erratically in my chest, as I watch her chest rise and fall with each heavy breath.

I don't know what I'm doing, she's not mine. However, right now, here in this small storage closet she feels as if she is.

"Declan." She breathes my name, and my control is ready to snap. I want nothing more than to strip her bare and fuck her against the door. Instead, I focus on controlling that urge, and whisper, "Careful. We can't have you falling." I play it off as if I was protecting her, and I was, and I still am. From me. If given the chance I would devour her.

I force myself to let go of her, and she slowly turns and peers up at me under long lashes. She licks her lips, and I can see a slight tremor in her hands as she fists them at her sides.

"T–Thank you."

Unable to help myself, I reach up and tuck a stray lock of hair behind her ear. "It was my pleasure." She has no idea how long it's been since I've held a woman in my arms. I know that I should take a step back giving us both some much-needed space, in the cramped room, but I can't do it. I watch as she inhales, and slowly exhales before her eyes bounce around the room, and land on the ice buckets at our feet.

"I should wash them out before we use them." She scrunches up her nose. "This room is dusty."

I don't want to step away from her, but I know I have to. Stepping back, I grab the other bucket. "Watch yourself," I tell her, nodding for her to lead the way. She has to move around me, and I should move, but where's the fun in that? She slides by, her chest rubbing against my back, her small hands resting on my shoulders as she maneuvers around me. The heat of her palm sizzles through the cotton of my long-sleeve T-shirt.

She turns when she reaches the door. "Let me take one of those."

"I've got it. If you can get the light."

She steps out of the room, giving me space to do the same before turning off the light and closing the door. "Thank you for your help," she says as she leads me to the kitchen.

"You're welcome."

Once in the kitchen, I place the buckets in the large steel industrial sink and turn on the water before pushing my sleeves up to my elbows.

"Declan, I can do that," she says, coming to stand next to me.

"I've got it."

"Fine." She pushes up her sleeves as well. "You wash, and I'll dry." She's trying to act as if she's irritated, but the small smile that lifts her lips tells me otherwise. It could also be that playful gleam in her eye.

I lean into her so that we're shoulder to shoulder. "Are you always this stubborn?"

"Oh, hush." She leans into me as if she could actually knock me over while her sweet laughter surrounds us.

My cell rings in my back pocket. "Can you get that? It might be about Blakely. Back pocket, right side," I tell her.

Since her hands are still dry, she steps back and lifts up my shirt, retrieving my phone. "It says FaceTime call from Mom."

"Accept it. I'm sure it's Blake." Doing as I ask, she hits Accept, and the video call connects.

"Daddy!" Blakely cheers. "What's you doing?"

"I'm washing a couple of ice buckets." Kennedy turns the phone so that she can see that my hands are in sudsy water.

"How'd you show me?" Her little brow furrows, and I swear she's smarter than the average four-year-old. Sure, she's going on five, but my little girl doesn't miss anything.

"Do you remember Kennedy?" I ask, knowing she does.

"Is she there?" She gets her face close to the screen, where we can only see her blurry nose. "I can't see her."

I chuckle. "Baby girl, you need to hold the phone back." She does as I ask. I nod, and Kennedy turns the phone toward her.

"Hi, Blakely." She waves and smiles at the screen.

"Are you at the party too?" Blakely asks.

"I am. I'm filling in for my grandma."

"Her leg is still hurt?"

"Yes. She's going to need to take it easy for several weeks."

"Are you having a sleepover?" she asks.

"No. I'll be home later."

"Daddy, are you having a sleepover?" she asks.

Kennedy turns the phone back toward me. "No. I'll be home tonight missing you," I tell her.

"Kennedy, you should have a sleepover with my daddy, so he's not lonely. I'm staying with Mamaw and Papaw, and he's going to miss me."

I grin, and Kennedy chuckles softly and steps closer to me so that we're both in the frame. "I think maybe one of your uncles might stay with him."

She has no idea if that's true, but it's a good save to distract Blakely from her original question. "All my uncles are there?" she asks.

"They are." Kennedy smiles.

Blakely gets a serious look on her face. "Kenny, my uncles are trouble." She nods her little head.

I can't help it. I burst out in laughter. "You're trouble," I tell my daughter.

"I'm not trouble, Daddy. I'm your princess." She shakes her head as if this is information I should have already known.

"Well, princess, I need to finish washing these up so we can have ice for the parties. I love you. Be good for Mamaw and Papaw."

"I will. Love you, Daddy. Bye, Kenny." Blakely waves her little hand at the screen, and the call ends.

"She's adorable, Declan."

"Thank you. She's a handful, but I wouldn't trade her for anything." I glance over, and she holds up my phone. "You can just shove it back in my pocket." I angle toward her, and she once again lifts my shirt and slides my phone into my back pocket as I ask. When she lowers my shirt I feel her fingers ghost across my back, and my fucking cock is ready to go yet again. What is it about this woman?

"Done." Her voice is low and husky, and damn it all to hell it takes more effort than I knew that I possessed not to lift her onto the counter and kiss the breath from her lungs.

I clear my throat. "Okay, I think this one is ready." I put one of the freezer buckets in the second of the three areas of the industrial sink, and she gets to work rinsing and drying it while I wash the other. The sexual tension cackles between us, but we both choose to ignore it.

"I think we should go ahead and fill these up." Kennedy pulls her phone out of her pocket and checks the time. "The caterers will be here soon." She grabs one of the two buckets and carries it to the ice machine. She scoops ice until it's full, and I slide the other one next to her, placing the lid on the first.

Once she's finished with the second, I take them both and nod for her to lead the way to the banquet room.

"Let me have one of those." She reaches for one, but my grip is firm. Her soft hands land over mine, and it takes every ounce of self-control that I can muster not to toss the buckets and beg her to put those soft hands all over me.

"Kennedy?" She stops, and her eyes find mine. "Show me where you want me."

"What?" she asks, swallowing hard. Damn, I wish my words meant how they sounded. It's been way too long since I've enjoyed the company of a woman. Way. Too. Damn. Long. I raise the buckets full of ice. "Where do you want me to put them?"

"Oh, yeah, um, that." She places her hand on her chest over her heart. I wonder if it's racing like mine is just from being near her. "I can take one to the women's side, and you can take one to the men's side."

"I've got them, Kens." The nickname rolls off my tongue with ease.

A slow smile tugs at the corner of her mouth. "No one has ever called me that before."

"Good. That can be just for me." Why does the thought of having something with her no man before me ever has excite me so much?

She gives me a slow nod. "I think I like that."

"Show me where you want me."

"This way." She turns and walks back toward the banquet room, and I force myself not to stare at her ass the entire way. Not that I could see it with her long sweater, but I can imagine it, and that's enough for me. I can't get involved. She doesn't even live here, and I have a daughter to think about.

"I thought you got lost," Archer says when we step back into the room.

The caterers are setting up, and all my brothers and all of the ladies are already here. I ignore my little brother and follow Kennedy like a puppy to where she wants the bucket placed.

"Thank you."

I nod. "I'll take this one to the other side."

She places her hand on my arm. "I appreciate your help, Declan." I nod and walk away, trying to commit to memory the heat of her touch.

I keep my head down as I make my way to the opposite side of the banquet hall and place the ice bucket in the same place on this side. The food smells incredible, and I realize it's been a while since I've eaten. I had a longtime customer call for a quick fix, and I rushed to get Blakely ready for Archer to pick her up and take her to our parents' place, back to the shop, and then back home again to shower and get ready for tonight.

"I don't know why we need this damn divider," Brooks grumbles from behind me.

I turn to look at him, and he's scowling at the partition that makes the large room into two. "It's your bachelor party."

"I don't need a damn bachelor party. What I need is to be with Palmer."

"She's in the same damn building as you," I remind him.

"It's not the same." He crosses his arms over his chest and scowls.

"How's she been feeling?"

His scowl is instantly gone and replaced with a smile. "Good. Little nauseous but other than that, she's been a fucking rock star. She's tired a lot, but I've been keeping up with the house, and laundry, and groceries and all that shit on my days off so she doesn't have to worry about it." He looks to the right at the room divider.

I want to give him shit, but to be honest, I can't. I can't ride him for loving her and their unborn baby. I know what it feels like to become a dad for the first time, and it's a rush like nothing else I've ever felt. Sure, my situation was different, but the fact that Blakely is my daughter and she made me a dad is still the same.

"It's the best feeling," I tell him, and he turns back to face me. "Holding your baby for the first time. It's like nothing else I've ever felt."

"I can't fucking wait." He moves to the refrigerator and grabs a bottle of water.

"Not drinking?"

"Nope. Palmer can't, so neither am I. Besides, what if something happens and she needs me? I don't want to be drunk off my ass."

"You're a nurse, Brooks. You know that she's going to be just fine."

"Shit happens. I see it every damn day, and I will not be that guy. I want to be the man who's there to support her, not have to phone a fucking friend because I've had too much to drink and can't drive her to the hospital."

"She still has months yet before you need to worry about that."

He shrugs and takes a sip of his water. "Don't care. I didn't want to do this anyway."

"The twins pushed for it," I tell him.

"I don't understand why. They're babies." He chuckles. We both know that if Maverick or Merrick heard him referring to them as babies, they'd give him hell. "They shouldn't worry about bachelor parties."

"Yeah, well, Dad told them they could drink. He's going to stop by later and drive them home."

"Ah." He nods. "That explains it."

"I'm surprised you didn't know that."

"The details didn't matter to me."

I know that what he says is true. He just wants to marry the love of his life. He was insistent that they didn't start another year with her not being a Kincaid, and honestly, I can't say I blame him. If I'm ever lucky enough to find that kind of love, I can see myself being the same way. I loved Blakely's mom. She was my best friend, but I wasn't in love with her. I've watched two of my brothers fall ass over heels for the women who are perfect for them. That gives me hope that mine is still out there waiting. Maybe when Blakely is a little older and understands the concept of dating, I'll try my hand at finding the love of my life. Until then, my nights at home cuddling with my little girl are more than enough for me.

I've been fine for the last five years. A few more won't kill me.

Chapter 5

KENNEDY

I'M SITTING IN GRANDMA'S OFFICE, staring at the manuscript on the screen. I haven't been able to focus. Not because it's too loud, but because Declan Kincaid sets my body on fire. There were a couple of times earlier, I was sure he was going to kiss me, but he never did. Not that I need to be worrying about that. I'm newly divorced. I don't need to jump back into a relationship. Besides, nothing could come of it even if we did do something. I don't live here. I have a home and a life back in Florida. That's where my parents are, and that's what I know. I don't need to be forming any kind of attachments while I'm in Willow River.

"What are you doing hiding?"

I look up from where I've been staring at my computer screen to find Ramsey leaning against the door frame. "Not hiding. Staring off into space," I admit.

"Why are you in here all by yourself? We're celebrating."

"I don't want to impose."

She waves me off. "Please, you're more than welcome. Put that away and come hang out with us. I'll formally introduce you to everyone."

"You don't need to do that."

"I know I don't need to. I want to. Besides, this is my best friend's bachelorette party. My best friend that is about to become my sister. Are you really going to tell me no?" she asks, batting her lashes.

I chuckle. "Does that work with your fiancé?"

"Every damn time." She grins. "Come on."

"Why not." I shrug. After saving my file, I close the document, power down my laptop, and put it back into my bag, so I'm ready to go at the end of the night. "I'm not getting anything done anyway."

"What is it that you do?" she asks. "No, wait. The girls will want to know. Might as well wait until we're all together."

I stand from the desk, and she links her arm through mine and leads me back to the ladies' side of the banquet hall. "There they are." One of the women raises her drink in the air and the rest cheer.

"Ladies, this is Kennedy. Her grandma Maureen owns this fine establishment," Ramsey slurs.

"Hi." I wave awkwardly.

"That's Palmer, the bride to be." She points out the woman wearing a veil. "This is Piper, who is Palmer's older sister." She moves on down the line. "Jade"—she points at a redhead—"she's dating Orrin Kincaid. Alyssa, she's Sterling's best friend."

"It's nice to meet all of you."

"What are you drinking?" Jade asks me.

"Oh, I'm not. I still have to close up when y'all leave, and drive home."

"That's not going to work," Ramsey says, tugging me toward the refrigerator for a drink.

"Really, I'm good." I laugh. "How about you have one for me?" I suggest.

"Party pooper."

"I'll stay sober with the bride," I tell her.

Palmer cheers. "My girl." She stands and rushes to give me a high five. "Let it go on the record that if I wasn't preggers right now, I'd be indulging," she tells me.

"Noted." I nod, biting my cheek to keep from laughing. Palmer pats the open seat next to her, and I take it.

"Okay, now, tell us about you," Ramsey says, taking her seat at the round table.

"Not much to tell. Recently divorced after four years of marriage to a man I probably never should have married in the first place. I live in Florida, and I'm a book editor. Mostly romance novels for independent authors."

"Maureen is your grandmother?" Piper asks.

"She is. When she fell and broke her leg, I volunteered to come and help take care of the manor while she recovers. I can work anywhere, so it made sense. Not to mention my parents are empty nesters and do lots of traveling these days."

"Well," Palmer sits up in her chair, "I'm Palmer. Brooks Kincaid is my baby daddy, and future husband." She stops to smile, and it lights up her face. "I'm a photographer. I have a studio in town."

"My turn. I'm Piper, sister to the bride, and sister to that one's fiancé." She points at Ramsey.

"Oh, me too." Palmer laughs. "I forgot to mention that."

"Should I be taking notes?" I ask them, humor in my tone.

"Maybe." Palmer nods.

"Anyway, I'm Piper. Heath is my man. He's not a Kincaid or a Setty, but he's mine." She flashes me a grin that matches her sister's. "I'm a schoolteacher, and I teach here in Willow River."

Jade raises her hand and introduces herself. "I'm Jade, and I'm dating Orrin Kincaid, the oldest of the nine brothers. I'm a radiology tech, and I work at the hospital in Harris, the next town over."

"My turn." Ramsey smiles. "I'm Ramsey, soon-to-be Setty. The Kincaid boys are my cousins but might as well be my brothers. Their brother"—she points at Palmer and Piper—"Deacon and I are getting married in June. It's our two-year anniversary of the day we met. I work at the local law office with my future hubby."

I turn my head to the only one left. "I'm Alyssa. I work as a receptionist at a doctor's office in town. I'm Sterling's best friend. And yes, we're just friends." She laughs.

"Thanks for having me," I tell them. "It's nice to meet all of you."

Before they can answer, there is commotion by the door. We all turn to look, and my mouth drops open at what I see. There is a large group of men who all look like they could appear in a woman's fantasy. I lift my hand to make sure there's no drool on my chin.

"It's a lot when you see them all together for the first time." Palmer leans in close to whisper.

"Wow." I'm at a loss for words. What do they feed the men in Willow River?

They all start walking our way, and Brooks is leading the pack. He makes a beeline for Palmer. She jumps from her chair and rushes toward him. She leaps into his arms, and he catches her easily, pressing his mouth to hers.

"Enjoy that while you can," Ramsey calls out to them. "It won't be long before my niece or nephew will keep that from happening."

Palmer tosses her head back in laughter. "You just worry about making me an aunt again, so we can have two Palmers in the family."

The group laughs. Well, everyone except for me. "I think I missed something."

"Palmer gets the credit for Deacon and me meeting. She organized a blind date photo shoot. She didn't tell us who we were going to be meeting. Anyway, she claims that our firstborn should be named after her." Ramsey grins. "And since she's marrying my cousin, I figure they can name their baby Ramsey. I always wanted to be a Kincaid." Something flashes in her eyes, and I can tell that there's a story there, but I'm not going to push.

Archer takes the seat next to me that Palmer vacated. "We tried to hold him off as long as we could, ladies." He rolls his eyes.

"Why would you do that?" Piper asks him. "Look at them."

We all turn to look at the happy couple. Brooks has one arm around Palmer's waist, holding her close, and the other rests over her baby bump. We can't see it, but it's the intimacy of the moment that has me feeling all warm and gooey inside.

Music gets turned up, and everyone starts to dance. "You coming?" Archer asks me.

"I think I'll sit this one out," I tell him.

He nods and joins the others in making some silly dance moves that the guys who are not attached to their ladies are doing. My eyes search for Declan, but I don't see him. "You don't dance?" I hear his voice from beside me.

I turn to my right, to the chair that Archer vacated, and see

Declan watching me intently. "No, I mean yes, I do, but I'm just sitting this one out."

"Didn't you hear that we're celebrating?" His grin tilts the corner of his lips.

I turn to look back at the happy couple. "They look good together," I say.

Declan makes a humming noise in the back of his throat as an agreement. When I hear the chair slide against the floor, I turn to see him standing, holding his hand out for me. "This is a party, Kens."

Not gonna lie. I love the way he calls me Kens. It's personal and intimate and something that Lyle would never have done. It was Kennedy to him, and that's just how it was. When I don't take his hand, he reaches down and grabs mine, tugging me from my chair.

He leads me to the edge of the group of his friends and family who are dancing and begins to move. I laugh at him when he mimics his brothers and breaks out into some weird dance, flapping his arms in the air and gyrating his hips.

"Get it, Dec!" one of the guys calls out. There are too many of them for me to know who it was. I recognize Archer, Brooks, Deacon, and of course, Declan. After that, I'm lost.

Declan winks at me and pulls me closer, and I copy him move for move. What the hell... if you can't beat them, join them. I'm laughing so hard that I can hardly stand when the song changes and slows down. The couples wrap around each other, and I smile at Declan and turn to grab water before going back to my seat when I feel a hand on my wrist.

"Dance with me," he says softly.

"Yo, Kennedy, I got next," Archer calls out.

Declan steps in close. "He's going to be disappointed," he says once his arms are wrapped around my waist and my chest is pressed against his.

I peer up at him. "Oh, yeah? How so?"

"You've already found your dance partner for the night."

"Is that so?" I act as though his words don't affect me when the reality is that I feel like I have a swarm of butterflies fluttering around in my belly.

"I asked you first."

"Is that how this works? Kind of like finders keepers?" I joke.

He gives me a slow nod. "We can go with that if you want. As long as I'm the one you're dancing with, I don't care what you call it."

"Archer asked me first."

He pulls me closer, the warmth of his hand on the small of my back reaching my skin through my sweater.

"And what did you tell him?"

"I was sitting that one out."

He nods. "You waited for the right brother." He winks, and my heart stalls in my chest.

"I'm leaving," I blurt. "I'm only here until my grandma gets back on her feet. Literally." I laugh nervously.

I watch him as he looks away and swallows hard. "Just a dance, Kens," he finally replies. "Dances," he corrects. "All of your dances tonight are mine."

He says the words, but his facial expression and the way his body stiffens tells me it's more than just a dance, but I don't think he knows what this electric current is between us any more than I do.

"All my dances," I repeat.

He keeps one hand splayed on the small of my back while the other traces up and down my spine. We're barely swaying to the beat, and I'm sure that all eyes are on us. I should pull away, but I can't make myself step away from him. There undoubtedly will be questions from the ladies I met tonight. That still doesn't have me stepping away from him. There's this force that surrounds us, it's unlike anything I've ever felt, and I'm not willing to break it.

Not until he does.

We dance for two more slow songs in that very position. Barely swaying, his hand holding me close, while the other drives me insane from the warmth of his touch. When the song turns fast, I lift my head from his chest and peer up at him. He tucks my hair behind my ear and leans in. I lick my lips. This is it. He's going to kiss me. Except for a pair of hands land on my hips, and I'm lifted out of his arms.

"Archer," Declan growls.

"Mom and Dad taught you to share, Declan," Archer teases.

Archer carries me as if I weigh nothing, and I'm deposited into a circle of gorgeous men. "Kennedy, time to meet the rest of us," he says, slinging his arm over my shoulder.

I feel Declan. I know that sounds crazy, but when I look to my right, he's standing there, hands casually pushed into the pockets of his dark-washed jeans, his eyes bouncing around the group of his friends and family.

"Let's start at the top," Archer says. "You already know the ladies, so we'll go to the gents." He points at Ramsey and Deacon. "That's Deacon, Ramsey's fiancé. Brother to Palmer and Piper."

"We met," I tell Archer, but lift my hand to wave lamely anyway.

"Right, okay, then we have Heath. He's dating Piper, not that you couldn't figure that out on your own." He points at where Piper is currently hanging onto Heath's back as if he's ready to give her a piggyback ride. She's wrapped around him, and they're both all smiles. I wave at Heath, and he nods.

"Now, my bros. Big bro, Orrin, Jade's fella." He points at Orrin and Jade. "Then we have Declan." He looks over me to his brother and winks at him. Declan rolls his eyes. "Then we have the man of the hour, Brooks." He turns us a little and continues to point out his brothers. "Sterling, Rushton, and then there's me." He leans in close. "The best-looking out of the bunch." His brothers scoff, and he chuckles. "Ryder, and the twins, the babies of the family, Maverick and Merrick."

"It's nice to meet you all." I wave again. I'm sure that I look like a complete loser, but it's done, and I can't take it back.

I get a round of "heys" and "nice to meet yous," and I'm ready for the awkward to take over, but it never comes. Instead, the music is turned back up, and I find myself being pulled into a circle with just the women as we dance and jump around being silly. It's surprising how at ease I feel. They're all close, and I expected to feel like an outsider, which is why I hid in Grandma's office to begin with, but that's not the case at all.

We dance the night away. Several of the guys and the ladies, all except for Palmer and me, keep drinking, and two hours later, they're no longer able to walk in a straight line, and they're slurring their words.

"I think it's time to call it a night," Brooks speaks up.

"I can help take people home," I offer.

"Thank you, but we're all set. Our dad is coming to help, and Palmer and I are both taking a group."

"I'm happy to help," I tell Brooks and Palmer.

"That's sweet of you. I think we have it all worked out," Palmer tells me. "We planned it out before we got here. We like to have a good time, but we also like to be responsible and make sure everyone gets home safe."

"Well, it was nice to meet all of you." I allow my eyes to bounce around the group.

I step away and begin to pick up the tables and toss the trash. "We can help with that," Brooks speaks up.

"No way." I shake my head. "This is included in the fee. We actually have a cleaning crew that will come in tomorrow and take care of all of this and set up for the rehearsal. I was just getting a head start."

"Are you sure?" Palmer asks.

"I'm positive. Go. You have a lot of stops to make before you get home."

"Will you be at the rehearsal?" Palmer asks.

"Yes. I'll be taking over for Grandma for the next several weeks."

"I'll see you then." She steps out of Brooks's hold and opens her arms, coming toward me for a hug. I don't hesitate to hug her back.

"Congratulations, you two."

"Thank you." Brooks steps up behind her, wrapping her in his arms, his large hand resting over her belly.

Tears instantly well in my eyes. I wave, quickly turn my back to them, and head toward the food table, starting to clean up. I don't need to explain my woes to them. This is a happy time in their lives. I don't need to bring them down with my inability to carry a baby of my own. Instead, I busy myself covering the food. I'm going to have to find some containers from the kitchen for the leftovers from both rooms. I make a mental note to give the containers to Palmer tomorrow after the rehearsal. No point in all this food going to waste.

"Hey." I feel a hand press to the center of my back. I don't have to look to know that it's Declan. I can smell his cologne. "Kennedy?"

Composing myself, I turn to look at him. "Thank you for the dances," I tell him.

"You okay?" he asks, ignoring me.

"I'm good. Just been a long few days."

He studies me, lingering enough for me to shift my stance, feeling bare beneath his gaze. "What are you doing with this stuff?" he asks.

"I'm going to wrap it all up and put it in the fridge and then give it to Palmer tomorrow."

"Hey, Brooks!" he calls out.

"What's up?" Brooks calls back.

"Let's get this food all cleaned up, so we can take it home, and Kennedy doesn't have to deal with it."

"You don't have to do that," I tell him. "That's a part of the service they paid for."

Declan smiles. "There's plenty of us to make quick work of this. I don't want you walking out to your car by yourself."

"Willow River is safe." Not that I know that firsthand, but I have heard Grandma rave about the small town and how great everyone that lives here is since she moved here five years ago.

"That might be, but I'm still not leaving you here all alone to walk out that door by yourself."

I want to open my mouth to tell him that I'm a big girl and that I don't need a man to take care of me, but something stops me. It's the look in his eyes. They're full of nothing but sincerity, so I bite back my reply.

Declan's right. In a matter of minutes, all the food from both sides is packaged up, and Palmer expertly sends home containers with everyone. After grabbing my things from my office, Declan waits while I lock the door and then walks me to my car, which one of the twins started for me. They did it for everyone but for them to include me makes me feel as if I'm a part of their tight-knit group. Aside from my best friend, my circle is small. I'm an only child of two only children, so life is pretty quiet for me. I'm envious of the Kincaid family. I wonder what it would be like to be a part of a loud, loving family like that. Don't get me wrong, my family loves me, but it's small and, well, compared to this group, quiet.

Chapter 6

DECLAN

M Y BROTHER IS GETTING MARRIED today. He's the first of
the nine of us to take that step, and I couldn't be happier
for him. Palmer is his perfect match. The wedding is small, just
close friends and family. They kept things intimate, which fits
the two of them flawlessly. If Brooks were to include all of us, the
wedding party would have been huge. They settled on one
person for each of them. Palmer chose her sister, Piper, and
Brooks chose Orrin. I imagine by the time we're all married off,
we'll each have had our chance to stand at the altar as best man
for one of our brothers.

With Blakely on my lap, I watch as my brother promises to
love Palmer for all the days of forever. When he leans in and seals
the promise with a kiss, my daughter turns and smiles. "Now can
we have cake?" she asks.

I chuckle. "Not yet, squirt. We have to have dinner before we
eat cake."

"Aww, but, Daddy, it's a party."

"Come on you." I stand with her in my arms and carry her out of the wedding room, which is what I heard my mom refer to it as earlier, and to the banquet hall. The divider that was here just a couple of days ago is gone, making one large room. There are tables with centerpieces and tables and tables full of food.

"Oh, the cake looks yummy," Blakely says as I carry her past the cake to the line for the food to make her a plate.

"After you eat," I remind her.

She sighs as if she's fifteen, not less than half a year from turning five. "Fine."

Ignoring her sass, I fill her plate with everything she points at that she wants, grab her a juice box that I know is Palmer's doing, and a stack of napkins before leading her to a table. She climbs up on the chair and digs into the plate I place in front of her.

"Daddy, are you hungry?" she asks.

"I'll eat," I assure her. "I'm just waiting for someone to come and sit with you."

"I'm a big girl," she tells me.

I run my hand over her soft head of hair. "I know you are. But Daddy doesn't like to leave you alone." What I don't tell her is that as a single father, there are so many fears that I hold inside me it's not funny. One is, what if I walked away and she choked? Everyone is talking and laughing and celebrating, and what if we didn't see her? What if we didn't make it to her in time? This is just one of the many things that keep me up at night.

I worry that I'm not enough for her. That she's missing her mother in her life, a woman who, even though I didn't love, would have been an amazing mother to our little girl. She doesn't have that. Instead, she gets me, and I hope like hell that I'm doing right by her.

"Kenny!" Blakely calls out with her mouth full.

"Manners," I remind her. "Don't speak with your mouth full."

She visibly swallows the rest of her food, opens her mouth, sticks out her tongue, then calls out and waves to Kennedy a second time. This kid spends way too much time with my brothers and me.

"Blakely, you look beautiful." Kennedy stops by our table and gives my little girl all her attention.

"Jade did my hair." She turns in her chair to show Kennedy, and I hold my hands up to keep her from falling.

"She did a great job." She smiles at Blakely. Then her eyes find mine. "Declan."

My heart kicks up its rhythm. That's only ever happened when I'm near her. I hate it and love it all at the same time. "Kennedy. Everything looks great."

"Thanks." She smiles kindly. "I can't take credit for it. Palmer and my grandma had it all worked out. I'm just here to make sure it's executed." She notices I don't have a plate. "Are you not eating? You know they have enough food for three times this amount of people."

"I'm going to. Just waiting on someone to come sit with Miss Sassy Pants." I gently poke Blakely in the side, making her giggle. That sound is one I will carry with me for the rest of my life.

"I can sit with her. Is that okay with you?" she asks Blakely.

"Yeah, we're friends," Blakely replies.

"It's okay," I tell Kennedy.

She ignores me and pulls a chair out next to Blakely. I watch as she grabs a napkin and gently wipes at my daughter's mouth as if she's done it a million times before. "Go, we've got this, Daddy." She smiles at me, and it takes my breath away.

"I'll be right back." I point at Blakely. "Be good for Kennedy."

"Daddy," she shakes her head, "I'm an angel. Papaw told me so."

I huff out a laugh as I stand and drop a kiss on top of her head. "Thank you," I say, my eyes meeting Kennedy's. "Can I bring you back something?"

"Oh no, I'm fine."

I nod, but I plan to make her a plate anyway. I'll just grab her a little of everything. As she said, there's more than enough food for her to feed a damn army. I make my way toward the line.

"Where's Blake?" Rushton asks.

"She's already eating. Kennedy is sitting with her."

"She's cute."

"Of course she is. She's my daughter." I know he's not talking about Blakely. He's right about Kennedy, yet he's wrong. She's cute as hell, and sexy as fuck. I've never thought the two could be equally correct about one woman, but Kennedy has proven it's possible.

Rushton chuckles. "I wasn't talking about Blake, even though we all admit the kid is cute as hell. I was talking about Kennedy."

"No." I don't need another one of my brothers hitting on her. Not when she makes my heart race like no one ever has. His smirk tells me he knows exactly what I'm saying no to.

"What? I'm single. She's single. We're the same age too. Mom said she's twenty-five."

I'm six years her senior and a father. She needs someone other than me, but it won't be one of my brothers. "No."

Rushton grins. I ignore him. Instead, I grab two plates and begin to fill them.

"Hungry?" he asks.

"One is for Kennedy."

"Aww." Sterling steps up behind me. "He's even making her a plate. You've got it bad, brother."

"Fuck off," I quip with no heat behind the words. I ignore the rest of their ribbing as I continue to make our plates. I grab a handful of napkins, sure that Blakely will more than likely need them even with the stack I already grabbed.

When I reach the table, Blakely is talking a mile a minute, and Kennedy is giving my little girl her full attention. I place a plate in front of her and one on the other side of Blakely, where I was sitting. I walk away to grab us both a bottle of water.

"What's this?" she asks when I make it back to the table, handing her a bottle of water.

"Your dinner."

"I'm not a guest, Declan."

"You are now," Brooks says. I turn to look at him over my shoulder. "Enjoy, we have plenty, and we're celebrating my wife." His smile is bigger than his face as he bends down and blows a strawberry on Blakely's face, making her laugh. He stands and points at Kennedy. "Guest," he says, not leaving any room for argument.

"See." I'm smug, knowing I won. No one likes to lose.

"Kenny, it's really yummy," Blakely tells her once again with her mouth full.

"It's Kennedy," I remind my daughter at the same time Kennedy says, "Mouth closed, cutie," tapping my daughter on the nose.

Blakely swallows. "And there's cake. You hafta eat it all gone to get cake. Right, Daddy?" She turns to look at me.

"That's right."

"Well, we better get started." Kennedy holds her hand up for a high five, and Blakely doesn't leave her hanging. They both start to eat, all while carrying on a conversation. They're talking as if they are the best of friends. Blakely soaks up the attention, and it appears that Kennedy is fine with giving all of hers to my daughter.

Realizing that I'm staring, I start to eat, listening to their conversation. Blakely reaches for her juice box, and I go to hand it to her, but Kennedy beats me to it. I sit back in my chair and watch them. No one outside of my family ever steps in to help her. Sure, Palmer, Piper, and Jade do, but they're close with Ramsey, and Jade and Palmer are family now. It's only a matter of time until Orrin proposes.

So this woman, she's an anomaly in my world. She's beautiful and kind, and she treats my daughter like the amazing little girl that she is. She's not kissing her ass to try to get to me. She hasn't even looked at me. She's all eyes on my little girl.

I don't know what to do with that.

"Daddy, you's got to eat, or you don't get cake."

I shake out of my thoughts. Leaning over, I kiss Blakely on the cheek. "I'm eating."

"No, yous were doing this." She makes her impression of me, blank-faced and staring off into space. I laugh, as does Kennedy.

"Funny girl." I tap her nose.

She turns to Kennedy and shakes her head. "Daddys are weird," she says, making Kennedy laugh again, which in turn causes Blakely to crack up laughing as well.

"What's going on over here?" Archer takes a seat in the chair across the table from me.

"Uncle Arch, did you eat your food all gone so you could have cake?" Blakely asks.

He grins and pats his flat stomach. "Yep."

My little girl nods her approval and dives back into the small scoop of potato salad I put on her plate.

"Kennedy, it's good to see you again." Archer winks at her.

"Archer," Kennedy replies. I can hear the humor in her voice.

"You're going to save me a dance, right?" he asks. "Maybe at midnight?" He wags his eyebrows, and I kick his shin under the table. "OW. What the f-freak was that for?" he asks, reaching beneath the table to rub at his leg.

"I'm not even supposed to be eating, let alone dancing. Your brother insisted," she tells him. I don't have to look at her to know she's smiling. She's just giving me shit, and we both know it.

"Is that right?" Archer loses his scowl for a grin.

"Daddy made her a plate." Blakely spills the details.

"That was nice of your daddy," Archer tells her.

"He's nice. He made mine too," she tells him.

"So about that dance?" Archer turns his attention toward Kennedy.

"Her dance card is full," I answer for her. I can feel her eyes on me, but I don't dare look. I might as well just piss a circle around her at this point. I don't know what's gotten into me.

"And how would you know?" Archer challenges me.

"Because it's got my name all over it." I pop the last bite of my roll into my mouth and hold his stare as I chew.

Archer grins and taps the table with his hand. "My work here is done." He pushes back in his chair and stands. "Blake, you and me, dance floor as soon as you get your cake."

"You're on," she readily agrees.

I watch as my meddling little brother walks away, and I know I'm going to have to explain myself. I don't have an explanation, not one that I want to reveal. My reasoning is that I don't want anyone's hands on her but mine. I can't tell her that, so I need to think of something fast.

"Declan?" Her soft voice has my gaze snapping to hers. She's sitting back in her chair, peering at me behind Blakely.

"He's like a dog with a bone," I tell her. "I didn't want you to feel pressured." It's lame as far as excuses go, but outside of the truth, it's the best that I've got.

"He's harmless." The glint in her eyes tells me that she sees right through my line of bull shit.

She's right. He is harmless, which makes my reaction to him asking her to dance even worse. I know it. She knows it. However, neither one of us mentions it. Blakely's mom was the last woman I touched. That was the night she got pregnant. No one has gotten close to piquing my interest until now. I feel like I'm a fifteen-year-old all over again. The only difference is I now know what it feels like to be inside a woman. I know what it's like to run my hands over every inch of their skin as their pussy milks my cock.

Basically, I'm fucked.

"Daddy, look!" Blakely lifts her empty plate to show me that it's cleaned.

"Good job, baby girl," I tell her.

"Now we get cake?" she asks.

"We have to let Uncle Brooks and Aunt Palmer cut the cake first," I remind her.

"Uncle Brooks!" she calls out over the banquet hall.

"Blakely," I scold, and my dad voice that I've perfected comes out to play.

"Aunt Palmer!" she calls out, ignoring me.

"Blakely!" Palmer calls back with a huge smile on her face.

"Can we have cake?" my daughter calls back, and I'm beyond scolding her. How can I when Palmer is answering her?

"Of course we can. This is our party; we can do what we want!" Palmer hollers back. The room erupts in laughter because that's a classic Palmer reply.

My eyes scan to my brother, who is looking down at his new wife with hearts in his eyes, and nods. If it's within his power, he'll make it happen in regard to his wife and his niece. As soon as Blakely called out, we all knew how this was going to turn out.

"Kiss!" Maverick calls out.

Brooks grins, sliding his hand behind Palmer's neck, and kisses the hell out of her. I hear a sigh from beside me. Looking over, I see Kennedy watching them. She's smiling with her hands resting over her heart.

There is just something about a wedding. Maybe that's why I'm feeling all "she's mine" when it comes to this woman. She's not mine. Not even close, but even just thinking about it makes me want to turn that thought into reality.

"What?" Blakely shrieks. She turns to face me. "Daddy? Why did Aunt Palmer put cake all over Uncle Brooks's face?" She scrunches up her little nose in confusion.

"That's tradition."

"What's tradition?" She tilts her head to the side.

"A tradition is something you always do. Like we have Christmas Eve at Mamaw and Papaw's, and when Daddy goes fishing with Papaw and his brothers."

"That's a silly tradition." She shakes her head like adults are weird. She's right about that.

"Blake!" Brooks calls out. "Come here, sweetheart. You get the first piece," he tells her.

My daughter is quick to scramble from her chair and rush to my brother. He hands her a plate with a piece of cake. I scoot my chair from the table, ready to go help her, but Merrick scoops her up in his arms. He must ask for a bite because she shakes her head and moves her plate to the side out of his reach. My brother tosses his head back in laughter, and I grin. Don't mess with Blakely and her cake.

"She's such a sweet girl, Declan."

Turning toward Kennedy, I nod. "Thank you. She's a handful, but I couldn't ever picture my life without her in it."

"You're a good dad."

"Thank you. It's hard, you know? To be dad and mom at the same time. I worry she's not getting what she needs."

"That's the most absurd thing I've ever heard. She's a happy, healthy little girl. She's surrounded by love, and you can see that in her confidence. You're doing an incredible job with her."

"I appreciate you saying that. Some days I wonder."

"Well, don't." Her voice is firm. "She's lucky to have you."

Something flashes in her eyes, but it's masked before I can figure out what it means.

"Delivery," Merrick says, placing Blakely in her chair. He kisses the top of her head and moves to the table next to ours, where Ryder and Sterling are sitting.

I suddenly realize that my entire family has left us alone. Well, aside from Archer. Kennedy, Blakely, and I are occupying this table all on our own. It's as if they are intentionally giving us our space. Am I that obvious? Did Archer open his mouth? Either way, I'm happy to have this time with her. Even if I'll be fielding questions from my family for weeks to come, it'll be worth it.

"Daddy, you need to go get Kenny some cake."

"Oh no, you don't have to do that," Kennedy is quick to correct.

"My girls want cake. That's what they get." I wink at Kennedy as I stand from the table to grab her some cake. It's not until my mom hands me two plates with a small grin that I realize what I said.

My girls.

It's official. I've lost my damn mind over this woman.

Chapter 7

KENNEDY

*M*Y GIRLS.

Blakely is jabbering a mile a minute, but I'm not retaining any of her words. I keep hearing Declan's voice just before he left to grab us a piece of cake. Did I hear him right? Did he say "my girls"? He did. I know that he did. I should be put off by that, but I'm not. Instead, my heart flutters in my chest, and my palms are sweaty.

I don't know what it is about this man, but he seems to rile me up. I mean, come on, the ink is barely dry on my divorce decree, and here I am feeling some kind of way about a man who lives too far away for me to be entertaining anything with him.

"It's so good," Blakely says, shoving another bite of her cake into her mouth.

"Slow down, sweetie," I tell her. "You don't want to choke."

"Okay, Kenny," she says, taking a much smaller bite this time. I smile at her, calling me Kenny. I sort of love it when it comes from this adorable little girl. Almost as much as I love her father calling me Kens. They must be a nickname family.

My phone vibrates on the table. Grabbing it, I smile when I see a text from my best friend, Morgan.

Morgan: Happy New Year's Eve. How's the wedding?

Me: Happy New Year's Eve. It's good. It's at the dinner stage right now. Well, the cake, actually.

I snap a picture of Blakely's cake plate, being sure not to get her in the picture, and send it to Morgan. I'm not sure how Declan would feel about me sending pictures of his daughter to my best friend.

Morgan: You're eating cake??

Me: They insisted I join them. It's small, just close friends and family. You'd love them all.

Morgan: I'm glad you're not bored out of your mind. LOL.

Me: Definitely not bored.

Declan heads this way, so I snap a picture of him to send to her. He's wearing dark-washed jeans and a long-sleeve black button-up, with the sleeves rolled up to his elbows. I swallow hard before firing off his picture.

Morgan: Damn!

Morgan: Details.

Me: His parents live next to my grandma.

Morgan: Does he live there too?

Me: No.

Me: Gotta go.

Morgan: KENNEDY! You can't just go after sending me that. If he's single, you get to drive him as you stole him.

I can't stop the laugh that bubbles up in my chest. "For you," Declan says, leaning over my shoulder and whispering in my ear. All laughter ceases as my body heats at the close contact.

"Thank you." I tilt my head back to smile at him. He taps my nose just like he did earlier with Blakely. I should be offended, right? Or worried that he's putting me in the friend zone? I'm not. Because the heat in his eyes tells me he's thinking of me as anything but friendly.

"You're welcome." He takes his seat next to his daughter and dives into his cake like he didn't just set my body on fire by being so close.

My body has never reacted to a man like this. Not even my ex-husband. Just another glaring reminder that we never should have married. It seemed like the logical next step, but that's not always the best decision just because it seems logical. I was young and loved him. I still love him, but I'm not in love with him. In fact, I'm pretty sure I never was.

"Kenny, you need to eat your cake." Blakely's looking at me like she can't believe I'm not devouring the chocolate goodness sitting in front of me.

"Yes, ma'am," I tease, and she grins and nods when I take my first bite.

"Are you hiding?"

I turn to find Jade smiling at me. "Nope." I grin, and she chuckles.

"I get it. We can be a lot to take in."

"No. Not at all. I'm just soaking up all the happiness," I tell her.

"You should be out there dancing. My boyfriend still has seven single brothers." She winks.

"Are you playing matchmaker?" I ask.

"Depends. Is there one of them that you have your eye on?"

Declan. "Nope."

"Ah, the plot thickens." She moves to lean against the wall next to me. "Tell me which one."

"Stop." I shake my head. "They're all very nice-looking men."

"They are, and I know you have your eye on one of them. Don't feel bad. We all did. Well, Palmer and I did. Piper already had her eyes on Heath."

"You lost me." I have no idea what she's talking about.

"The day that Deacon proposed, all the guys were standing together, and Ramsey told us if we had our pick, who would we choose."

"You picked Orrin. I take it?"

"Yep." She grins. "Little did I know that a few minutes later, he'd follow me outside and ask me out on a date."

"What? No way. Did Ramsey know he was going to do that?"

"Nope. She didn't know that Deacon was proposing that very same day either."

"So Palmer?"

Jade nods. "She picked Brooks."

"What are the chances?" I ask with a chuckle.

"It's fate. You have to choose. The universe needs to hear you in order for it to happen."

"You don't really believe that, do you?" I ask, raising my eyebrows.

She shrugs. "I'm not really sure what I believe. I know that it could be coincidence, or it could be fate. What I do know is that

I'm in love with Orrin, and well, you know how things turned out for Palmer and Brooks."

"What's going on over here, ladies?" Ramsey asks, throwing her arm over Jade's shoulders.

"Just admiring the view." She nods to where most of the guys are standing around talking and laughing.

"Oh, did she pick one?" Ramsey asks excitedly.

"I am not picking one." No way in hell am I going to admit that if I had my choice, it would be Declan. Every single time I'm around him and his adorable little girl, I get this feeling in my chest. It's not something I've ever experienced. It's scary and tempting all at the same time.

"What? Why?" Ramsey's face falls.

"This looks like trouble." I look up to see Palmer and her sister, Piper, walking toward us. "I thought this was my party? I missed the invite to this little side bash," Palmer teases.

"We need all the juicy gossip, ladies," Piper tells us, sipping her drink.

"No gossip," Jade tells her.

"She won't pick," Ramsey tells them. Her nod toward the guys is the only explanation she needs to give them before they're caught up in the conversation.

"You really should. We all picked, well, except for Ramsey. She was already madly in love with Deacon at the time, but we're all still madly in love with our men that we chose."

"Come on. You realize how that sounds, right? I can't just say, hey, universe, I want insert name here." I wink at them, and they groan. "Send him my way."

"It doesn't work like that, and damn, I thought we had you." Palmer chuckles.

"She's right. But is it really worth the chance if that is how it works? Are you willing to miss out on your forever, Kennedy?"

"You all are too much." I laugh.

"So?" Jade asks.

"I'm not picking."

"You have to," Piper chimes in.

"It's tradition," Ramsey adds.

"Yes." Palmer points at her. "It's tradition. You're the only one of us who's unattached and hasn't picked."

"This is crazy," I say, already feeling myself start to fall under their pressure. "This is peer pressure." I try to give them a stern look, but we all end up falling into a fit of giggles.

"We'll help," Ramsey says. "Okay, we'll start at the top from eligibility down. Declan is the oldest of the seven available, but he's a single dad, and I can't let you pick him unless I know you're down with being second sometimes. That little girl is his world, and she's all that he has."

"I would never do anything to take Blakely away from her daddy. She's a precious little girl, and you can tell how much he loves her." I clamp my mouth shut, knowing that the conviction in my voice gave me away. Palmer links her arm with mine and places her head on my shoulder.

"Welcome to the family," she says.

I'd laugh off her antics, but she's not laughing, and neither are the rest of them. "I didn't pick," I remind them.

"Oh, you picked," Jade tells me.

They're all watching me, except for Palmer, who's still standing with our arms linked, and her head on my shoulder. "Fine." I roll my eyes. "Declan."

"What about me?" the man himself asks.

My head snaps to the left to seek out the voice. He stands with his hands shoved in his pockets, Brooks right beside him. "Nothing," I'm quick to deny. Damnit. I should have kept my mouth shut.

"Beautiful, our parents are leaving," Brooks tells Palmer. "Come say goodbye."

She nods and then turns, keeping her voice low just for me. "He's had a rough few years. I think you're exactly what he needs." With that, she releases me and allows her new husband to sweep her away.

"I should go find Heath," Piper says before skipping off.

"Have you seen Orrin?" Jade asks Declan.

Up to this point, his eyes have been locked on mine. He turns away to address her, and I take my first breath since he walked up to our little huddle. "He was helping Dad with packing some of the food and taking it to their car."

"Thanks." She rushes off.

"My fiancé promised me a dance that I need to collect." Ramsey reaches over and gives my hand a gentle squeeze before leaving me alone with Declan.

"Something you need to tell me, Kens?" He takes a step closer and links his hand with mine.

His back is to the room, so I know that they can't see us, which I'm grateful for. My heart thunders in my chest. "Nothing," I lie.

"You know you can tell me." His voice is low, keeping this conversation intimate and just between the two of us.

"They wanted me to choose," I tell him.

"Choose what?"

"One of you. The seven eligible Kincaid brothers."

He nods. "Palmer chose Brooks. Jade chose Orrin."

"What? You know about that?"

"Of course we do. The girls tell, and the guys fill us in."

"I should tell them this is happening."

"They know," he assures me. "They only share the stuff they don't care that anyone finds out. You can trust them. All of them." His eyes bore into mine as if he needs me to believe what he says is true.

"They're all really nice," I say lamely. It's my attempt to change the subject, but the look in his eye tells me it's not going to happen.

"Did you choose?"

He damn well knows that I did. He heard me say his name. He wants me to say it, but I'm not budging. "Maybe."

He steps closer. "Who did you choose?"

"Daddy!" Blakely calls.

Declan drops my hand and takes a giant step back, putting some much-needed space between us. I can't think clearly when he's that close to me.

"What's up, squirt?" he asks, lifting her into his arms, and setting her on his hip.

"Papaw said I can spend the night with him and Mamaw and watch his balls drop."

I bite down on my cheek to keep from laughing.

"We're going to watch the ball drop." Carol Kincaid steps next to Declan with a man who looks so much like his sons it's easy to know who he is. "Kennedy, this is my husband, Raymond. Ray, this is Maureen's granddaughter, Kennedy."

"It's nice to meet you." I offer him my hand.

He takes my hand and shakes it. "You too. How's your grandma feeling?"

"Ornery as ever." I laugh.

"She's on the mend then." Carol smiles.

"She is. The pain is controlled. She's just restless."

"Well, if she needs anything, you let us know," Carol tells me.

"I will, thank you."

"Now, how about you let our only granddaughter spend the night with us old folks so you young folk can bring in the New Year."

"You don't have to do that," Declan tells his mom.

"Blakely is going to make me some popcorn. No one adds the cheese flavoring like she does," Raymond says. He reaches for Blakely, and she goes willingly.

"He's right, Daddy. I'm real good at shaking the fake cheese."

"Give me a kiss," Declan says. He leans in, so does she, and she gives him a loud, smacking kiss. "Love you, baby girl," he says softly.

"I love you too, Daddy. Bye, Kenny." She waves, and I wave back, and then they're gone.

"Come on. I'll make you a drink."

"I'm driving," I remind him.

"I'll take you home." The look in his eyes tells me he wants to take me to his home instead of my grandma's.

"Water is fine," I tell him.

He nods. "After you." He motions toward the table of food and the same refrigerators we used for the bachelor and bachelorette parties to keep the drinks cool. Before we make it to the drinks, Merrick's voice—at least I think it's him; it's hard for me to tell the twins apart—telling everyone to hit the dance floor.

"The parentals are gone," he announces into the mic. "Time to let loose." He holds up a bottle of beer, and everyone cheers.

"They're staying with me tonight," he tells me. "I assumed I'd have Blake, so I told them I'd drive them to my place."

"Looks like you're going to have your hands full."

"That's exactly what it looks like. Remind me to thank my little brother."

"For what?"

"Change of plans," Declan says, guiding me to the dance floor. He slides an arm around my waist when Brooks calls out for him to slow it down so he can cuddle his baby momma. The song changes to "Spin You Around" by Morgan Wallen. "Come here," Declan whispers, pulling me into his chest.

I have no choice but to place my hands on his chest. He moves them to rest on his shoulders as we sway to the music. He holds pressure on the small of my back, holding me close. I'm glad he is because my knees are weak. He smells incredible and being this close to him has me feeling off balance.

"Who did you pick, Kennedy?" he rasps, his lips next to my ear.

My heart is beating so loud in my chest that I'm certain he can hear it. I lick my lips and debate telling him. He knows. I know that he knows. He just wants to hear me say it. "Girl talk," I tell him.

He pulls me closer, which I didn't think was possible. One hand rests low on my back. If he were to move it just an inch, maybe two, he'd be gripping my ass. The other runs up and down my back. I'm wearing a modest little black dress that flares at the hips. It's not sexy, but right now, I feel as though it's the sexiest outfit I've ever worn with the way he's looking at me.

"I want to hear you say it."

There it is. Confirmation that he already knows.

"You already heard me," I counter.

He dips his head. "Let me hear you say it, Kens." Pulling back, his eyes bore into mine.

"You, Declan. I chose you." He closes his eyes as the song changes. I go to step away, but he holds me tight. "Almost six years," he says cryptically. He places his lips on my forehead, holding them there for several thunderous heartbeats.

"My turn." Before I know what's happening, Archer tugs on my hand and pulls me away from Declan.

"Archer," he growls.

"Sorry, brother. You have to share. She's the only single lady here, and there are seven of us." Archer grins as he spins me around until we're standing several feet away from his brother.

That's how the next hour goes. I'm moved from one brother to the other and then sandwiched between the twins. It's weird but funny as hell. I laugh the entire time.

"I need a drink," I tell them.

"You want me to get it?" one of them asks. I think it's Maverick.

"No, you do your thing," I tell them, smiling. I walk to the refrigerator and grab a cold bottle of water. I stand off to the side, drinking it until it's gone. It's been a long time since I've been dancing.

"Penny for your thoughts?"

I turn to find Declan standing next to me. "Just thinking about how long it's been since I've been dancing. Tonight was fun. Thank you for including me."

"I'm glad you had a good time." He reaches up and tucks my hair behind my ear.

"I'm a sweaty mess." I laugh, because I'm sure I look like I've been rode hard and put up wet.

"You're beautiful." His words are softly spoken, almost as if he's hoping that I don't hear him, but I do, and so did my heart and the butterflies in my belly.

"One minute!" Orrin calls out.

"Come on." Declan laces his fingers with mine and pulls me to the crowd of his friends and family as we all start the countdown to the New Year. I close my eyes and send up a silent resolution that this year is going to be mine. I'm working on me and what makes me happy.

"Five." We start the countdown.

"Four."

"Three."

"Two."

I never get to one because Declan's lips are on mine. His hands cradle my cheeks, and he moves in close. I feel his hard length and gasp. He takes the opportunity to slide his tongue past my lips.

I've never been kissed like this.

I feel as though I'm consumed by this man.

His taste.

His scent.

His touch.

We're jostled, and he pulls away. He presses his forehead to mine, and that's when everything around us comes back into focus, and I realize he's breathing just as heavily as I am.

"Happy New Year, Kennedy."

"Happy New Year, Declan."

Chapter 8

DECLAN

"UNCLE MAV SAYS THAT I'M the prettiest," Blakely tells me.

It's Friday night, and after I picked her up from my parents,' I decided to go ahead and get next week's grocery shopping out of the way. I promised Blakely we could make cupcakes this weekend, and we don't have what we need. "I agree with Uncle Mav," I tell my daughter, stopping to add two gallons of milk to my cart.

"That's what Mamaw and Papaw said too." She smiles up at me from where she's sitting in the front seat of the cart. She's almost too big to do that anymore, and I hate how fast she's growing up.

"What do you want for dinner tonight?" I ask.

She taps her index finger against her chin. "I say dino nuggets and mac and cheese." She gives me a toothy grin, and even though that doesn't sound the least bit appetizing to me, it's quick and easy. Not to mention I can't say no to her. Not with something like this.

"Why don't we grab some chicken strips from the deli?" I compromise. I stop near the boxes of macaroni and toss in several boxes. She's not a super picky eater, but she'd live off mac and cheese if I were to let her, and it's a quick meal. Sometimes at night, I'm too exhausted to put much effort into dinner.

"Okay, Daddy." She agrees easily, and I'm once again reminded of how incredibly lucky I am. She's easy to love and care for. I've read countless books and forums online about single parenting, and the stories I've heard are terrifying.

"You know," I tell her, moving on down the aisle, "we should make pancakes for breakfast in the morning."

"Oh! Can we make the blue ones again? Those tasted real good." She's nodding her head and licking her lips.

I chuckle. "Sure can. I'll grab some food coloring just in case we're out. Don't let me forget when we get to the bakery aisle."

"Got it."

Believe it or not, she has a mind like a steel trap. That's something my brothers found out real fast. They had her saying the word *shit* when she was just over a year old. My mom laid into them good, which means I didn't have to. None of us ever want to disappoint our momma. Anyway, she doesn't forget anything, so anytime I have something big planned, I don't tell her right away because that's all I'll hear about until the day of the event.

I'm taking my time pushing the cart up and down every aisle. Not because I enjoy being at the grocery store, but because I enjoy this time with my daughter. When we get home, it will be unloading and putting away the groceries, starting dinner, laundry, dishes, and the list goes on and on. Here it's just my girl and me hanging out.

We turn down the cereal aisle, and I grab a box of pancake mix and a bottle of syrup. I think I have some at home, but these are two staples I don't like to run out of. I've been known to make pancakes for dinner, not just breakfast.

"Kenny!" Blakely leans to the right, looking behind me as she waves her little arms in the air.

Slowly, I turn to look, and sure enough, the beautiful Kennedy has just turned down the same aisle. I take her in. She's in a pair of leggings, a long sweater, and boots that come to her knees. Her hair is pulled back from her face, and her big brown eyes sparkle. She's not looking at me, though. Her eyes are on my daughter.

"Blakely, I've missed you." She wheels her cart next to ours and leans over, hugging my daughter.

My heart stutters in my chest at her easy affection for Blakely. I'm in all new territory with this woman. She's the first since I found out I was going to be a father to hold and keep my attention, and she knows my daughter. I've dated a couple of times, just dinner here and there. None of those dates ever led anywhere, and I only went on them at the insistence of my brothers and my mother. I wasn't interested, and they never got anywhere near my little girl.

Now, here I am, lusting after a woman who has not only met my daughter, but they have formed a quick friendship of sorts, and that throws me off balance. Even if I was willing to ask her out, knowing that she's leaving and that she's already formed some kind of attachment to Blakely complicates things.

Maybe it's just me who complicates things.

I seem to always have an excuse. Just ask my brothers. They seem to think I'm full of them when it comes to dating, and maybe they're right. My past has left me hesitant about relationships.

"Are you getting pancakes too?" Blakely asks her.

Kennedy smiles. "That does sound pretty good."

"Daddy makes blue ones." Her little eyes find mine. "Daddy, can Kenny spend the night and have blue pancakes?"

"Not tonight," I tell her. What I want to say is sure, I'll drop you off with Mamaw and Papaw or Ramsey or one of your other uncles, and Kennedy can spend the night with me. My cock begins to thicken at the thought.

"Wild Friday night?" I ask, changing the subject.

She laughs softly. "Grandma had company. The sewing club. They invited me to stay, but to be honest, I just needed to get some air."

"And this is where you decided to get it?"

She shrugs. "It's not like I have a long list of friends in the area."

"Kenny, you're my friend," Blakely tells her.

Kennedy's eyes soften. "I know. You are a sweet girl."

"Have you had dinner?" I find myself asking. I shouldn't go there, but I can't seem to help myself when it comes to her.

"No." She looks into her empty cart. "I don't even really need groceries." She laughs. "Just something to get me out of the house."

"Have dinner with us."

"Oh, I don't want to impose." She waves me off, politely declining.

"It's not an imposition if you're invited," I tell her.

"Yeah, Daddy's making mac and cheese." Blakely tries to sell the idea.

"Really?" Kennedy asks as if she's intrigued. "I love mac and cheese."

Blakely gasps. "You do? It's my favorite."

"You should join us. It's nothing exciting. Some chicken strips from the deli and some mac and cheese. We could go out to grab something too. Dorothy's Diner is open until nine."

"You don't have to change your plans for me."

"Dinner at our place?" I ask again.

"Please, Kenny?" Blakely bats those long eyelashes that cover her blue eyes that are the exact replica of mine.

"Are you sure I'm not imposing?"

"What's *im* what you said?" Blakely asks.

I start to answer her, but Kennedy does before I get the chance. "It means I don't want to ruin your plans."

"She won't. Right, Daddy?"

"No imposition. We'd love to have you."

"Well, all right then. Let me put this cart back and call and check on my grandma."

"We have a few more things to get. Join us when you're ready. We're working our way through the aisles," I tell her. I don't want to rush this tradition that Blakely and I have. Besides, I also don't want to have to make another trip to the store this week. I'm getting what we need to get us through to next weekend when we do this all over again.

"Are you sure you don't mind?" This time her eyes hold mine.

"I insist. It's not gourmet, but the company is top-notch."

She smiles. "I'll find you." With that, she pushes her empty cart back to the front of the store.

"Are we leaving?" Blakely asks.

"No. We still have some shopping to do."

"Is Kenny leaving?"

"No. She's going to follow us home."

Blakely tosses her little arms in the air. "Yes!"

I know how you feel, baby girl. I know how you feel.

I move on down the aisle, tossing in what we need before moving on to the next. I said I didn't want to rush this, but I don't linger like I would have before running into Kennedy. I tell myself it's because I don't want her to wait on us. It's my story, and I'm sticking to it.

"She's out," Kennedy says softly.

We're sitting in the living room. Blakely is curled up on my lap where we were watching her favorite princess movie in the chair, and Kennedy is sitting on the couch. Her boots are off, and her legs are beneath her, the throw from the back of the couch tossed over her lap.

"She's usually in bed before nine. She didn't want to miss a minute with you."

"She's really great, Declan."

"Yeah, she is." I smile at her. "Let me put her to bed, and I'll be right back."

"I should go." She says the words but makes no move to leave the comfort of my couch.

"Stay." There's a plea in my voice that I don't recognize, but she nods, so I'm calling it a win. "I'll be right back." Standing without waking Blakely, I head down the hall to her room. I'm grateful I had her change into her jammies and use the bathroom before we started the movie. Placing her on her bed, I pull back the covers, tucking her in tight. "Sweet dreams," I whisper.

"Daddy loves you." Reaching over, I turn on her small night-light and pull the door mostly shut and make my way back to Kennedy.

"Can I get you something to drink? Beer? I think there is a bottle of wine in the fridge from the last time that Ramsey was here."

"I'm good." She smiles.

I sit on the couch, closer than I should but still leaving some space between us. "All right, adult movie it is." I reach for the remote and begin to browse. "What are you in the mood for?"

"You watch porn with your daughter just down the hall?" She places her hand over her chest and pretends to be offended, but she loses the battle with her laughter as it sputters from her soft lips.

"Ha ha, funny girl." I tickle her side and she squirms.

"I thought so." She reaches behind her and pats herself on the back.

"I don't really watch many movies, so you pick."

I can't seem to find anything, and I know it's because I'd rather talk to her than watch a movie. Turning off the television, I stand and turn on the small Bluetooth speaker connecting my phone and choose a general country playlist. "Country music?" I ask her.

"Yep. Actually, I like a lot of different genres, but I find that I listen to country more often."

"Me too." I make my way back to the couch and sit. This time, I turn to face her. "Tell me about you."

"Me? Why do I have to go first?" she counters.

I chuckle. "Fair enough. Declan Kincaid. Thirty-one years old. Never married. Single father to Blakely Kincaid, who is going to be five in May, but she talks and acts like she's fifteen." That gets a chuckle out of her. "I own Kincaid's Auto Repair in town. I went to trade school in high school and worked there as a part of the program. Old Man Jennings hired me on after graduation, and five years later, I bought the place from him and changed the name."

"Impressive."

"Your turn."

She wiggles in her seat. "Okay. Kennedy Edwards. Recently divorced from my college boyfriend. We were married for just over four years. I'm a self-employed literary editor. My client base is primarily independent romance authors. I prefer books to movies and TV. The books are always better." She grins. "I live in Tallahassee, Florida, where my parents, who are empty nesters and spend most of their time traveling, live as well."

"Divorce is tough."

"It is," she admits. "However, it's what needed to happen. Looking back, I can see it now. We never should have gotten married. We were best friends in college. Met freshman year and hit it off. It was quite some time before we started to date. We were graduating from college, he was a year older than me, and marriage seemed like the next logical step."

"No kids?"

Something changes. Her eyes turn sad. "No. I can't have kids."

"Kennedy." I breathe her name. "I'm so sorry."

She gives me a watery smile. "It's okay. I've come to terms with it. When I was sixteen, my appendix ruptured. There was a lot of damage to my fallopian tubes. I was told I'd never be able to conceive." A tear slides over her cheek, and I can't handle it.

I move in close and pull her into my arms. She comes willingly. "I'm sorry," she whispers. "You didn't need me to lay all that out for you."

"Hey." I wait for her to lift her head and look at me. "I want to know you." I wipe at her tears with my thumbs. "This is a part of you, and I'm glad that you told me." She nods and sits back, blowing out a breath.

"Blakely's mom, she died in a car accident when Blake was just a month old. Cassie and I were best friends too." I give her a sad smile.

"Declan, you don't have to share just because I did."

I reach out and lace her fingers with mine. I bring her hand to my lips and kiss her knuckles. "I want to know you, and I want you to know me. For the first time, I want that more than anything."

She nods, so I keep going. "She was in a relationship. His name was Boyd. Cassie and I had been friends since high school. Small town and all that. Anyway, Cassie and Boyd were on again and off again. One night she showed up at my place with a bottle of vodka and a gallon of orange juice and told me it was over for good, and she wanted to get drunk. Who was I to stop her? Their relationship was toxic, and I was glad she'd finally kicked him to the curb."

"I hate that for them. Sometimes it's hard to do the right thing, even when you know what that is."

"Yeah," I agree. "So we drank. A lot. As in, neither one of us remember most of the details of the night. The next morning we woke up naked in bed together. There was a condom in the trash and a wrapper on the floor. We swore to never talk about it again and went on with our lives. It was a drunken mistake. That's until about two months later when she landed back on my doorstep. This time she had a gallon of orange juice sans vodka. That night changed my life.

"She found out she was pregnant.

"She was on birth control but had been on medication a couple of weeks before for a sinus infection. Neither one of us thought anything about it. We'd used protection, but the proof was there in the ultrasound picture she handed me. What was worse is that she didn't know if the baby was mine or Boyd's."

"Oh, Declan." She squeezes my hand, which is still laced with hers.

"I had to tell my family that I might be a father. There was a fifty-fifty chance that her baby was mine. As you can imagine, Boyd was furious. He was always pissed off and accusing us of being more than friends, and there was nothing between us. Well, not until that night. Even afterward, it was the same between us. I didn't see her that way, and she didn't see me that way either."

"That had to be so hard for you."

I nod. "Boyd was convinced it was his baby. He insisted on a prenatal paternity test. Cassie fought him about it for a few weeks. The doctor assured her that she and the baby were perfectly safe, so she finally agreed."

"She was yours."

"She was mine.

"Boyd and Cassie fought all the time. She spent more nights in my spare room than she did in the home that she shared with him. After Blakely was born, the fighting continued. He had a hard time with the woman he loved being the mother to another man's baby. I get it. I understand, but I'd like to think if I was in that situation... if the situation were reversed, and I was broken up with my girlfriend, and this happened, I would love that baby because it was a part of her. Boyd, however, didn't feel that way. To be honest, I don't know how I would feel, but I know how much I love my daughter. Any baby is innocent in all of this."

"How could you not love an innocent child?"

"It's hard to say how I would react or feel. I'd be pissed and hurt, I'm sure, but to turn her and the baby away. If I truly loved her? I don't think I could do that. Hell, if I loved her that much,

I never would have pushed her into a breakup to be in that kind of position to begin with."

"You're a good man, Declan Kincaid."

"I'm a father," I correct her.

"And a damn good one. She's lucky to have you."

"Anyway, Cassie was here dropping Blake off for my weekend. Boyd called. He was drunk. He was ranting and raving and told her to meet him at home. I hated my daughter being there with him. I remember being thankful that it was my weekend with Blake. Cassie left to pick him up. He was at a buddy's house just outside of Willow River. She never made it. A drunk driver hit her."

"Oh my god," she breathes. I look up to find tears in her eyes, this time for my little girl and me and the mother she will never know.

I take a deep breath and keep going. I need to finish this. "It was Boyd. The drunk driver that hit her was Boyd. He took Blake's mom from her."

"I don't even know what to say," she confesses.

"I've never told anyone that story who I wasn't related to."

"Thank you for trusting me."

"It's a small town. Everyone knew, but I never talk about it. I was too busy trying to be mom and dad to a little girl who was robbed of the chance of knowing an incredible woman."

"I'm so sorry for your loss. What happened was tragic, but, Declan, I need you to hear me when I say that I'm an outsider looking in, and you're an incredible father. Blakely is happy and healthy, and that's because of you. You are giving her everything that she needs."

"Thanks. Okay, that turn was longer than I imagined. Your turn."

She smiles and begins to tell me her own story.

Chapter 9

KENNEDY

DECLAN TRACES HIS THUMB OVER my wrist. The movement is soothing. I feel like such a failure as a woman, and I don't like to talk about my divorce and what led up to it. However, after he gave me his history, it's only fair that I give him mine too.

"Lyle never wanted children. Sometimes I think that's why he asked me to marry him. He thought it was the perfect scenario. Anytime I brought it up before the wedding, he would always say he just wanted some time with me and that we would talk about our options when we were ready. I was ready, and he wasn't."

"He doesn't know what he's missing. Being a dad is the hardest yet most rewarding thing I've ever done in my entire life."

I smile at that. Everything about Declan is the opposite of my ex-husband. "About a year ago, I brought it up, and he blew me off. I kept bringing it up until one day, a few months later, he decided we needed a break. He moved out."

"Damn," he mutters.

"We talked on the phone, texted a lot, but he wasn't budging, and neither was I. I might not be able to get pregnant, but that doesn't mean there isn't a little boy or little girl out there who doesn't need a mommy." Hot tears prick my eyes, but I blink them away. "I was open to anything. Adoption, surrogacy, IVF, even fostering, but Lyle wanted no part of it. We decided mutually that divorce was our next course of action. I wasn't willing to give up my dream of one day being a mother, even if it wasn't the conventional way. He wasn't willing to budge either. He didn't want kids. There was no changing his mind."

"I'm sorry. He's an idiot."

I laugh at that. "He's settled on what he wants out of life, and sadly, that doesn't include me, but I'm okay with it. When we made the decision to divorce, I was sad, but I wasn't torn up about it, you know? I was okay. I'm young. Twenty-five. I still have a chance to be a mom, even if I have to do it on my own."

"Kens." His voice is low and deep. He waits until I give him my eyes. "He didn't deserve you. I feel sorry for him because he doesn't know what he's missing. Sure, kids are a lot of work, and you give up a lot of yourself for them, but I wouldn't change it. I wish Cassie could be here every day. Not because we'd be together, that's just not who we were. But I do wish that she could be here for our little girl and to see her grow up. The way Blakely came into my life wasn't conventional, but given a chance, I wouldn't change anything except for stopping Cassie from going after Boyd that night."

"I don't begrudge him what he wants, you know? I just wish I had seen it all sooner. I was young and wrapped up in the fairy tale."

"The fairy tale he didn't give you."

"He's out there," I tell him, forcing a smile. "My prince charming is out there, and one day, I'll be a mom."

"Come here." He pulls me into his arms, and I go willingly. His embrace is warm and comforting, and I realize I've missed the comfort of someone to hold me. Things were off with Lyle and me for a very long time. I wanted it to work. I wanted *us* to work, but I'm glad that we didn't have a baby. Everything happens for a reason, and I'm convinced the best is yet to come.

"Movie?" Declan asks.

"Definitely." I try to move, but he keeps his hold on me. He shifts to get more comfortable and, in turn, makes me more so as well. He chooses a movie, but I can't tell you one single thing about it. All I can think about is how good he smells and how being wrapped in his arms feels right. I barely know this man, but it's as if we just fit.

"I should get going." I sit up and stretch my arms over my head once the movie comes to an end.

"You okay to drive?"

"Yes." I smile at him. "Thank you for tonight. It was unexpected and exactly what I needed."

"You're welcome to join us anytime." He stands and offers me his hand, helping me stand as well. "Where are your keys?"

"Um." I look around. "I think I left them on the table by the door."

He nods. "I'll go start your car."

"You don't have to do that."

"I'll be back." He leans in and presses his lips to my cheek before moving toward the door. I watch him slip on some boots and a coat and grab my keys before he disappears outside.

My hand covers where his lips just rested. I shouldn't be having these kinds of feelings. My belly shouldn't be fluttering, and I shouldn't be melting from a single press of his lips to my cheek, but here I am, swooning like a teenage girl and her first crush.

Shaking out of my fog, I fold the blanket I was using and place it on the back of the couch before making my way to the front door, sliding into my boots, and pulling on my coat.

When Declan walks back inside, my breath stalls in my lungs. He's rugged and sexy and the complete opposite of any man I've ever dated. He reminds me of the men in the novels that I spend my days with.

Declan Kincaid is definitely book boyfriend material.

"You sure you're good to drive?" he asks.

"Promise." I look up at him.

"Will you text me when you get home?"

"I'm a big girl, Declan." I will admit that his concern is nice. It's been way too long since a man cared about me getting home safely.

"Trust me, Kens, I know. I won't sleep until I know you're home."

Reaching into the pocket of my leggings, I pull my phone out. I get to the new contact screen and hand it to him. "Add your number."

He does as I ask and taps the screen. When I hear a beep from somewhere in the house, I give him a puzzled look as he grins. "Now I have yours too."

"Do you plan on using it?" I ask boldly.

He runs his index finger over my cheek. "You all right with that?"

"I'm only here for a couple of months. Max."

He nods. "While you're here." He doesn't say more, but he doesn't have to. The look on his face tells me what he's thinking.

"Do you think that's a good idea?" I know for certain I'll fall for him. It's too soon after my divorce to even be entertaining the idea, but I know myself, and no way can I keep feelings out of the equation. Not with a man like Declan.

He takes a step closer, and his hands land on my hips. "I think it's the best idea I've ever had. I like spending time with you. I want to do more of that."

"I don't live here, Declan."

"I know." He pulls me into a hug. "I know you don't live here, and I know that you're only going to be here for a couple of months at most, but I also have this gut feeling that if I pass up the chance to spend more time with you, I'll regret it for the rest of my life."

"You have these gut feelings often?"

"No. That's why I trust them when I do."

"So... we hang out?"

"Yeah," he says, pulling back. He keeps his hands on my hips as he smiles down at me. "We spend time together."

"The ink is barely dry on my divorce papers," I voice my earlier thoughts.

"Are you still in love with him?"

"No." My answer is instant.

"If he were standing here asking you to take him back, would you?"

"No."

"What if he begged?"

"No."

"Then let's do this. Me and you."

"Casual."

"Sure, as long as I'm the only man you're spending time with."

I laugh, but his face remains serious. "How is that casual?"

"I don't really do the casual thing."

"Then why do this?"

"Because I like you. I like the time we've spent together." My belly flops at his confession and the look on his face. He's not playing. This is what he wants.

"Let's start with hanging out. I'm not... this is crazy, Declan."

"Just me?"

"What do you mean?" I'm being coy, and we both know it.

"I'll agree to hanging out, but I don't want you hanging out with any other guys while you're here."

"Are you one of those possessive types?" I don't hate it, but I can't let him know that. I refuse to let him know that even though internally I'm screaming *yes* at the top of my lungs.

"No. Well, I haven't been in the past."

"Oh, I see how it is. You're getting greedy in your old age," I tease.

"I'm six years older than you," he reminds me.

"Is that gray?" I lift my hands to run my fingers through his hair.

"Funny girl." He pulls me closer. "Me and you, Kens. While you're here, it's you and me."

"And what am I getting out of this deal?" My heart races. In fact, it's thumping so loudly I'm sure that he can hear it.

"Me."

"Meh." I scrunch up my nose, and he tosses his head back in laughter.

"I'm not letting you leave until you agree."

"You mean I get to spend the night with a man who treats his little girl like a princess and wants all my time? That's not very threatening."

"Kennedy."

"Oh, the full name." I pretend to shiver in fear, but my grin that matches his gives me away. "Yes, Declan Kincaid. I'd love to spend more time with you. Just... don't break my heart. Okay?"

"Never." There is so much conviction in his voice I almost believe him. However, I know the truth. I agree to a short-term friendship, or whatever you want to call it, with a man who is not a short-term anything. I can already feel the first crack in my fragile heart, but I'm not going to let that stop me. I want this for me. I deserve to spend some time with a man. It's time that I stop waiting for things to happen and start living. This is my time away to cleanse my life of my past.

I'll move back home in a couple of months and take the first steps to make my dreams come true. Being a mom.

"I should go."

"Be safe. I'll walk you out."

"You don't have to do that. You already went out in the cold to start my car." He gives me a look telling me I'm being ridiculous for thinking he shouldn't walk me and opens the door.

When we reach my car, he turns me and places a soft kiss on my cheek. "Don't forget to text me."

"I don't want to wake Blakely."

"You won't."

"Night, Declan. Thank you for dinner and for your company."

"What are you doing tomorrow?"

"Uh, nothing that I know of. Unless Grandma has plans for me."

"Let me know. I want to see you."

"We're really doing this, huh?"

"Yeah, Kens, we're really doing this." He pulls open my door and waits for me to be settled inside and strapped in before closing the door and stepping back.

I wave, but I'm not sure he can see me since it's dark. I back out of the driveway and smile all the way back to my grandma's place. Tonight turned out not at all as I expected. I'm giddy with the idea of getting to spend more time with him.

When I walk into the house, I hear the TV on, and I hope that she's asleep in the chair. Walking into the living room quietly, I stop when I see Grandma sitting in her recliner with a big ole grin on her face.

"What's that?" I point toward her face.

"What?" She feigns innocence.

"That grin. What's with the grin? You hiding a man in here or something?" I'm pushing the heat from her to me. At least I'm attempting to. I know my grandma too well to know that she's not going to fall for it.

"Oh, my dear granddaughter, I wouldn't hide him." She winks, and I can't stop the laughter that bubbles up in my chest.

"I have no doubt." I smile at her, taking a seat on the couch.

"So how was dinner?"

"Good. We had chicken tenders from the deli, macaroni and cheese, and applesauce."

"Sounds like a meal planned with a little girl in mind."

"Most definitely. He'd already promised her. He offered something else, but I insisted he not change his plans."

"And it was good?"

"Yeah, I mean nothing fancy, but it was good."

"And Declan?"

"He was good too. He and his daughter, who was there, was also good," I say, as a reminder that tonight nothing happened. Well, not nothing, but nothing like her perverted mind is alluding to.

"Tell me everything." There is so much excitement in her voice. I hate to disappoint her.

"There's nothing to tell. I ran into them at the store, and they invited me to dinner. I followed them to their place, we had dinner, watched a princess movie with Blakely, then Declan and I watched another movie, and I came home."

"Is that what you kids are calling it these days?" She's practically giddy at the idea of her granddaughter doing adult things with Declan.

"Adult things? Do tell."

Shit. I said that out loud. "Nothing happened. We talked and got to know one another better. He started my car for me to warm it up before I left, which I thought was sweet. That was it."

"I see getting details out of you is like pulling teeth. Did he kiss you? Did you hold hands? Are you going to see him again? I need to know all the things, Kennedy."

"No, you don't."

"He's the one," she tells me.

"What are you yammering on about?"

"I told you I wasn't going to tell you which Kincaid brother you were going to marry, but I changed my mind. It's going to be Declan."

"Grandma, I think you're delirious from lack of sleep. Let me help you to your room." I don't know why she's so hooked on me marrying again so soon, let alone one of the Kincaid brothers. Then again, I stopped trying to understand Grandma's reasoning for things years ago. She definitely dances to the beat of her own drum.

"I have a bum leg. I'm not crippled. I can do just fine and I have that stupid scooter you insist I use. Besides, I'm not going to bed yet. I still need to pry the details out of you."

"He gave me a hug. He talked about Blakely's mom, and I told him about Lyle and the divorce. He kissed me on the cheek and suggested we get together again."

"There it is." She rubs her hands together. "Was that so hard?"

I just shake my head and smile. "I'm going to bed. Let me help you."

"Oh, all right," she concedes.

I help her up and with her scooter. I bring her phone and a bottle of water that I know she likes to keep on her nightstand. Once she's settled in bed, I kiss her weathered cheek good night. I make sure the night-light in the bathroom is on, and when I walk by the outlet, her motion night-light comes on as well. I don't want her to fall in the dark.

I make my way through the house, checking the door is locked and all the lights are off. Once I'm in my room, I strip out of my clothes. I'm in the middle of sliding the oversized T-shirt over my head when my phone beeps with a message.

Morgan: Happy New Year.

Me: Happy New Year. Just got home from an event at the manor.

Morgan: Any hot guys there?

She follows her message with a winking face emoji, and I smile.

Me: Several.

I smile when I think about my company for the evening.

Morgan: Did you get a midnight kiss?

Me: I did.

Morgan: I want details.

Me: I'll call you tomorrow and we can catch up. Kiss Iris for me. Tell Mitch Happy New Year.

Morgan: Will do. Tell Maureen the same.

I toss my phone on the bed only for it to ring. I scramble to answer it before Grandma has a chance to hear it.

"Hello."

"Kennedy."

"Declan, hi, I'm so sorry I forgot to text you. Grandma was up when I got home, and we've been chatting. I just got her in bed. I made it safe and sound." I rush to get the words out, blowing out a heavy breath.

"Why are you breathing so heavy?" he asks in his deep sexy voice.

"I was changing into my pajamas and scrambled to get to the phone."

"Are you changed?"

I look down at my naked chest. "No. Hold on a second." I drop the phone to the mattress and pull the T-shirt over my head. "I'm back." I move to turn out the lamp and slide under the covers.

"Now, what are you doing?"

"Getting under the covers. My legs and feet are cold."

"What are you sleeping in?"

Is it me or is his voice deeper? "An oversized T-shirt." My

reply is all breathy, and I'm sure I sound like an idiot, but he affects me in ways I've never experienced.

He makes this humming sound that sends my heart racing. "I should have made you stay with me."

"What? Why? I'm fine."

"Yeah, but I could have kept you warm."

"Oh." I don't know what to say to that. Lyle never said those kinds of things to me. I'm out of my depth here.

"Next time."

"I did agree to a next time," I manage to reply without sounding like a phone sex operator.

"You did. Did you ask your grandma about tomorrow?"

"No, but I will. I'll text you."

"That works. Night, Kens."

"Night, Declan."

I wait for the call to end before pulling my phone from my ear. I feel giddy and excited at the possibilities of what the future might hold. I hate to admit this, but Declan is a big part of that. He makes me feel wanted and sexy. It's been a damn long time since I've felt either of those things. Lyle wasn't much for displays of affection. Declan is his complete opposite, and I have a feeling he's exactly what I need during my stay in Willow River.

Chapter 10

DECLAN

"DADDY'S GRUMPY," BLAKELY ANNOUNCES AS we walk into my parents' house for Sunday dinner.

"He is?" Dad lifts her into his arms and places a loud smacking kiss on her cheek.

"Yep. He said I couldn't wear my flipper-floppers," she tells him.

"Blake." I sigh. "It's the middle of winter. We save flip-flops for the summer."

"See," she tells my dad.

"Sorry, princess, I think your dad's right with this one. What would you do if your toes froze off?"

She gasps. "I thought Daddy was joking me."

The room erupts with laughter, and the little ham that she is, my daughter grins and soaks up the attention. "Still grumpy," she says, smiling over Dad's shoulder at me. I blow her a kiss, and she catches it and holds it next to her heart.

"Are Brooks and Palmer home yet?" I ask.

"Yeah," Sterling answers. "They're on their way."

"Newlyweds," Archer jokes.

"Just wait, son." Dad points at him.

"Not for a long time, old man," Archer replies.

Archer is twenty-three and is in no hurry to settle down. None of us have been in any kind of hurry. Well, besides Orrin. I'm still shocked he hasn't proposed to Jade yet. We all know he's crazy about her. I'm sure he's just giving Brooks and Palmer their time in the spotlight.

"Where are the twins?" I ask Rushton.

"They went to some kind of indoor swim park or something." He shrugs. "They're not going to be home until late. Apparently, it's the best place to pick up girls." I can hear the sarcasm in his voice. At twenty-five, Rushton has had his fill of chasing women. We all grow out of it at some point in our lives.

"That explains why the house is so quiet." Rushton chuckles, as do Sterling and Archer.

"That smells amazing, Mom," Ryder says, stepping into the kitchen. "Can we eat now?" He sticks his bottom lip out in a pout. That would have worked for him fifteen years ago. He's all grown up now, and Mom stopped giving into us years ago. Well, unless we're with her on our own or just with a few of us. Never when we're all together. She thinks she's being sly, but we all know she's a sucker for her boys.

"We have to wait on your brothers and their wives."

"Did Orrin and Jade get married, and I wasn't invited?" I tease.

"Oh, hush." She waves me off. "We all know it's going to happen. It's easier to bundle her in with Palmer." Mom grins. She can't hide the fact that she's thrilled that her sons are settling down and finding the loves of their lives.

"Ramsey and Deacon will be here soon too. So no, you can't eat now." She gives Ryder a pointed look, and he carries on with the pout, knowing it's not doing him a damn bit of good.

The front door opens, and I hear my daughter yell, "My girls," and I laugh. The house gets louder as Ramsey, Deacon, Brooks, Palmer, Orrin, and Jade all filter into the room.

"Did you all carpool or something?" Sterling asks them.

"No, but we couldn't do that again if we tried," Orrin comments.

"Come eat." Mom waves to the Crock-Pot of baked steak and the counter full of fixings to go with it.

"Ladies first," Dad says as if we need a reminder.

We all hang back while Mom, Jade, Ramsey, and Palmer make their plates. I'm right behind them with a plate for Blakely, carrying it to the table so she can sit beside my mom as she requested.

The rest of us make our plates, and we spread them out all over the house. Brooks, Declan, and Orrin are all sitting at the table with the women, while Dad and the rest of us sit at the island and the couch, basically anywhere we can find a seat. Our parents have a dining table that seats twelve, but we've long since outgrown that. I heard Mom talking to Dad a few weeks ago that their next project might be adding on a larger dining room so that everyone can sit together. I hate to break it to her, but with nine boys, potentially nine wives, and future kids, that's gonna have to be a big-ass table.

Conversation and laughter fill the house just as it always does when we all get together. For such a big family, we are all getting along really well. Sure, there were arguments between us growing up, but no matter what, we've always got each other's back.

"That was delicious, Momma," Ryder says, stopping by the table to drop a kiss on her cheek.

"What about me, Uncle Ryder? Don't I get a kiss?"

"Blake, you're going to be a high-maintenance girlfriend one day," he teases.

She nods and smiles like he just gave her the best compliment of her life. "And a wife too. Like Palmer and Ramsey." She turns and looks over at Jade. "Are you gonna be a wife? I told Daddy we need one of those," she rambles on.

Jade opens her mouth to speak, but Orrin beats her to it. "Yes, she is." He sets his plate on the coffee table and moves to stand behind her chair. Jade tilts her head back to smile at him, and something tells me that this is it. This is his moment.

"Stand for me." His voice is soft. The same voice he uses with Blakely or our mom.

Jade pushes back from the table and stands as he asks her to. "Orrin?" There's a quiver in her voice. She knows just like we do what's about to happen. He didn't tell any of us, yet we all knew it was inevitable. We all remain not only silent but still, even Blakely. We don't want to miss this.

"I wanted to do this when we were all together—" he starts, just as the sound of the front door opens.

"We're home," Maverick calls out.

"Damn, that smells good," Merrick mutters. "We should have just stayed home."

They walk into the room and still. "What's going on?" Maverick asks.

Orrin laughs. "As I was saying, I wanted to do this when we were all together, and it looks like my little brothers had some kind of ESP today." He smiles at Jade and drops to one knee. "I love you." His voice is strong. Clear. "I know that I don't want to live this life without you by my side." His voice cracks.

"Yes," Jade says. She leans over and kisses him.

"Babe, I haven't asked you yet."

"Sorry." She laughs, as do the rest of us.

"Jade Sanders, will you do me the incredible honor of being my wife? Will you marry me?" He opens up the ring box, and I'm not close enough to get a good look at it, but I can see the sparkle and shine from here. I'm guessing from the gasp that leaves the ladies, my big bro made a good choice on the ring.

Jade nods, tears racing down her cheeks. "Now's the time to say yes," Ramsey reminds her.

She wipes at her cheeks as Orrin stands. "Yes. Yes. Yes." She throws her arms around his neck, and he twirls her around.

"Uncle O, I'm next," Blakely calls out.

I just shake my head at my daughter and my brother, who obliges her by lifting her in the air and spinning her around. "She said yes."

When he puts Blakely on her feet, she giggles and stumbles over to where I'm sitting on the couch. She crawls up into my lap, and I hug her tight. I relish these moments. She's growing up so fast that I know that it won't be long before hugging me will be the last thing she wants to do.

"Daddy?"

"Yeah, baby?"

"We'll find ours." She pats my shoulder.

"Our what?"

"Our wife. Mamaw says that love takes time, so we just have to be potent."

"Patient," I correct her.

"Yeah, that."

"I love you, Blakely. You are the only woman I need." It's not a lie, but flashes of Kennedy float through my mind. I've done nothing but think about her, and I don't know how I feel about that.

We all take turns congratulating the happy couple when Mom announces that she's taking dinner next door to Maureen and Kennedy. "I'll take it," I offer quietly.

"Thank you." Mom smiles at me. It's not just a smile. It's one of those mom smiles that tells you they know more than what you want them to know, but they're staying quiet and giving you time to come clean. Yeah, it's one of those.

She packs up everything, and I slip into my coat and boots. I call out for my daughter, telling her to be good, and make sure they all know I'm stepping out for Mom, of course, and pull the door closed behind me.

I opt to walk to clear my head instead of driving. The distance between the two places isn't more than about five hundred feet or so. I had hoped that Kennedy and I could get together yesterday, but Maureen wasn't feeling well, so she opted to stay in. I get it. That's why she's here, but I was also disappointed. Thankfully I didn't mention the possibility of seeing her to Blakely. She would have been disappointed.

Stepping onto the porch, I rap my knuckles on the door and take a step back. I rock back on my heels as I wait for her to answer the door. When it finally opens, I smile and wave.

"Declan?" Kennedy pushes open the storm door. "What are you doing here?"

I lift the bag of food my mom packed up. "I brought dinner. Mom made baked steak, and she asked me to deliver this." I hold the bag up again. It's one little white lie.

"That's so sweet of her." She pushes the door open wider and steps back. "Come in out of the cold."

"Kennedy? Who's there?" Maureen calls out.

"Before you go in there, I just want to apologize in advance for anything that she might say that's offensive or presumptuous."

"I've met Maureen many times," I remind her.

"I know, but not since she's convinced that I'm destined to be with you or one of your brothers. The seven that aren't attached, of course." She playfully rolls her eyes.

"What?" I choke out.

"You know how she is, or if you don't, I can only tell you that my grandma, she gets these crazy ideas in her head and won't let them go. One of them was selling her home in Florida and moving to Willow River. Well, that one actually turned out okay." She waves her hand in the air. "Anyway, she's got herself convinced that I'm destined to be with a Kincaid brother. Just ignore her, and I'm sorry in advance."

"Me." I don't even think before I say it. I stand here with my heart beating out of my chest waiting for her to reply. I didn't think before I spoke, but that doesn't mean I wasn't serious.

"What?" She tilts her head to the side, her brown locks moving over her shoulder.

"Me. If she wants you with a Kincaid brother, it's going to be me." She opens her mouth as if she's going to respond but quickly shuts it. I lean in and press my lips to her cheek. Her skin is soft, and smooth, and I have to push down the desire to kiss every inch of her skin. "I missed seeing you yesterday." With that, I walk away and head to the living room. I act as if my own words haven't caused a riot inside my chest. I've been here several times to pick Blakely up when she's here visiting with my mom, so I know the way.

"Declan. What a nice surprise." Maureen's smile is wide and genuine, and since I know her plan, maybe a little devious.

"It's good to see you, Maureen." I hold up the bag of food. "Mom sent dinner. You know she cooks for our small army every Sunday."

"Oh, that was nice of her."

"I'll just put it in the kitchen. Are you hungry now?" I ask.

"I think I'll save it for later. Kennedy made a late lunch of soup and grilled cheese. One of her favorites and one of mine as well."

"That's a staple in my house as well. Blakely is all about grilled cheese and dipping it into her soup."

"How is that sweet girl of yours?"

"Rotten as ever." I laugh.

"Oh, she's a sweet thing." She waves off my comment.

"That she is, but she's sweet and rotten."

"Sit. Sit. How have you been?"

"Doing well. How are you feeling?"

"Kennedy has been taking great care of me. She's a good one to have around."

"I bet she is." I rub my hand over my face to hide my smile.

"What's this I hear about you and my granddaughter having dinner?"

"There's not much to tell. We had dinner, watched a movie with Blake, and then another after she went to bed."

"You need a good woman in your life," she tells me.

It's cracking me up that she's not even trying to be subtle about it. I decide to play her game. "You think so, Maureen? Do you have anyone in mind?" I ask, already knowing her answer.

"Possibly. How do you feel about marriage?" she asks.

"I think marriage is great if you can find someone you want to spend the rest of your life with. In fact, my brother Orrin just asked Jade to marry him earlier."

"Did he?" Maureen asks.

"That's incredible," Kennedy speaks up. "I'm so happy for them." The sincerity in her voice tugs at something in my chest.

"It was a spur-of-the-moment kind of thing, but we were all there to witness it."

"Oh, I love a good wedding," Maureen says. "I'm sorry I missed Brooks and Palmer's. Kennedy assured me, as did your mom, that everything was perfect."

"It was perfect, and they couldn't be happier. Your manor was the perfect place for them to marry."

"What about you? Have you ever thought about where you'll get married?" she asks.

I laugh. "Can't say that I have."

"Any plans to leave Willow River?"

"No, ma'am. My business is here. My family is here, and as a single father, I rely on them more than I care to admit. Blake needs family around her, and frankly, so do I."

"Kennedy, did you hear that? He's a family man."

"I heard." Kennedy playfully rolls her eyes and sticks her tongue out at me.

"I'm famished. Declan, be a dear and help Kennedy make me a plate. She's been feeling unwell today."

My head snaps to Kennedy. "What's wrong?"

"Nothing. I'm perfectly fine."

"She has a headache. She's needs a nice strong man to take care of her." Maureen nods slowly.

"Grandma!" Kennedy shrieks. "Where is your filter?"

Maureen shrugs. "What's a filter?"

"You sit. I'll make you both a plate." I won't comment on how just minutes ago, when I arrived, Maureen was still full from lunch.

"Oh, Kennedy, you better go make sure he doesn't need any help."

"No." I stand and look at Kennedy. "I can do this without help." I then turn to face Maureen. "What kind of man would I be if I let her help me when I'm capable on my own and she's not feeling well? I can manage to pop the two dishes into the microwave." I don't wait for her to reply as my feet carry me back to the kitchen.

I can hear hushed voices, but I tune them out. I busy myself warming the two plates Mom sent with me. Once one is finished, I pop in the next and carry the first to Maureen. "Miss Maureen," I say, charming her. At least, I hope that I am. "This one is for you. Would you like something to drink?"

"Declan, she's fine."

"Oh, dear, I'd love a glass of sweet tea. Kennedy just made a fresh pitcher. Pour a glass for yourself," she says, digging into the dinner I place on the TV tray in front of her.

"Kens? Sweet tea?" I ask.

"I can get it." She starts to stand, but I hold my hand up to stop her. "Let me do this for you."

"Declan, she's exaggerating. I'm fine."

"Regardless, let me take care of you." I bop her on the nose, but what I really want to do is kiss her. I won't have my second taste of her to be with Maureen as a witness. She would never let us live it down, and the entire town of Willow River would know by morning.

By the time I deliver Kennedy her meal and pour three glasses of sweet tea, I realize I've been here for longer than anticipated. It's not a problem, my family knows where I am, and I know that my daughter is in good hands. But it is a problem because my brothers are never going to let me hear the end of this. At least I can say that Maureen was chatty from being cooped up in the house from her broken leg.

I doubt they'll buy it, but it's my story, and I'm sticking to it. Besides, it's not a complete lie. She is a Chatty Cathy tonight, but I don't mind. I get to see Kennedy, even if it is with her grandma telling me about her menstrual cycle. Women sure did get the short end of the stick as far as that goes. I shudder at the thought of dealing with what they have to endure on a monthly basis. I'm man enough to admit that men, as a species, couldn't handle it. That's why God shouldered the task to the woman.

"Why don't you kids go grab some dessert or something?" Maureen suggests, pulling me out of my thoughts.

"I have to get back." I stand from my seat on the couch. I down the remainder of my tea and rinse my glass before placing it in the sink. "If you ladies need anything, just call me."

"We're fine, but thank you for dinner. Please tell your mom it was delicious," Kennedy says politely. "I'll walk you to the door."

Once we reach the door, I pull her into my arms. "You doing okay?"

"You mean other than being embarrassed? Yeah, I'm fine."

I rest my palm against her cheek. "Call me if you need me."

"I'll be just fine. I have everything I need."

"Yeah, but if you don't, it's me who takes care of that for you."

"You're... a lot to take on."

"You'll get used to it." I press a kiss on her forehead. "Lock up behind me."

"Yes, Dad," she teases.

I chuckle under my breath as I cut back across the yard back to my parents' place. Suddenly, I'm no longer grumpy, as Blakely claimed. I just needed a little Kennedy in my life, it seems.

Chapter 11

KENNEDY

"OH, PHOOEY," GRANDMA SAYS FROM her chair as soon as I enter the room. I just finished cleaning up the kitchen from breakfast.

I raise my eyebrow in question, and she grins. She holds my gaze, and I know she's waiting for me to respond. "What is it?" I ask, afraid of what the answer will be.

She places her phone facedown on her lap. I raise my eyebrows in suspicion but wait for her to release whatever bomb she's about to drop on me.

"I forgot that my car is due for an oil change. I just got my confirmation text." She nods toward where her phone lies in her lap.

"Oh." That's not at all what I was expecting. "I can take care of that. Where does it need to go?"

"Kincaid's Auto Repair." She smirks. "You know where that's at in town, right?"

"I'm sure I can figure it out," I tell her. I'm proud of myself for keeping my voice steady when I'm quivering inside at the mere thought of getting to see Declan.

"Oh, good. You have to be there at noon."

"Noon. Got it. I'm going to get in the shower. Do you need anything?"

"No. Thank you, Kennedy. I'm so glad that you're here."

My shoulders fall. Now I feel guilty for thinking the worst of her. But in my defense, meddling should have been her middle name. It's her favorite pastime. "I'm glad I'm here too. We have a baby shower at the manor Sunday, but nothing else, right?" I just want to make sure I stay on top of the manor's schedule, along with taking care of Grandma and maintaining my editing schedule. It's a lot more to juggle than I'm used to.

I take my time in the shower and let my mind drift to Declan. I haven't seen him since Sunday. We've texted a few times, but that's it. He did ask me to dinner on Wednesday night with the two of them, but Grandma had a late doctor's appointment, and we stopped to eat afterward. She's been cooped up in the house.

He asked about this weekend, and I said maybe. I know that I'm divorced, but it feels wrong to have these kinds of feelings for a man so soon after a divorce. And not I'm-in-love-with-him feelings, although Declan would be easy to fall in love with if the time I've already spent with him is any indication.

It's the chemistry between us. It's unlike anything I've ever felt. If he's close, I want to be next to him. And the blushing. Dear lord, I'm a grown woman. I should not be blushing, yet when Declan is around, I can't seem to control it.

Then there's the way my heart races, my palms break out in a sweat, and there is an ache between my thighs. These are all new concepts for me when it comes to a man. Just another glaring reminder that Lyle and I never should have married.

Speaking of my ex-husband. Well, the papers are filed. It's just a formality from the courts at this point. I haven't spoken to him since the night he dropped by with the papers for me to sign. I should be upset about that, right? Instead, all I can think about is Declan and how I feel like my younger self anytime he's nearby.

After finishing my shower, I take extra time to get ready. I tell myself it's because I've been lounging around all week, but it's a lie. I don't know if I'll get to see Declan today, but I'm going to his shop, and that's more than enough motivation to put a little extra into my appearance.

I find Grandma in the living room crocheting. "Whatcha making?"

"A baby blanket."

"For Palmer?"

"Not yet. I don't know what they're having. Do you?" she asks.

"No. I don't think they know yet."

She nods. "This one is for the hospital. I like to make them and donate them to the new families."

"That's really sweet of you, Grandma."

She smiles. "I love to crochet, but I can only make you so many scarfs, sweaters, and blankets before your house is overflowing."

"Good point." She's not wrong. I have so many items that she's made for me, but I can't part with any of them. I love them all so much, knowing they were made with love from her. Not only that, but I know she's not going to be with us forever. There will come a day that she passes, and I'll have every single item she's made me to remember her by. Not that I'll need them. Grandma Maureen is not someone you can easily forget, but I'll feel like she's there with me. I already do when I'm at home, and she's here. Her presence is all over my house.

"Do you need anything from town?" I ask her.

"Not that I can think of. Take your time, dear. The key's on the hook by the door."

"Thanks, Grandma. I'm sure an oil change won't take long. Call me or text me if you think of something." I bend down to kiss her cheek before grabbing my purse, sliding into my coat and boots, and heading out the door.

To Declan.

I find his shop easy enough. Willow River is a small town, and his garage is right on the main strip. I also found Orrin's body shop and Palmer's photography studio. The Kincaid family has roots all over this town.

The lot of Kincaid's Auto Repair is jam-packed, but I'm able to find a spot in the back. Pulling down the visor, I check my hair and the light makeup I put on. I don't want to look eager, but I also want him to take notice. Making sure I have my purse, my phone, and my keys, I climb out of the car and head inside.

The chime on the door alerts whoever needs to know of my presence. A tall guy with shaggy brown hair and his face covered in something black that looks a lot like grease pulls open a service door and peeks his head inside.

"Can I help you?" he asks.

"Hi." I wave. "I'm Kennedy Edwards. My grandma Maureen Hoffman has an appointment for an oil change today."

He wipes his hand on a red shop towel that he produces from his back pocket. "I thought all the cars on the schedule had already been dropped off. Let me take a look." Shoving the towel back into his pocket, he wiggles the mouse and begins to hit a few keys on the keyboard. "What's the name again?" he asks.

"I've got this, Gus," a voice I know all too well says from behind me.

"Oh, is this the add-in?" the guy I know now as Gus asks.

"She is. I've got it."

"Sure thing, boss." He winks at me before disappearing behind the service door once again.

"It's good to see you, Kennedy."

"You too." Then something he said registers. "Did he say that you worked me in today?"

He nods. "Yeah, Maureen said her car was making some kind of grinding noise, and she didn't feel comfortable with you driving it."

"Unbelievable." I blow out an exasperated breath. "I'm sorry, Declan. She lied to you."

A slow, sexy grin lifts his lips. "Her car's not making a grinding noise?"

"No. She told me it was an oil change appointment that she forgot about." Hiking my purse up on my shoulder, I look out at the full lot and realize he was adding us into his already packed schedule. "I'm sorry," I say, my eyes going back to him. "You're slammed today, and you were obviously making an exception for us. I didn't mean to waste your time. I'll talk to her." I turn to walk away, but he grabs my wrist, halting me.

"Hey, it's not a big deal. We could have made it happen."

"She has to stop this meddling."

"She really does want to marry you off, huh?" He grins.

"Not just marry me off, but apparently, she's decided it's going to be you."

His grin grows wider. "She has good taste."

"I'm not debating that. But she can't just will something to happen, and it comes true. Not only that, but this is your business. This is how you put a roof over your head and food in your daughter's belly. She's messing with that."

"By giving me more work?" He quirks an eyebrow. "Kennedy, I'm telling you it's fine. In fact, it's more than fine. It's been too damn long since I've laid eyes on you."

He takes a step closer and gently tugs at one of my curls that I spent extra time with the curling iron for this morning. "Have lunch with me."

Before I have a chance to answer, the door chimes. On instinct, we both turn to look and see a smiling Brooks. "Fancy seeing you here." He leans in and kisses my cheek.

"Brooks, good to see you. How's married life?"

"Fucking fantastic." The smile that lights up his face could light up every single house in Willow River with how electric it is.

"How's Palmer been feeling?" I ask.

"She's perfect. No nausea. Just perfect." My heart swells and cracks a little at the same time. I'm happy for the two of them, but I'm sad for myself. I want a partner in my life who will be thrilled to be a parent with me. No matter how we have to go about it.

"What's up?" Declan asks.

"I came to see if we can have Blakely tomorrow?"

"Sure, you know she loves spending time with you all."

"I promised Palmer, the last time we were there, that I'd take her back to the aquarium so she could bring her camera. I thought Blakely would enjoy it too. Give me some practice for what's to come."

"Like you need practice," Declan scoffs. "You've been there every step of the way with Blakely. You all have. You're going to rock being a dad, B."

"It seems like it's so far away," Brooks comments.

"Trust me. The baby will be here before you know it. Blakely will love spending the day with the two of you. Thank you for taking her."

"I was thinking we'd come and get her tonight. Let her spend the night, and then we'll head out in the morning. If that's all right with you."

"Sure." Declan looks at me and smirks.

"Thanks, man. I know you'll want to see her after working all day. Just shoot me a text when you're ready, and we'll come and pick her up."

"I can drop her off to you."

"Nah, you know she likes riding in my truck. Besides, I have a car seat, and you need a night off. You're always in dad mode, man. Take a night for yourself." He looks over at me. "Kennedy, good to see you again." With that, he waves and walks out the door.

"Well, it looks as though I find myself needing some company this evening. Dinner?"

"Dinner sounds nice. Let me know when and where." On the outside, I'm cool as a cucumber. On the inside, I'm shaking like a leaf. I've been out of the dating game so long that I'm not even really sure how this is supposed to work anymore, but I'm rolling with it. I might be recently divorced, but it's been months since my marriage ended. Declan is the perfect man for me to jump back into the dating scene with. He'll be like my practice run for when I get home and start focusing on the rest of my life.

"When, let's say seven or so. I'll head out of here right at five to get Blake from my parents.' I'll spend a little time with her, help her pack her bag, and once Brooks picks her up, I'll head your way."

"Okay."

"That was a hell of a lot easier than I anticipated." He steps closer until we're standing nose to nose. "You and me," he says huskily.

"While I'm here," I agree.

He places a tender kiss on the corner of my mouth. "Lunch?"

"I should let you get back to work."

"Not until you have lunch with me. You have to eat, right? Is Maureen expecting you?"

"Right." I chuckle. "You know she's not."

"Then have lunch with me." His hand lands on my hip, giving it a soft squeeze.

"How about I run to the diner and grab us something? We can eat it here. In your office?"

"Are you trying to get out of spending time with me?"

"I literally just agreed to dinner tonight."

"And lunch today?"

"Let me bring something back for us. That way I'm not taking up more of your already booked day. That's the least I can do with Grandma calling and forcing you to add me into your schedule."

"She didn't force me, Kens. And it's not just Maureen. This is my town. I grew up here, and although Maureen might not be a lifelong resident like the rest of us, she's still a citizen of Willow River. I'd take care of any of them the way I offered to your grandmother this morning."

"And it has nothing to do with me?"

"Nope. However, don't mistake that to mean that I didn't want to see you. My day got a whole hell of a lot brighter when I found out I'd be seeing you today. It's been too damn long."

"Not even a full seven days," I remind him.

"Too. Damn. Long."

I melt at his words, my body feeling all warm and gooey on the inside. "What do you want from the diner?" I ask him, pretending his words didn't affect me like they did.

"Whatever is on special is fine. I have drinks here. I keep the fridge in my office stocked."

"Should I see if any of the guys want anything?"

"Nah, they like to go down as a group and eat together."

"Well, all right then. I'll be back."

He engulfs me in a hug and whispers, "Hurry."

When he releases me, it's on shaky legs, but I manage to maintain my composure as I walk back out in the frigid January air. Sliding behind the wheel, I let the engine warm up a little before I pull out on the road and head a few blocks down to Dorothy's Diner. It's a short drive and would have been a great walk on a warmer day.

When I pull open the door, the warmth and the smells of home cooking wash over me like a warm embrace. Taking a seat at the counter, I grab a menu and begin to look at my options.

"Hey, darlin,' what can I get you?" an older lady asks, pulling a pen out from behind her ear.

"What's on special today?"

"We have meatloaf, mashed potatoes, green beans, and dinner roll."

"I'll take two of those, please. To go."

"You're new in town?"

"I am. I'm Maureen Hoffman's granddaughter. I'm staying with her while she's healing from her broken leg."

"Oh, well, you don't want two meatloaf dinners. Maureen swears hers is better than mine. You'll never hear the end of it." She laughs, and it shakes her entire body.

"Oh, this isn't for her. It's for a friend and me."

"A friend, you say? Anyone I know?"

"I'm guessing my little brother." I hear from behind me.

Turning to look over my shoulder, I see Orrin smiling. "How are you doing, Kennedy?"

"I'm doing well. How about you?"

"Living the dream." He nods to the older lady. "That for Dec?"

"Yes. He— Yes." There is no point in trying to explain how I ended up at his shop today.

"Do I need to have a talk with my little brother about him making you get him lunch?" he asks, crossing his arms over his chest.

"Little?" I laugh. All nine of the Kincaid boys are built like brick houses.

"I'm the oldest."

"I bet there was never a dull moment growing up in your house."

"Nope." Orrin grins.

"I offered to pick up lunch for him. I was there, and he looked busy, and well, we all gotta eat."

"That we do, little lady. I'll get this right out for you. Orrin, you want the same?"

"Yes, ma'am."

"Congratulations on your engagement."

He nods. "Thanks. We'll be reaching out to you or your grandma about the manor."

"Oh, is this going to be soon?" I ask him.

"Damn, I hope so. We haven't set a date, but the sooner, the better."

"Here you go." Dorothy sets two bags on the counter. One for me and one for Orrin.

"Thank you." I hand her my card. "I've got him too."

"No. You are not buying my lunch."

"Too late. Consider it a happy engagement lunch."

"My fiancée isn't here."

"Does she need to be for you to celebrate the fact that she's agreed to be your wife?"

"No. No, she does not. Thank you for lunch, Kennedy. Next time it's on me."

"You've got a deal."

He holds the door for me as we walk outside and head to our cars. "Kennedy!" he calls out.

I stop. "Yeah?"

"Tell my little brother I said hello." He winks, climbs in his truck, and pulls out onto the road.

I've only been in Willow River for a few weeks, but it feels like I've lived here all my life. No wonder Grandma fell in love with this place. The charm isn't just the area or this little town. It's the people in it.

Chapter 12

DECLAN

AS SOON AS BROOKS AND Palmer back out of my driveway, I grab my keys and my phone and head to the garage. I've dated a few times over the years, and I can't ever remember being this excited about any of them.

They weren't with Kennedy.

The more time I spend with her, the more of her time that I crave. That's why when I pull into her grandma's driveway, I leave the truck running and rush to the door, rapping my knuckles against the metal three times. I'm eager to see her, to soak up more of her time.

"Hey." She pulls open the door.

"Gorgeous." The word falls from my lips easily. She smiles shyly.

"Let me grab my coat. Do you want to come in?" she offers.

"I'll just wait here. I love Maureen, but I'm a selfish bastard tonight when it comes to you. I want you all to myself."

"I'll be right back." She closes the door and reappears, calling "Goodbye" over her shoulder. She steps out onto the porch, and I wrap my arms around her in a hug.

"Damn, you smell good." I put just a little space between us. Lacing her fingers with mine, I lead her to my Tahoe. I help her inside and rush around to the driver's side, sliding behind the wheel.

"So where are we headed?" she asks as we pull out of the driveway.

"I thought we could drive to Harris. There are several restaurants and steak houses to choose from, and then maybe a movie? Sterling and his best friend, Alyssa, are at the Willow Tavern tonight. We could go there if you want."

"Honestly, I don't care what we do. It's just nice to get out. I love my grandma, but she can be a lot. She has a few friends from her sewing club coming over and bringing dinner tonight. I swear she assumed we would end up with plans tonight."

"She's a riot." I shake my head. "I didn't know she was this sneaky until you came to town."

"She's a hot mess, Declan."

I can't help but laugh softly at her exasperation. My phone rings and I accept the call on the dash. "Hey, Sterling. You're on speaker. I have Kennedy with me."

"Hey, Kennedy," Sterling says.

"Hi." She waves at the dash as if she can see him. Cute as hell.

"Did you decide if you want to meet up?" Sterling asks.

"We were just talking about it." I don't voice that I want her to myself. I'm hoping she chooses for it just to be us. "Kinda thinking getting out of Willow River is where we're headed." I drop a hint.

"Why don't you all join us?" Kennedy asks.

I bite back a groan. We were almost home free. "Dinner and a movie," she adds helpfully.

"I'm almost at Alyssa's place. Let me ask her. She had plans with some douche who canceled on her last minute hence the best friend rescue. Let me see where her head is, and I'll call you right back."

"Sounds good." I end the call on my steering wheel. "How about we just cruise around town until we hear from them?" I suggest.

"Sounds good to me. So Sterling and Alyssa are just friends?"

"Yeah. They've been friends forever. Hell, kindergarten, maybe? I don't really remember. I just know Alyssa has always been around."

"And they've never dated?"

"Not that I'm aware of. They're both adamant that it's platonic between them. Sometimes they act like a couple, but I think it's just because they've been friends for so long."

"What about you? I know about you and Cassie. Anyone before or after her worth mentioning?"

"No. I've dated here and there. It's never gone past one date. I don't know if it's because I just wasn't interested or if I was too focused on being a single father to give any of them a real shot."

"Pappa Bear," she teases as my phone rings again.

"What's up?" I say, after accepting the call on the dash.

"We're in. Alyssa is all about getting out of Willow River for the night. Where do you want to meet?"

"I'll just swing by her place. Kens and I are just riding around town right now anyway."

"Sounds good. See you in a few." The call ends.

"I guess we have guests for the night."

"You don't sound happy about that?"

"Is it selfish that I want you all to myself?"

"Not selfish. Sweet. It's been a long time since anyone has wanted me all to themselves."

"Lyle?" I ask her.

"He was good to me. He loved me, but I don't think either one of us were ever in love. You know that deep 'feel the other person in your soul' kind of love. We just stayed together because it was comfortable." She releases a heavy sigh. "Lesson learned. I'll never settle for less than the kind of love you only see on the big screen or read about in books. Maybe it's because I work mostly with romance authors, and I made myself believe that kind of love was fictional."

"It's not. Look at my parents, hell, two of my brothers, and my sister, well, Ramsey," I amend, "have found that kind of love. And your parents, they're still together, right?"

"They are. They're still madly in love. I guess I just lost my way. I went with easy."

"No judgment here. I got drunk, slept with my best friend, and got her pregnant." I chuckle under my breath. I can laugh about it now. It still hurts that Cassie is gone, but I have the best part of her still with me. She lives through our daughter every single day.

"What is it with you Kincaid men having women as best friends?" Her voice is lighter, and I'm glad that the heavy of the conversation has passed.

I chuckle. "Just Sterling and me. Maybe we're just big ole softies?" I've already got a soft spot for her, so it's a valid assumption.

"Oh, that's a given. Have you seen all of you with your daughter? So soft," she teases as I turn into Alyssa's driveway.

Sterling and Alyssa come out of the house. He opens the back door, and Alyssa steps in, moving to the passenger seat while Sterling sits behind me. "Good to see you again, Kennedy," he says. "You remember Alyssa?"

Kennedy turns in her seat to look at them. "Hi, yes. Good to see you both."

"So where are we headed? I'm starving," he asks.

"You're always starving," Alyssa reminds him.

"Hush, woman. It takes a lot to fuel this." I don't have to glance in the rearview mirror to know that he's motioning toward his body. We all like to stay fit, and we've all been known to boast about it from time to time.

"So cocky," Alyssa replies, and it's a line I've heard her say to him. Hell, she's said that same line to all of us many times over the years.

"What are you in the mood for?" Kennedy turns in her seat again, and I can tell from the angle she's asking Alyssa. Sterling and I both keep our mouths shut because we know damn well if the ladies make a decision, that's where we're going.

"What about Mexican? I'm craving some chicken maxi and a margarita."

"Yes! Oh, nachos." Kennedy hums, and my cock thickens at the sound. She turns back around and settles into her seat. I glance over, making sure she's still buckled in, before putting my eyes back on the road.

"What do you think, Declan? Mexican."

"Done."

"Sterling?" Kennedy turns her head to ask his opinion.

"The ladies have spoken," he quips, making her laugh.

I love the way the sound wraps around me. I've been on a few dates where the woman was fake, from her tits to the pound of makeup on her face, to her laugh. There is nothing fake about Kennedy. She is who she is, and she embraces that. I love that about her.

"Just like that? No arguments?"

I can feel her gaze. "No arguments. We like Mexican, so why would we?" I ask her.

I watch her out of the corner of my eye as she shrugs. "Just not something I'm used to."

Reaching over, I take her hand in mine, lacing our fingers together and resting our joined hands on her thigh. "Looking forward," I say softly, hoping my brother and his best friend are ignoring us. They're chattering back and forth, so I'd say my chances of that are good.

"Looking forward." She nods.

I know that she said that they never should have married, but he doesn't sound like he was very loving or romantic. The selfish bastard didn't appreciate what he had.

"All you want is nachos?" I ask Kennedy.

"Have you seen a plate of nachos? They're huge, and I won't be able to eat it all, but I'm craving them."

"She's right," Alyssa chimes in. "It's a huge plate of chips and beans, and chicken, and sour cream, and lettuce, and all the wonderful things."

Kennedy raises her hand over the table for a high five, and Alyssa slaps her palm. "I'll share them with you," she assures her.

"Maybe just one," Alyssa agrees.

"You and I both know you can't have just one."

"Damn you. Now I want nachos." Sterling laughs as our server drops off our drinks. "Can we add another nacho supreme, please?"

"Yes, sir," the server agrees and scurries off to add it to our order.

"You could have had some of mine," Kennedy tells him.

"Trust me, Kennedy, it's better that he has his own. This guy"—Alyssa points her thumb at Sterling—"can put away the food."

The four of us fall into easy conversation throughout dinner. Kennedy fits in with us as if she's been a part of our lives just as long as Alyssa has. There are a few times we have to explain what we're talking about, but that's all a part of the getting-to-know-each-other process.

"Now what?" Alyssa asks as we exit the restaurant.

"I just checked on Grandma." Kennedy holds up her phone. "She's still sewing her little heart away with her sewing club, so I'm good with whatever."

"Why don't we just go back to my place?" Alyssa suggests. "That way, we're close if Maureen needs you. We can watch a movie or play cards."

"Wait. Kennedy, your answer to this is important. Are you ready?" Sterling asks her.

"Oh, boy," she says, and I can hear the smile in her voice.

"Do you know how to play euchre?"

"Yep."

"Are you any good?" he counters.

"I do all right."

"Do you know the left from the right bowers?" he challenges.

"I guess you're just going to have to wait and find out."

"Dec, take us back to Alyssa's. We have to find out how well your girl plays. This is important."

"Did you ask Palmer the same?" Kennedy teases.

"I didn't have to. I knew she could play."

I reach over the console and place my hand on her thigh. I can't seem to help myself where she's concerned. If she's close, I want to be touching her. "We'll show them how it's done, Kens."

"Damn right," she easily agrees, resting her hand over mine. Using her thumb, she traces over my knuckles, and it's driving me wild. How is it such a simple touch can have my cock painfully pressing behind my zipper?

Eventually, she entwines her fingers with mine, and that's how we remain until I pull my Tahoe into Alyssa's driveway and park behind Sterling.

"Come on." Alyssa links her arm through Kennedy's and leads her into the house while Sterling and I trail behind them.

"What's up with the two of you?" he asks me.

"Honestly, I don't know."

"I like her."

"I do too." I rest my hand on his shoulder as we make our way up the steps of Alyssa's front porch. "I do too."

"So we decided we're partners," Alyssa announces when we walk into the kitchen.

"Nope." Sterling walks behind her and wraps his arms around her, lifting her into the air. "You're always my partner."

"Maybe it's time to change things up," Alyssa tells him.

"Not happening, Tink."

"Tink?" Kennedy asks.

Alyssa rolls her eyes dramatically. "He calls me Tink." She points over her shoulder where Sterling still has her wrapped up in his arms. "Because I'm smaller than him."

"Come on. You're a tiny thing, not just standing next to me."

"I'm built low for stability," she counters. "Besides, five foot five is not that short."

"Babe, I'm six foot three. That's almost a full foot taller than you."

"Oh, hush." She swats at his hands that are clasped at her chest but makes no move to get free.

"Kennedy and I already had plans to hand your asses to you anyway, right, Kens?" I slide my arm around her waist, letting my hand rest on her hip.

"Yep."

"Fine, but next time, it's me and you," Alyssa tells Kennedy. "Girl power and all that."

Kennedy chuckles. "Deal."

Sterling digs the cards out of the drawer in the kitchen while Alyssa grabs us all a bottle of water from the fridge. We settle around her small four-person kitchen table as Sterling deals the cards.

We laugh, trash talk, and chat about anything and everything. I tell Sterling that Brooks and Palmer are taking Blakely to the aquarium tomorrow. Alyssa complains about her job at the local doctor's office.

"I've been there for five years, and that witch, Tamara, keeps promoting everyone but me. I bust my ass for her," Alyssa complains.

"What does she have against you?" Kennedy asks.

"Is it that obvious?" Alyssa replies with a heavy sigh. "We were all at the Willow Tavern one night, and her then fiancé, now husband, was there. He was hitting on me, and she caught him. She claims it was my fault. That I was coming onto him. She's hated me and made my life miserable ever since."

"Why don't you find another job?"

Alyssa shrugs. "I went to the vocational school for secretarial. I love what I do, just not who I do it for, if that makes sense."

"It does, but you deserve better. If you're not going to go to her boss about the way she's treating you, maybe you should look for a new job. You can still work in the same capacity, just in a different environment."

"You're right," Alyssa agrees as her cell rings.

She answers the call, and her shoulders drop. By the sound of it, someone is canceling plans on her.

"Well, Kristy and Jerry canceled on us for tomorrow night," Alyssa tells Sterling. "I guess he did something to his back at work today and going to a concert no longer sounds like a good time."

"Damn," Sterling mutters before his gaze finds mine. "Why don't the two of you go with us?"

"Where?" Kennedy asks.

"Brett Young."

I watch her closely, and her eyes light up. "You want to go?" I ask her. I'd need to ask my parents or one of my brothers to watch Blakely, and I hate that because Brooks has her tonight, but maybe this one time won't hurt? I never leave her two nights in a row.

"I can't leave my grandma again."

"Mom will help," Sterling is quick to offer. He pulls his phone out of his pocket and dials our mom, putting the phone on speaker.

"Sterling? Is everything okay?" Mom answers. "You never call this late."

"Yes. You're on speaker with Tink, Dec, and Kennedy."

"Oh, hello, kids," she replies. It doesn't matter how old we are. She still calls us kids. As a father, I get it. Blakely will always be my little girl.

"We have a question."

"This should be good." Mom chuckles.

"Tink and I had plans to go to a concert tomorrow night."

"I remember."

"Kristy and Jerry backed out. We asked Dec and Kennedy to come with us, but she doesn't want to leave Maureen two nights in a row." Sterling smiles and winks at Kennedy.

"That's easy. I'll spend the evening with her."

"Are you sure?" Kennedy speaks up.

"Of course. I've been wanting her to help me with a blanket I'm going to make for Brooks and Palmer's baby. This will be the perfect opportunity to do that. And, Declan, Blakely will stay with us. And before you start feeling guilty like we know that you will, you need this. It's perfectly fine to have a life outside of your daughter."

"Thank you, Carol. I appreciate that very much."

"Thanks, Mom. Are you sure you don't mind? You have her during the week." I ask. I don't want her to feel as though she's raising my daughter. That's my job.

"No thanks needed. You know I love having her, and so does your dad. She'll love visiting with Maureen. I only have a small amount of time before my second grandbaby gets here. I need to get busy. This gives me the push that I need. You kids be safe and have fun. Love you."

"Love you," Sterling, Alyssa, and I all reply before Sterling ends the call and pushes his phone off to the side.

"So you're in?" I ask Kennedy.

"I'm in." She smiles at me from across the table, and my heart does this weird thing where it stalls and then starts with a faster beat inside my chest.

"Whoop!" Alyssa cheers. "I'm so excited."

"Me too," Kennedy agrees. "It's been years since I've been to a concert. In fact, I think I was a sophomore in college."

"Seriously?" Alyssa asks.

"Yep."

"Oh, girl. This is going to be epic. Sterling is going to be our designated driver, so you and me, we're going to let loose."

"Is that what we're doing?" Kennedy laughs.

"Definitely. And it's the best way because these two"—she points a finger at me and my brother—"won't let anything happen to us. We can drink and have a good time, knowing that they're going to get us home safe. I don't ever drink more than a couple unless I'm with Sterling."

I watch as my brother's chest expands, and his eyes soften as he looks at his best friend. I know he cares about her, but that look, there's something there, and I make a mental note to ask him about it. Then again, maybe I'll just let it go for now. Besides, he didn't push me earlier when it came to Kennedy. I'm sure it's just the effect that Kennedy has on me. She's got me thinking everyone feels this way, or that they need to.

Chapter 13

KENNEDY

I FELL ASLEEP LAST NIGHT with the feel of Declan's lips pressed against my cheek. I was hoping that he would kiss me, but he didn't. What he did do was spend two hours laughing and talking to me in his Tahoe as we sat in my grandma's driveway. All the lights were out when we got back, and neither one of us were ready to end the night.

I could barely keep my eyes open when he finally walked me to the front door. He gave me the best hug I've ever received, then promptly kissed my cheek and told me to lock up. I might have stood at the window and watched as he drove away.

Luckily for me, as I was getting ready for bed, Morgan texted me. She was up feeding Iris and wanted to say hi. Which was quickly followed by an "I hope I didn't wake you" text. I called her immediately and spilled all that's been happening in my life to my best friend. It was sometime in the early morning hours when I finally succumbed to exhaustion.

"How was dinner last night?" Grandma asks.

"Good. We actually met up with Sterling and his best friend, Alyssa. We went to Harris and had Mexican. Then we went back to Alyssa's and played euchre."

"That sounds like a good night to me," she says, chipper as ever.

"How are you feeling?"

"Great. No pain, just this damn cast." She huffs. "We made progress of squares for the Memorial Day quilt we're going to donate at the parade this year. Now it's time to start sewing on it."

"That's great. Hey, I have a question. Sterling and Alyssa have concert tickets, and the couple they were going with backed out last night. Do you mind if I go? Carol said she would come and stay with you. She wants you to help her make a blanket for the new baby."

"First of all, you're an adult and don't need my permission. Second, is Declan going to be your date? And third, I'd be happy to help Carol make a blanket for the new baby Kincaid."

"I know. I just feel bad. I'm here to help you. Yes, Declan will be going as well, but we didn't really discuss that it was a date, and Carol is really excited about the new baby. Blakely will be with her."

"That Blakely is a fun one." She grins.

"She's pretty cute."

"So Declan?" Grandma asks, wagging her eyebrows.

"Stop." I point an index finger at her.

"Maybe I should start a pool? We can all place bets."

"What? You're an insane woman. What could you possibly be betting on?"

"You, of course. You're going to get it right this time, my dear. I feel it in here." She places her hand over her heart. "You deserve special, and that man is it. He's already put that smile back in your eyes, and it's lighting up your face. Good things, Kennedy dear. Good things. Now, you better go shopping. I know you didn't bring a single thing to wear to a concert. You want to look good for your man."

"He's not my man." I say the words but wish that hers were true. It's too soon to be falling by society's standards, but my heart has been lonely for far too long. My phone beeps and I see his name on my screen.

> **Declan:** Alyssa asked for your number. She's going to be calling you. Something about an outfit.
>
> **Me:** Grandma and I were just talking about what I was going to wear tonight.
>
> **Declan:** You're beautiful in a burlap sack.

My face heats as my fingers fly across the screen.

> **Me:** How do you know? You've never seen me in a burlap sack.
>
> **Declan:** Your beauty has no limits.

"What? What's he saying?" Grandma asks.

"How do you know that it's him?"

"The look on your face. The happiness I was talking about, it's coming off you in waves."

"He's just telling me that Alyssa, who is Sterling's best friend, is going to call me about what we're wearing tonight."

"Good. Go shopping. Enjoy yourself."

"I'm here to take care of you," I remind her.

"You are. And maybe, just maybe, you'll be able to take care of yourself while you're here as well. Besides, I'm going to nap and read a little of my book. Nothing exciting to see here. Go enjoy your day with your new friend."

Declan: Don't shy away from me, Kens.

Me: Sorry, Grandma was talking to me.

Declan: Can't wait to see you.

Me: Me too.

I feel giddy. It's been years since I've felt this way, and honestly, I'm not really sure I ever have. Sure, I've been excited about a guy's attention when I was younger, but this is different. More intense.

My phone rings, and it's a local number. "Hello," I answer.

"Hey, Kennedy, it's Alyssa. What are you doing today?"

"Not much. You?"

"I want to go shopping for tonight. Are you available to come with me? I know you're taking care of your grandma, but no pressure."

"Sure. She's good for now. Where should I meet you?"

"My place? An hour?"

"That works for me."

"Great. I'm excited about tonight. See you soon."

"That was Alyssa. I'm going to meet her to go shopping. Are you sure you don't mind?"

"Kennedy, I needed help the first few days. The pain is gone, and I can get around just fine on the scooter. You're helping at the manor, which was my biggest concern when this happened." She points at her foot. "Go. Live. Have fun."

"You make it sound as if I lived in a dungeon."

"You might as well have. He worked all the time and was never home. The two of you didn't have a marriage. One day when you marry Declan, you'll realize what you've been missing."

"You're out of your mind." I laugh. "Just because you will it to happen doesn't mean that it will."

She taps her temple with her index finger. "I know things. I've been around a long time. I can see it."

"Care to share with the class?"

"I already did. Declan Kincaid is your future."

"You have no way of knowing that. And what I meant was how do you know things? What am I not seeing that you are?"

"Comes with age, my dear. It's a trade secret I cannot set free." She grins wildly.

"I'm going to get ready."

"Make sure you trim... um, the forest," she calls after me.

"Grandma!" I gasp as I stop and turn to face her.

She nods. "Go on now."

I continue to the spare bedroom, all while shaking my head. She's eccentric, but I love her, and I've missed her more than I realized.

I've barely pulled into Alyssa's driveway when she comes bouncing out of the house. She taps on my window, and I roll it down for her. "Want me to drive?" she offers.

"My car's already warm. You can be my copilot."

She grins and makes her way to the passenger side and climbs inside.

"All right, where are we headed?" I ask her.

"How much time do we have?"

"All day. Grandma assures me she's fine and she's doing really well. She insisted I come, so however long we need."

"Perfect. Let's drive to Harris and go to the mall. We'll find something there for sure."

"Are you looking for something in particular?" I ask.

"Not sure. Just something new. I was looking at my closet this morning, and nothing stood out to me. I figured a night out deserves a new outfit."

"I didn't really pack anything enticing either, so I'm glad that you called."

"Okay, I have to ask. What's up with you and Declan? I've known him for years, and I've never seen him look at anyone the way he looks at you."

"What's up with you and Sterling?" I counter.

"Touché." She chuckles. "Nothing is the sad truth. He's been my best friend since we were kids, and that's all we've ever been."

"Really? Not even a kiss?"

"Nope. Sure, on the cheek. We hold hands, especially at big events, so he doesn't lose me in the crowd, but nothing but friends."

"Wow. The way the two of you are with each other, it feels like you're a couple. That's from an outsider looking in."

"Yeah, I sometimes guess it kind of feels that way too, but that's only because we're so close. He's always been there for me and me for him. That's just who we are. We've each dated people who didn't understand our relationship, but that's okay. I want someone in my life who is going to be okay with Sterling and me being close. If not, they can hit the road. He feels the same way."

"Have you ever considered exploring more with him?"

"No. Never. Now that I've answered all your questions, it's time for you to answer mine. Take a right up here," she instructs me.

"Nothing to tell, really."

"Lies."

"Fine. We've hung out a few times."

"And?" she prompts. "Come on. It's more than that."

"He asked me to hang out with him while I'm here."

"Hang out, like last night, or hang out as in mattress dancing?" she asks.

"Mattress dancing?" I laugh. "How old are you again?" I tease. It's as if we've known each other for years.

"Hey, I've learned to keep it clean since Blakely came on the scene. She gets enough of that trash talk from her uncles. Aunt Alyssa is not going to be the cause."

"Aunt Alyssa, huh?"

"Stop. It's just easier than explaining to a little girl that I'm her uncle's best friend. Sure, she could probably figure that out now, but when she was smaller, it was just easier. Sterling told her to call me that, and we all kind of just accepted it."

I watch as she shrugs out of the corner of my eye. "Aunt Alyssa has a nice ring to it," I tell her.

"Annyywayyy, tell me more. Declan. Let's hear it."

"I don't know. I'm recently divorced, and I don't live here."

"So that's what's stopping you? Take the distance out of the equation and the divorce too. Do you still love him? Your ex?"

"No."

"So without either of those two things, tell me what you're thinking?"

"If neither were an issue, I'm thinking I'd like to see more of him."

"Then do it. You can work anywhere, right? That's why you were able to be here to help your grandma?"

"Yes."

"Is there something back home that's keeping you there? I know it's not your job."

"My parents live there." Not that I see much of them. They spend a lot of time traveling and going to dinner with friends. They're empty nesters and enjoying life, as they should be.

"How often are they home? How often do you see them?"

"Are you a mind reader?" I ask.

"No, but I'm not as close to the situation as you are, either. I can look at it more objectively than you can."

"Not as much as I'd like."

"And your job? You just admitted that you can work anywhere, right?"

"Yes."

"Anything else?"

"My best friend, Morgan."

"How often do you see her?"

"She's married and has a little girl, so not as much as we used to."

Alyssa nods. "That's a tough one. I'd have one hell of a hard time moving away from Sterling. However, if there was a man who looked at me the way Declan is looking at you, then I'd do it. That's a once in a lifetime."

"Do you not see how Sterling looks at you?"

"Pft." She waves me off. "He's a big goofball, and it doesn't mean anything. Declan, on the other hand, he's all about taking you mattress dancing." She laughs as she speaks. "I can't say it now without laughing, thanks to you." She sniggers.

I pull into the parking lot of the mall and turn to face her. "Is it really that simple?" I ask her. "Because to be honest, I'm not sure. I married a man who was my best friend, then lover, and look where I am. I don't have the best track history."

"Does it feel different? When you're with Declan, does it feel different? I mean, I know comparing this is kind of a shit thing to do, but it's important for you to do it even internally. That's how you'll know. Trust your heart and your gut. Tell your head to fuck off."

"Hey, what happened to cleaning up your mouth?" I ask.

"The conversation warranted it. Now, let's go get us a couple of kick-ass outfits," she says as my phone alerts me to a message. The car is still running, and my Bluetooth system is set to read messages automatically.

"*Text Message from Declan,*" the radio announces. "*I should have kissed you last night. I won't make that same mistake twice. This is your chance to think about if that's what you want because it's all I can think about.*"

"Wow," Alyssa breathes. "That's a side of Declan I've never seen. He's got it bad."

"I-I really wanted him to kiss me."

"Well, my friend, it appears that tonight you're going to get your wish. Come on." She climbs out while I text Declan back.

Me: Yes.

Grabbing my keys and shoving my phone into my purse, I exit the car, and we make our way inside the mall. On the outside, I appear calm, but on the inside, my heart is thrashing against my chest. I know it's that one simple word that is going to change our relationship.

"You should come back to my place so we can get ready together," Alyssa suggests.

"Sure. I just need to run to Grandma's, grab a few things, and check on her, and then I'll be over. Thanks."

"It's always more fun to get ready together. That's one of the sucky parts of having a guy as a best friend. He rolls out of bed looking hot as hell." I raise my eyebrows, and she rolls her eyes. "I said nothing was going on, not that I was blind. Sterling is fine as hell, and so are his brothers."

"Are you close to Ramsey and the others?" I ask.

"I am. They include me, but I still feel like I'm on the outside. You know, since I'm not a cousin, wife, fiancée, or baby momma to one of the brothers."

"Well, now you have me."

"My girl." She gives me a high five before reaching into the back for her bags and getting out of the car. She waves as I pull away to check on my grandma and spend a little time with her before I need to head back to Alyssa's to get ready for tonight. I admit I'm really excited. I love going to concerts, and it's been way too long since I've been to one. Not to mention the promise that Declan made in his text message, and my simple reply.

Grandma's resting when I get home. She's insisted she's been fine and that her friend Mary stopped and brought lunch.

"Now, don't you come rushing home because of me," Grandma says as I lean down and kiss her cheek. She actively encouraged me to get packed and head on out to Alyssa's sooner rather than later. "Stay out all night, get a little wild and crazy. You're young. Enjoy it while you can."

"What if you need me?"

"I'm just fine. Carol and Raymond are right next door, and they have these things called telephones, and I can call for help."

"Are you sure? I mean, not that I want to stay out all night, but I want you to be sure you'll be okay."

"I'll be fine," she assures me.

"Okay, well, I guess don't wait up."

She grins. "That's the spirit."

"Behave." I point at her before grabbing my bag and heading to Alyssa's.

Just as I'm pulling into her driveway, my phone rings, and I smile when I see it's Declan. "Hey," I answer.

"Hey, yourself. You ready for tonight?" he asks.

"Actually, I'm getting there. Alyssa and I made plans to get ready at her place. I just pulled in."

"I just dropped Blake off with my parents. I'm heading back home to shower. I wanted to tell you I'd be at your place to pick you up around six, but I guess you're not there."

"Nope. I think Alyssa was going to text Sterling to pass on the information."

"I see how it is. I don't warrant a phone call?"

"No. I mean, that's not why. She just said she would, and I rolled with it. It's something new I'm trying. Not to overthink and overanalyze just... live in the moment."

"As long as those moments are with me."

"Demanding," I tease. Warmth spreads through me just from hearing his voice. Butterflies dance in my belly, knowing he wanted to hear from me.

"Not usually, but I guess I am when it comes to you."

"Not sure if I should be worried or flattered," I tell him honestly.

"The latter. Listen, I have a question."

"Sure, what's up?"

"Do I have to wait until the end of the night to claim my kiss? Is there a kiss limit?"

"Do you want to wait?" I don't want him to wait. And a limit? Hell no. There is no limit when it comes to Declan and his lips against mine.

"No."

"Do you want there to be a limit?"

"No."

"Okay."

"Okay, what? I need you to spell it out for me, Kens. You have to tell me it's okay."

"It's okay. You don't have to wait, and there is no limit," I say softly. He sucks in a breath, and even though it's through the phone, that sound sends a quiver of desire through my veins.

"One more question."

I can't help it. I laugh. "And that is?"

"Do I have to wait until six to see you?"

"Yes. Us ladies need time to prepare."

"You just need to breathe, Kens. You don't need anything other than the breath in your lungs."

"You've already got me. You don't need all the sweet words."

"Do I? Do I have you? I feel like I'm chasing you."

"Well, maybe you don't have to chase me anymore."

"Fuck," he mutters. "I'm not waiting for that kiss. I don't care who is there to witness it. I'm claiming those lips of yours."

"Promises, promises."

"Damn right. See you soon, Kens."

"See you soon."

Tossing my phone in my purse, I grab the bag that I packed and the ones from our earlier shopping trip and, on shaking legs, make my way to the front door. Alyssa is there, pulling me inside and straight to her room, where we start getting ready for our night with two of the Kincaid brothers.

I'm excited about the concert and hanging out with Sterling and Alyssa, but what I want even more than that is my kiss.

Chapter 14

DECLAN

I 'VE CIRCLED THE BLOCK FIVE times. I'm early. I couldn't just sit at home and stare at the walls thinking about Kennedy, about kissing Kennedy. So I got in my Tahoe and drove past Alyssa's place. I thought maybe Sterling was early since he and Alyssa are attached at the hip. However, he's not there, and I'm still early.

Finally, on my sixth pass, I see his truck parked in her driveway, and I pull in behind him. I don't bother with my keys since I've volunteered to drive tonight. I do take my phone just in case my parents need to get ahold of me and jog up the steps. I don't get a chance to knock on the door before it opens.

"The girls are still getting ready," he says, stepping back so I can enter.

I want to dart down the hall where I hear their excited voices and kiss the hell out of her. Instead, I somehow manage to take a seat across from Sterling at the kitchen table and wait.

"I'm proud of you, man. Going out two nights in a row." My little brother gives me a nod of approval.

"This isn't something I can do, nor am I willing to do all the time. I'm a dad first. Always." No matter how excited I am about tonight, the guilt of leaving Blakely two nights in a row is heavy. Now, my daughter, on the other hand, is thrilled to be spending the night with Mamaw and Papaw, and she talked my head off the few hours I got to see her today about spending the night with Uncle Brooks and Aunt Palmer and their trip to the aquarium. I'm lucky, so incredibly fortunate, to have my family helping me raise my little girl. I couldn't do this without them.

"You're also a man. You bust your ass owning your own business, and you're raising my niece, who is cool as fuck. You're allowed to have a life."

"Yeah," I agree. Not much else to say. Sterling knows I'm feeling the guilt of leaving her without me telling him. I look down the hall, hoping to get a glimpse of Kennedy, but no such luck. She's the only one I'd leave my daughter two nights in a row for.

"You sure you don't want me to drive tonight?" he offers. "That way, you can chill with your girl in the back?"

"I'm sure." Part of me wants to say yes, but the bigger part of me wants to control the narrative. Like who gets dropped off first. If I drive, the decision will be up to me. That kind of thing. Alyssa talked about the girls drinking, and I want to be the one who makes sure she's home tucked in safely to her bed tonight. Or mine, as long as I'm the one to take care of her.

I've never had a woman spend the night at my place. I bought it right after Cassie told me she was pregnant. I knew my life was about to change, and the tiny-ass bachelor-pad apartment I was living in was no longer going to cut it. I needed a house and a yard for my kid to play in. Life was busy after that. Moving, and planning for Blakely, then we lost Cass, and I was a single dad in the blink of an eye. I made a promise to my little girl. The house was our home, and I wouldn't use it as a place to get my rocks off.

Kennedy is the first to be there because I wanted her to be. The rest have been family or friends of the family, like Alyssa.

Sterling starts to ask me something else, but his words are cut off when the ladies enter the kitchen. My eyes rake over Kennedy like a starving man placed in front of a steak dinner. My heart stalls in my chest as I take her in. She's wearing a dark-burgundy dress with a design of brown and light beige around the hem, neck, and sleeves. My eyes keep going as I take in her bare legs, which disappear into a pair of brown cowboy boots.

"Look!" Alyssa sticks her cowboy-booted foot out toward Sterling. "Aren't they cute?"

"They look great, Tink." He chuckles at his best friend.

"Of course they do. Kennedy and I decided we wanted to go all out for the concert," she explains.

At the sound of her name, Kennedy mimics Alyssa showing Sterling and me her boots as well. That action pulls me out of my stupor. Standing with purpose, I move around the table and slide my arm around her waist.

"Kens," I say, my head already bending to be closer to her.

"Declan," she whispers.

"I think I made you a promise."

She smiles. It's slow and sultry. "I'm waiting," she murmurs as my lips press to hers.

I expect her to be hesitant, but she's anything but. Her arms surround my neck, and she buries her hands in my hair. My grip on her intensifies as she opens for me, allowing my tongue to glide past her lips, finally tasting her. It's all I've been able to think about.

A throat clearing brings me back to the moment. I kiss her one more time, just a soft peck, before pulling her into my chest and hugging her tight. My heart is racing, and I know she can feel it where her head rests. Good. I want her to know what she does to me.

"Damn," Alyssa mutters. "Told you he'd love the dress," she quips.

Kennedy's body shakes in laughter, and just like that, the intensity of the moment is lifted. I still want her with the fire of a thousand suns, but I got my kiss and the girl. I didn't mean to maul her in front of them, but I've waited what feels like a lifetime to kiss her.

"Are we ready?" Sterling asks.

Thankfully, he's not giving me shit right now. "Ready?" I ask the beauty in my arms.

"Definitely."

Reluctantly, I release her so she can slide into her coat, and we can hit the road. No matter what else happens tonight, it's already been the best date I've been on in years. I have Kennedy's lips to thank for that.

"Sterling!" Alyssa gasps when she sees where our seats are. "These are incredible."

We're sitting lower level, row one directly beside the stage. We have a clear view of anything that might happen on that stage tonight, and Alyssa is pumped about it. She throws her arms around my brother and hugs him tight. He just smiles and returns her hug with a shrug. I know him. I know what he's not saying: that he would do anything for her.

Sterling takes his seat, Alyssa beside him, then Kennedy and me sitting in the aisle seat. Without discussing it, we make sure the ladies are between us. Not that I think anything would happen to them, but it's how we were raised. If we were taught anything growing up, it was to respect women. They can take care of themselves, but with Sterling and me surrounding them, they can let loose and have a good time with no worries. We've got them.

The opening act, a band I've never heard of, comes out and immediately starts to play. No fanfare or hyping up the crowd, just a woman and her guitar. Alyssa and Kennedy are on their feet swaying to the beat and even sing along to a few of the songs, none of which I've ever heard. Not that it matters. Kennedy's having a good time, and that's all that matters.

By the end of the first act, they've finished their drinks and need refills and a bathroom break. Sterling and I go with them, not because we don't trust them. We're just protective assholes. At least I am. Hell, so is my brother. Alyssa might not be his, but that doesn't make him any less protective over her. We pick a beer booth right outside of the ladies' restroom. I grab this round while Sterling waits outside the door for them.

Conner Smith is next on stage. I've heard a few of his songs, and I'm a fan. I sing along to the ones that I know. The crowd is starting to fill in as we get closer to Brett Young coming on. Alyssa and Kennedy pull us to our feet when he starts to sing "I Hate Alabama." This one plays in the shop all the time. It's a slow beat, which makes it easy for me to draw Kennedy into my arms. Her back is to my chest as we sway to the beat, and she sings along at the top of her lungs.

My eyes seek out my brother. He has his arm around Alyssa, and they're singing and laughing too. I watch as he smiles down at his best friend, and he can keep denying it all he wants. They both can. There's something there. I just hope one day they're both brave enough to have that conversation. They're missing out on something, that from the outside looking in, could be epic.

Another bathroom break and a refill for the ladies, we've just gotten back to our seats, and Alyssa pulls her phone out of Sterling's pocket. She hands it to Kennedy, who knows to take a couple of different poses of Alyssa and Sterling.

"My turn." Kennedy looks over her shoulder at me. I smile and pull her phone out of my pocket and hand it to her. Apparently, her dress has pockets, but they're worthless. Her words, not mine. Alyssa agreed wholeheartedly, which is how Sterling and I ended up holding their phones for them. I've passed it to her multiple times for her to take pictures tonight, but I don't mind.

Alyssa takes our picture a few times, just as the lights go down. The crowd goes wild, including the four of us. We sing every word at the top of our lungs, dancing in our small space. When Brett slows things down, and I hear the beginning strings of "In Case You Didn't Know," I pull Kennedy into my arms once again.

I hold her tightly as I sing the words to her. I am crazy about this woman, and I don't want to hide that from her, from my family, from her grandma, not even from my daughter. That's the thought that knocks the breath from my lungs. I would never let Blakely get involved if I didn't think it was more.

Kennedy is more.

We have obstacles to face. The biggest is that she lives in Florida, but that won't stop me from pursuing her. The other isn't really an obstacle for us. Not anymore. I know she was worried about getting involved so soon after her divorce, but that kiss earlier told me she's smashed that concern.

As the song ends, she turns in my arms and places her hand on my cheek. The lights are low, but there is enough from the stage that I can see the intensity in her eyes. This time it's Kennedy who stands on her tippy-toes and kisses me. It's soft and slow but no less fierce than our first.

That kiss sets the tone for the rest of the night. We dance and steal kisses, and sing our hearts out. It's the best night I've had in a long damn time.

"Thank you for today and tonight," Kennedy tells Alyssa. She's looking over her shoulder into the back seat. "Are you sure you don't want anything for the tickets?" she asks.

"Nah, it's all good," Sterling tells her. "Thanks for driving," he tells me.

"Yeah, that." Alyssa leans between the seats and kisses my cheek. "Take care of our girl, yeah?"

"I'll take care of her."

"Catch you later." Sterling ushers Alyssa out of the back seat of the Tahoe and lifts her into his arms, carrying her into her house.

"They're cute together," Kennedy says, resting back against the seat.

"They could be."

"What do you mean?"

"They're both stubborn. We can all see it."

"Sometimes going all in is scary."

I reach over and place my hand on her bare thigh. "Are you scared?"

"I was."

"And now?"

"You're hard to resist, Declan Kincaid."

"I don't want you to resist me."

"I'm not. Not anymore," she says softly as we pull up to the traffic light. I hit my blinker to turn right. "I don't want to go home."

"Okay. What did you have in mind?"

She rolls her head to the side to look at me. "More kissing."

"How drunk are you?"

"Buzzed."

I hesitate, checking the rearview mirror to make sure I'm not holding up traffic, but Willow River is quiet this time of night. She must sense my hesitation.

"If you don't want to, you can take me home."

"It's not that I don't want to. I don't want you to regret me."

"Never."

"It's been a long damn time since I've had a woman in my bed."

"Let's not talk about you and other women." She scrunches up her nose.

"I kind of have to. I have a little girl to think about."

"You can take me home."

"I don't want to take you home. I want to take you to my house and take all those kisses you're offering." I want more than that, but it's been a long damn time for me. Not just that, but I refuse to fuck her after she's been drinking. When that happens, we'll both be sober.

"Let's do that," she says, making me chuckle.

"You want to stay at my place? I can bring you back tomorrow to get your car?"

"Hmm, depends?"

"On what?" I'm not sure there's much I won't agree to in order to get her to spend the night in my arms.

"What is your stance on cuddling?"

"Cuddling?" I ask, not hiding my smile.

"Yeah." She reaches over and squeezes my bicep. "I like when these are wrapped around me."

"Done."

"That easy?"

"Yeah, Kens. It's that easy." Changing my blinker to turn left, I check my surroundings and head toward home. When we make it to my place, she's passed out. She wakes when I lift her into my arms.

"A girl could get used to this." She smiles sleepily.

"That's the plan," I tell her.

"What? You want to carry me everywhere?"

"I could, but no, I want you to get used to it. To get used to me. To us."

"That will make it hurt worse when I leave," she says, her brow furrowing.

"Maybe you can stay." I let the words hang between us as I carry her to my room.

"My life is in Florida."

I swallow hard. I know what she's saying is true, but she doesn't realize that I can see her here. With my daughter and me, building our life together. Of course I don't tell her that. This thing between us has barely started, and scaring her away is not at the top of my to-do list.

Instead of talking about it like I know that we need to, I place her on my bed and lean over her. My lips find hers, and I try to put all the words I'm not saying into this kiss. When my lips trail down her neck, she groans.

"I'm all sweaty," she complains.

Lifting my lips from her neck, I peck her lips once more before pushing off the bed and standing. I take a minute to memorize her lying on my bed. Her hair is mussed, her lips are pink and swollen, and she's sexy as hell. I never want to forget this moment.

I blink hard before telling her, "Bathroom." I point at the door to my master bath. "Towels are in the closet. I'll grab you a T-shirt to sleep in."

She moves toward the bathroom but stops to look at me over her shoulder. "Thank you for taking care of me."

A lump forms in the back of my throat. What about this woman has me wanting to beg her to let me take care of her forever? "It's my pleasure, Kens."

"Not yet." She winks and disappears into the bathroom, my laughter following along behind her.

Pulling open my drawer, I dig until I find the shirt I'm looking for. It's one with my shop's logo on the chest and on the back. If she's wearing my clothes, I want my name on her. It's ridiculous, but I pull it from the bottom of the drawer and slam it closed anyway. Opening another drawer, I find a pair of my boxer briefs. They're going to fall off her, but she can roll them up or forgo them altogether. My shirt will hang off her, so she'll be covered. Besides, it's just the two of us.

Grabbing a pair of boxer briefs for myself, I rush down the hall to shower in Blakely's bathroom. By the time I get back to my room, Kennedy is standing in nothing but one of my towels wrapped around her. Her wet hair hangs down her back.

"Hey." She swallows hard.

"Those are for you." I nod toward the pile of clothes on the edge of the bed. "I didn't trust myself to bring them into the bathroom for you." I keep my feet planted where they are. I'm afraid if I move, I'll rip the towel from her body. My arms hang at my sides, my hands fisted to keep from doing exactly that.

She smiles. "I'm sure you could have restrained yourself," she says as her eyes drop to my cock. It's hard and clearly outlined beneath my tight boxer briefs.

"Doubtful," I mutter. "I'll just step out so that you can change. That's the least I can do," I tell her.

"This is perfect. Thank you, Dec."

I nod, loving the way she shortens my name with familiarity. Closing the door behind me, I rest my forehead against it. She's naked in my room without me. Forcing myself to stand, I move to Blakely's bathroom and grab the hairdryer, a comb, and a hair tie. I'm not sure she'll want any of them, but my guess is she will.

When I get back, my door is open. "Hey, I brought supplies," I tell her.

"I'm too tired to mess with it." She covers a yawn.

"Sit on the bed and face the door." I plug the hairdryer in behind the nightstand and sit on the bed behind her. "Come back," I instruct softly. She does as I ask, and I begin to comb her hair.

"I've never had a man comb my hair," she tells me. Her voice is soft. I can't see her eyes, but I can hear what I think is happiness and longing.

"Yeah? I can do a mean braid if you're interested. Of course, Blake would tell you that I'm not all that great." I laugh, thinking about my daughter.

"You're a good daddy, Declan."

"Thank you. She's my world." I spend the next ten minutes blow-drying her hair. I comb through it and then braid it for her. It's not going to win any competitions, but at least she's not going to sleep with wet hair. That's the dad in me, I guess.

"I'm going to put this stuff away. Get comfortable. I'll be right back."

I make a pit stop in the kitchen for a bottle of water and a couple of painkillers. When I hand them to her, she takes them without question, sucking down half the bottle. Turning off the bedside lamp, I crawl into bed over the top of her. I could have walked around the bed, but this made her giggle just as I hoped that it would.

"You promised me kisses," she says as I pull her into my arms.

"That I did." My lips find hers in the dark. It's not just our lips; our hands are everywhere. We're both battling to touch every piece of exposed skin, memorizing every dip and valley.

My hand slides under the Kincaid Auto Repair T-shirt and cups her breast. She moans into my mouth, and the sound goes straight to my cock. I take my time kissing her and teasing one nipple then the other, both hard peaks getting equal amounts of my attention.

My hands travel their way to the waistband of my boxer briefs. I never imagined I would ever in my life consider them sexy, but I'd never imagined them on Kennedy.

"This okay?" I ask her.

"Please."

I slip my hand beneath the rolled-up waistband and find her hot and wet for me. I take my time running my fingers through her folds, feeling the silk of her desire for me coating my fingers. When my thumb glides over her clit, her back arches off the bed.

"Declan."

"Tell me, Kens."

"More."

"More of this?" I kiss her softly.

"That too."

I chuckle. "Talk to me."

"I ache," she whispers huskily. That's good enough for me. I'm just about to slide one long digit inside her when she adds, "For you."

"Fuck." I push my finger inside, and we both hiss out a breath. I need more of her. More of this. I slide in another finger without breaking my pace, and she rewards me with a sexy as fuck moan from deep within her chest.

"Give it to me," I command. I need her to come all over my hand. And I need it now. I mold my lips to hers and pump my hand faster. Within a few breaths, she's calling out my name and coming. I don't stop until I feel her body relax. Lifting my hands to my mouth, I taste her and groan, knowing this one sample will never be enough.

"You." She reaches for my hard cock, but my hand on her wrist stops her.

"You, Kens. This was all for you. Now. I think I have a promise of kisses to uphold."

I fulfill my promise. We kiss until we're both too tired to keep our eyes open. Then I wrap her in my arms and fall into the best night's sleep I've had in my entire life.

Chapter 15

KENNEDY

"THANK YOU FOR CHOOSING WILLOW Manor," I tell Mrs. Wilson. She's just scheduled the banquet hall for her fiftieth wedding anniversary in August.

"This place is perfect, and I just love your grandmother. How is she?"

"She's doing well. Thank you for asking. She's still in a cast, but she's not letting it keep her down."

"Oh, I bet not. Maureen is lively," she says, smiling kindly. "Please tell her I said hello."

"I will," I assure her as I escort her to the door. My phone rings as soon as it shuts, and I smile when I see Morgan's name on the screen.

"I miss you," I answer.

"I miss you too. How are you? How is your grandma?"

"We're both doing well. I'm at the manor now. Just booked a fiftieth wedding anniversary party."

"Nice. How's that man of yours?"

"He's not mine."

"Are you sure about that?" she asks.

I release a heavy sigh. "I don't know. I've never felt this way about anyone." I don't need to elaborate because I know my bestie can read between the lines.

"Then grab it with both hands and never let go."

"I'm barely divorced."

"Doesn't matter. You're divorced and free to do as you please. Don't let fear or the expectations that society has put into your head keep you from experiencing greatness."

"How do you know it's greatness?" I ask her.

"The sound of your voice."

"How are Iris and Mitch?" I change the subject.

We spend the next fifteen minutes getting each other caught up before agreeing to talk again soon. I make a quick trip through the building, checking all the doors are locked and the lights are turned off before grabbing my stuff and heading home.

I'm not even pulled out of the lot when my cell phone rings. I smile when I see it's Declan. "Hey, you. Shouldn't you be working?"

"I'm the boss."

"There is that." I chuckle. "What's up?" We've talked on the phone every night this week. Sunday morning, he took me back to Alyssa's for my car and tried to convince me to come to Sunday dinner with his family, but I declined. I needed to spend time with Grandma. He even invited her, but I still declined. He called that night, and we talked for hours, and it's been that way every night since. He usually texts me during the day while he's working, which is why his call, although welcome, is unexpected.

"You said you would be done around three."

I look at the clock on the dash, and it's two minutes after. "I just got into my car to head home."

"What are your plans tonight?"

"Nothing."

"Come to my place. Have dinner with us. I'll have Blakely. I hope that's okay. I just—I can't leave her again after two nights last weekend."

"Declan, I would never expect you to. You're her daddy before anything else. That's how it should be."

"I've never had to worry about splitting my time with her before."

"If this is too much..." I leave my words hanging.

"No. No, Kens, that's not what I'm saying. It's different for me, but I'll adjust. I want to spend time with you. Please say you'll come. I know it's not a romantic date, but I promise good company."

"Stop. I don't need romantic gestures. You're real, Declan. Real surpasses putting on a show anytime."

"Oh, babe, trust me, my romance is not a show."

My smile is huge. I'm glad he can't see me. "It's the small things," I tell him. "Like dinner on the couch on Friday night with you and your little girl. It's the time spent, not where and how."

"He's a fucking moron," he mutters.

"Who?"

"Lyle. He lost the best thing that ever happened to him. I don't plan to make that same mistake." He rattles off the code to his garage. "Head over whenever you want. I won't get out of here until five thirty or a little later, and I still need to go pick Blake up from my parents.'"

"Do you want me to do that?"

"You'd do that?"

"Yes." I don't hesitate. "I'm done for the day. Grandma is meeting with her sewing club. What sounds good for dinner? I'll go home and change, pick Blake up, and she and I can go to the store. She's literally right next door to me, Declan."

"You'll need a car seat."

"I'm just now leaving the manor. I'll stop and grab yours."

"I can grab something for dinner on my way home," he offers.

"Nope. Blake and I are making dinner. No complaints. I'll be there in a few. I have one small stop to make before I get there."

"Be safe, Kens."

"Always. I'll see you in a few." Ending the call, I pull out of the lot. I stop at Dorothy's Diner and order him a large sweet tea as an afternoon pick-me-up. I grab one for myself and briefly consider ice cream for Blakely as well. I decide to grab that at the store so we can all indulge before making my way to his shop.

After parking my car, I head inside. Declan is sitting at the desk with the phone at his ear. He smiles when he sees me and waves me over. I place his tea on the desk in front of him, and he grips the back of my thigh, holding me next to him.

"Monday will work. Thank you." He hangs up the phone and wraps his other hand around my waist. "I missed you."

"It's only been a few days," I tell him.

"Five, Kens. It's been five days since I laid eyes on you."

"How else am I supposed to keep you interested?" I tease.

"Just exist."

Bending my head, I press a kiss to his lips. "You make my heart race when you say things like that."

"Good."

"Come on, Daddy. I need to get the car seat." I try to step back, but he keeps his arms around me, holding me close.

"Just take the Tahoe. It will be easier than moving the seat back and forth. Leave me your keys."

"Are you sure?"

"Yes."

"Don't men have an issue with women driving their vehicles?" Lyle hated it when I would ask to take his SUV over my car. I hated the bitching, so I quit asking. If I needed a bigger vehicle, I just had it delivered or asked Morgan to use hers.

"Not this one."

I raise an eyebrow.

"Not when it's you," he amends.

"Sorry to interrupt, boss," a guy I now know as Gus says, sticking his head into the office from the garage area. "Those parts you've been waiting on were just delivered." He waves at me and grins at our position.

"Thanks, Gus. I'll be right there." He stands from the chair, which causes me to step back. Reaching into his pocket, he produces a key fob. "Just use the garage door opener to let yourself in. The door from the garage to the house is unlocked."

"Got it." My words are muffled against his lips. "Here are mine," I say, stepping back and placing them in his hand. "Any requests for dinner?"

"You."

I can feel my face heat, and my body responds to his reply. A rush of warmth pools between my thighs. "Something a little more Blakely friendly?"

"I told you I can just pick something up."

"Nope. Blakely and I are going to cook. Speak up now, or no complaints later."

"Babe, as long as both of my girls are there when I get home from work, I'll eat anything you put in front of me."

"Again, with the pretty words." My poor heart is getting a workout with this visit the way it pumps furiously inside my chest.

"Do your parents know that I'm picking her up?"

"Yes, and so does she. To say she's excited is an understatement. I called them right after we talked."

"I feel a little weird going to your parents' to get her, but I'm excited to hang out with her."

"You have nothing to feel weird about. They know we're seeing each other."

"Is that what this is?" I tilt my head to the side, pretending to decide whether I like that description.

"It's a damn good start." He kisses me once more and steps back. "I need to finish this car so I can get out of here."

I point at his iced tea. "An afternoon pick-me-up."

"Thank you. Be safe. Text me when you get home."

"I'll be fine. I'll text you when Blakely and I get to your place."

"That's what I meant." He flashes me a knowing grin, and my heart takes off, galloping once again. He kisses me one more time, this one just a peck, before grabbing his tea and walking backward toward the door that leads to the garage. "See you soon, baby." He winks and disappears behind the door.

I take a minute for my heartbeat to regulate before climbing behind the wheel of his Tahoe and heading home.

"Kenny!" Blakely rushes toward where I stand, just inside the entry of Declan's parents' house. "Are we having a girls' day?"

"Well, until Daddy gets home from work. We're going to make dinner." I smile down at her.

"Come on in," Carol says.

I step farther into the room as Blakely continues to chatter. "What are we cooking?" she asks.

"That's up to us. What do you want to make?"

She taps her chin with her index finger, and it's cute as hell. "Cookies?"

I laugh. "We can make cookies, but I think we need something else. The cookies will be our dessert."

"Pancakes?" she asks.

"How about we go to the grocery store and see what we can find?"

"Do you have a seat in your car? Daddy says I have to have a seat even though I'm a big girl."

"I have your daddy's Tahoe, and he has my car."

"Blakely, go grab your things," Carol tells her.

"Okay!" She shoots off across the room to gather her coat and shove toys into her backpack.

"She has things she leaves here, but she loves having a backpack to take back and forth," Carol explains.

"She's adorable." My eyes watch as Blakely pushes items into her book bag. I'm grateful that Carol seems to be acting as if me picking up her granddaughter in her son's SUV to make them dinner is normal. I don't know if I could handle her asking questions about what's going on between us since I don't have the answers.

"Thank you," she replies.

"Ready!" Blakely says with her backpack half on and her coat in her arms.

I kneel to her height. "How about we put the coat on? We don't want you to freeze."

"Okay," she easily agrees. I help her with her coat and back into her backpack. "Bye, Mamaw. Will you tell Papaw that I'll be back soon and don't work on the puzzle without me?"

"I'll tell him," Carol assures her. "It was good to see you again, Kennedy."

"You too." I wave and lead Blakely out to the Tahoe.

"Ready?" I ask once I'm behind the wheel. Glancing in the rearview mirror, I see her head bob.

"Ready. This is the best day."

My heart squeezes in my chest. This little girl is such a joy to be around. My heart breaks for the loss of her mother and the relationship I'm sure they would have had. She's lucky to have so many people who love her.

"I don't know if I like it." Blakely scrunches up her nose. "Chicken pie don't sound like dino nuggets."

I smile at her. She's sitting cross-legged on the kitchen island. "It's chicken pot pie, and I promise you'll love it. I need you to pour the soup into the pan, help me mix the topping, and drop it on top."

"I'm good at pouring."

"Perfect." I grab the three cans of Progresso Chicken Pot Pie Style Soup and remove the lids. "Now, take this with both hands." I hand her one of the cans. "Slowly pour it into the casserole dish." She does as I ask, and I keep my hand close to help her.

"I did it!" she cheers once the can is empty.

"Great job, kiddo. Now, we have two more." We repeat the process two more times. "This is not truly homemade. We're kind of cheating."

"Is that bad?" she asks.

"Not when it comes to cooking. Sometimes you just don't have time, so you have to cut corners."

"I'm not allowed to use knives. You'll hafta do the cutting."

"Deal." I don't bother explaining. I'd probably just confuse her even more.

"Now, salt and pepper. We're going to do this together." I place the shaker in her hand and then use my own to shake out the desired amount of each into the casserole dish.

"Now, the fun part."

"We put pancakes in chicken pie?" she asks.

"No, we're making a homemade biscuit mix. This is Bisquick. It can be used for pancakes, but that's not what we're going to do with it."

"I might maybe like this," she tells me.

"I think because you helped me make it, it's going to be extra tasty."

"Will Daddy like it?"

"I hope so."

"He will. He likes all kinds of food."

We chat while I mix up the biscuit mixture. Grabbing another fork, I show her how to fork up a scoop and drop it carefully on top of the soup. "This is fun." She giggles as another scoop of biscuit plops on top of the soup mixture.

"All done." She smiles at me a few minutes later. "My hands are icky." She holds up her biscuit-mixture-covered fingers.

"Nothing a little soap and water can't fix." Lifting her into my arms, I move her to the sink so she can wash her hands before placing her back on her feet. "Let me get this cleaned up and in the oven, and we can start on the cookie dough."

"Yay!" She watches my every move and listens when I ask her to step back so I can open the oven. "Now, cookie time!"

She hugs me around my legs and smiles up at me. Something about the moment allows her little hands to reach inside my chest and wrap around my heart. This little girl and her daddy are weaving themselves into a place inside me that they'll never be able to be set free from.

Shaking out of my thoughts, I get busy measuring ingredients for chocolate chip cookies and handing them to Blakely to pour into a bowl when Blakely asks if she can stir. I know it's going to be a lot for her, but I hand over the spoon, knowing I'll need to help her.

"My arm's gonna fall off." She giggles with a pant of frustration at the same time.

"Want me to take a turn?"

"Yes." She drops the spoon into the bowl and exhales dramatically. "Daddy gets the kind you break off," she tells me. "This is funner but harder."

"It is more fun," I say, correcting her. "And harder, but nothing worth having in life is easy."

"You sound like my papaw. He talks all funny like that."

I bop her on the nose. "Your papaw is a very wise man."

"He's old." She laughs.

"Blake!" I whisper-shout. "Don't let him hear you say that."

She falls back on the counter. Luckily, the island is large enough that she's now lying back, her little body shaking with laughter.

"You're silly," I tell her, smiling.

Blakely cackles even harder, and I move to stand next to her to make sure she doesn't laugh herself off the island onto the kitchen floor.

"This is something to come home to."

I freeze and look up to find Declan standing, arms crossed, shoulder leaning against the wall.

"This one"—I point at Blakely—"has a case of the giggles."

"Daddy, Kenny worked me so hard."

"Did she?"

"Her cookies are harder to make than yours."

"These are from scratch," I remind her.

"Daddy, did you know you can scratch cookies?"

Declan chuckles. Stepping away from the wall, he makes his way toward us. He scoops Blakely up into his arms and rains kisses all over her face, making her laugh even harder.

"Daddy, I gots to pee," she cries. "S-S-Stop." She laughs. He places her on her feet, and she takes off, racing for the bathroom down the hall.

He steps around the counter and pulls me into his arms, kissing me softly. "I like coming home to both of you."

No matter how many times I've told myself not to, I'm falling for him. I'm setting myself up for heartbreak when I go back to Florida, but I can't seem to stop myself from letting it happen.

"How was your day?"

"Good, this beautiful woman came to visit me, and then I thought about her and her goodbye kiss all afternoon. So much so that I busted my ass to get out of there on time for once."

"She thought about you too. And there are more kisses available whenever you want them." I wink. "Dinner will be ready in about five more minutes."

"I'll grab a quick shower." He kisses me again. I look over his shoulder for Blakely, not wanting her to catch us. "Hey." He guides my chin until he has my full attention. "I'm not hiding this from her. She's smart. I want this with you, and she's already invested."

"I know you don't let women meet her."

"What women, Kennedy? I've been on a handful of dates that consisted of dinner. A few we had drinks after, and then I dropped them off. You're not just any woman to me. You understand that, right?"

"It's so soon."

He shrugs. "We've spent a lot of time talking and getting to know each other. I don't want to stop that, and I'm not hiding you. My brother did that with Palmer and almost lost her. I won't make that mistake."

"I'm going back to Florida."

"We'll work it out." He kisses me and strides off down the hall.

I don't know what he means by that, but I don't have time to dwell on it. Blakely comes racing back into the room, and the timer on the oven dings, letting me know that dinner is ready. I pull out the chicken pot pie and slide in the first tray of cookies.

Ten minutes later, we're sitting around the table having dinner while the first batch of cookies is cooling.

"This is family dinner," Blakely tells us. "And chicken pie is good, Kenny."

"Of course it is. You made it," I tell her. I take a drink of my water, and it goes down wrong, making me cough.

"Daddy, do we have any cock drops?" she asks, only making me cough harder.

Declan bites his cheek to keep from laughing. "Cough drops," he corrects her.

"That's what I said. Cock drops."

"I'm okay," I tell her. "I just swallowed wrong." I find Declan's eyes across the table, and instead of the laughter from a few seconds ago, it's now heat in his eyes. My body flushes when I think about his cock. How can I not? I'm going to hell using the innocence of a child to fuel my dirty thoughts about her dad. At least he seems to be doing the same.

After dinner, I make the rest of the cookies while Declan cleans the kitchen and Blakely plays with her dolls in the living room. Declan finds every excuse to touch me and kiss me while we share the space in the kitchen. Once we're finished, the three of us cuddle together on the couch and watch a movie. It's the perfect night. It's very domestic and one of the greatest nights of my life.

Chapter 16

DECLAN

KENNEDY AND I MADE PLANS to go to dinner tonight. Jade and Orrin were going to keep Blakely, but she woke up not feeling well, and I can't leave her. I won't leave her. Not when she needs and wants me. She's running a low-grade fever and just wants to cuddle. We're sitting on the couch, watching one of her princess movies. She's sipping on a cup of Pedialyte.

Grabbing my phone, I dial Kennedy.

"Good morning," she answers cheerfully.

"Hey, Kens," I greet softly.

"What's wrong?"

How is it that she can already read me so well? "I can't go to dinner tonight. Blake woke up with a fever."

"Oh no. Do you need anything?"

"No. I think we have what we need. We're just snuggling on the couch."

"Poor thing."

"Yeah. I'm sorry to cancel on you."

"You have nothing to be sorry for. She's your number one priority. I understand that, Declan."

"You could come over and cuddle with us," I offer. I know that's a risk that she could get whatever Blakely has, but I really want to see her.

"Are you sure?"

"Yes. Unless you're worried about getting sick too."

"Cuddles are worth it," she tells me.

Just another reason this woman has been able to push past all my defenses. She's an incredible human inside and out. "I agree," I tell her.

"I'll bring dinner. Anything else you need? Tissues? Cock drops?" she asks with a chuckle.

"We're good, babe." I snicker.

"Okay. Well, if you think of something, just text me."

"Who's that?" Blakely asks.

"It's Kennedy, sweetheart."

"Can I say hi?" she asks.

"Kens, Blake wants to say hi." I hit the speakerphone button so I can hear them. "Hi, Kenny," Blakely says without her usual flair.

"Hey, sweetie. Your daddy said you aren't feeling well."

"I gots a fever."

"I'm sorry you're sick." Kennedy speaks with so much empathy in her voice I feel myself getting choked up. "I'm going to stop by in a little while and see you."

"That will make me feel better," my daughter says.

"I'll see you soon, kiddo."

"Bye, Kenny."

I take the phone off speaker. "We'll be here," I tell her.

"Okay. What about you? Anything you need?"

"Not off the top of my head. Just you."

Her voice is soft when she replies, "I'll be there soon." The call ends, and I place my phone back on the end table and snuggle in with my little girl.

A couple of hours later, Blakely is sleeping in her bed, and I'm taking the opportunity to straighten up the house and do a couple of loads of laundry. I really need to run the vacuum, but that can wait. I don't want to do anything that will wake her up. I'm wiping the kitchen counters when my phone beeps with a message.

Kennedy: I'm here.

Me: I'll open the garage, and you can pull in.

Kennedy: Okay. I didn't want to wake Blakely if she was sleeping.

I don't reply. Instead, I slide my phone into my pocket and rush to the garage to open the door for her. She pulls in and climbs out of her car. When she reaches the back, I close the garage door and step off the steps to help her.

"What is all of this?" I ask.

"Well, I wanted to make Blakely homemade chicken noodle soup, then I thought she might not like it. So I grabbed some canned chicken noodles, some dino nuggets, and mac and cheese. I got more Pedialyte and some Motrin and Tylenol for her fever and some tissues."

"Kens..." I'm at a loss for words.

"I just wanted to help you and her."

I lean in and kiss her before taking the bags from her hands and carrying them inside. "I'll pay you back for all of this," I tell her.

"You will do no such thing. I wanted to do this." She holds up another bag. "I found this too, and I couldn't pass it up."

"What is that?"

"It's a super soft blanket with stars and the moon. They glow in the dark." She smiles, and I don't know if the gesture or her thoughtfulness has my heart flipping in my chest. Probably a combination of both.

"She's going to love that."

"Is she sleeping?"

"She is."

"Okay. Well, let me get the chicken on for the soup."

"What can I do to help?"

"Just relax, Daddy," she tells me. "It can't be easy taking care of a sick little girl on your own."

"She's just been clingy today. We've been through worse, that's for sure."

"Regardless, you never know what the rest of the day and night might hold. Why don't you go rest while she is?"

"Can we put the chicken in a Crock-Pot?" I ask her.

"Sure. It takes a little longer, but it's not even noon yet, so it should still be ready by dinnertime. And I bought canned just in case she hates it."

Going into the pantry, I grab the Crock-Pot and place it on the counter, plugging it in. I retrieve a liner from the drawer. "Use this. You can lie with me."

"I—Okay." She nods and gets to work placing the chicken and broth into the Crock-Pot. Ten minutes later, we're checking on Blakely, who is still sound asleep. I point the touchless thermometer at her head and see that she's still running a low fever, but she's resting peacefully. Then I take Kennedy by the hand and lead her to my room, closing and locking the door. I turn the baby monitor on that I still sometimes use when she's sick or if I'm outside working early or after she's in bed in case she wakes up and needs me.

I release Kennedy's hands as I make my way to the windows to close the blinds. It's a dreary winter's day anyway. I'm already in a pair of lounge pants and a T-shirt. Pulling back the covers, I pat the space next to me.

"What about Blakely?"

"She's resting. I turned on the monitor, and she'll knock on the door if she needs me. Right now, I need you." We've not really had any time together other than kissing like teenagers on the couch after my daughter falls asleep. I need to change that. Now.

Her eyes visibly soften even in the dimly lit room. She sits on the edge of the bed and pulls off her boots before climbing under the covers next to me.

"Much better," I say, pulling her close. "I've missed you."

"I was here last night."

"I know. It's been hours." I slide my hand up the back of her shirt and press my lips to hers. It's meant to be just a soft peck, but it turns into me pulling her on top of me. My cock is throbbing with need, but I ignore it like I do every other time I'm with her. We can't go there. Not right now. Instead, I kiss her soft and slow. Taking my time to taste her. I already know the curve of her lips and the slope of her tongue as it dances with mine. I kiss her until our lips are swollen and our lungs are screaming for air.

I end up turning us so that her back is pressed against the

mattress while I hover over her. Breaking the kiss, I lift her shirt, tugging it off and tossing it to the side. Kennedy's chest rises and falls with each labored breath.

My mouth twitches with the need to pull her hard nipples into my mouth. Bending my head as I shimmy down the mattress, I do just that, sucking the pebbled bud through the white lace of her bra.

"Dec," she breathes.

"Yeah, baby?"

"I need—" She bites her lips when I press my lips to her quivering belly, staring up at her through hooded eyes.

"What do you need, Kens?"

"More. I need more."

Sitting back on my knees, I work her leggings and her panties over her hips and down her thighs. One leg, then the other is freed as I toss them with her shirt. She's lying in nothing but her thin white lace bra, making her appear angelic.

Knowing that our time is limited before my daughter wakes and needs us, I get busy. I settle back onto the mattress, tossing her legs over my shoulders. I dive in, tasting her pussy. My mouth covers her clit at the same time as I slip one long digit inside her. Her back arches off the bed. I move my free hand to press on her belly to keep her still while my mouth devours her.

Kennedy's soft moans of pleasure have my cock throbbing against the mattress, but I don't dare stop. I work her over, devouring her with my mouth. I slide in a second finger, and the moan that fills the room is the most erotic sound I've ever heard.

I pump my fingers faster and suck on her clit a little harder, and that's all it takes for her orgasm to reach its peak. Her soft cry of my name fills the room. I won't stop until every ounce of pleasure has been wrung from her body, and she falls against the mattress, exhausted and sated.

Carefully, I remove her quivering legs from my shoulders as I make my way back up her body to lie next to her. I pull her into my arms, her head resting against my chest. We're both breathing heavily. My cock is standing tall, but I ignore it. This was for her. That is until her soft hand grips the base.

"Kens." I don't know if her name is a warning or a plea at this point.

"Your turn."

"That's not how this works, baby. I got just as much out of that as you did."

"Well, now I'm going to get as much out of this as you do." She glances at the monitor on the nightstand, and my heart hammers in my chest. "She's still sleeping. I have time." How is it possible that her checking on the well-being of my little girl has me craving her more than my mouth on her pussy?

"Too many clothes, Kincaid," she teases.

Not needing to be told twice, I stand and strip out of my clothes before sliding back under the covers next to her and pulling her into my arms.

She kisses me, her tongue tracing my lips, before her mouth trails over my jaw, down my neck, my chest, and over my abs. When she reaches my cock, she wastes no time taking the tip into her mouth, giving both an initial first taste.

She works my cock with one hand while the other grips my thigh as she takes me deep into the back of her throat. My eyes roll to the back of my head at the feeling of her hot, wet mouth. I force myself to lock my gaze on her. This is a moment I'll remember for the rest of my life. The room is dimly lit, just the bare amount of daylight peeking through the closed blinds, but it's enough light for me to see that her eyes are closed as she works me over.

As if she can sense my stare, her eyes open and catch mine. She never breaks her rhythm as she stares at me. When she does finally slow, it's to take me deeper. I grab her hair in my hand so that I don't miss a single second. She gags, releasing me, then goes right back for me.

"I'm close," I whisper harshly. I'm more than close. Watching her take me to the back of her throat has me barely maintaining control. "Kens, baby, you have to stop," I say the words, but I make no move to pull her off me. I'm warning her. It's her choice if she wants to stay the course.

I'm still holding her hair out of her face as she increases her efforts, not heeding my warning. Her gaze is still on mine, and there's a challenge in her eyes. That's what does it. That sends me over the edge as I release into her mouth. She takes all of me, swallowing every drop that I give her.

My cock is barely free before I pull her up my body and crash my mouth with hers. My taste lingers with her own on our lips. It's erotic and sexy and, dare I say, life-changing. I've never felt this way about a woman. I've never had a woman strip me bare. Not just physically but also emotionally.

I don't know if it's the high of my orgasm or the woman who has words I've never uttered fighting to pass my lips. "You're my every fantasy come true," I say instead.

She doesn't reply, but she does snuggle into my chest. "Baby, let's get cleaned up and get dressed, and we can nap until Blake needs us."

"I like this plan." She crawls over me, collects her clothes, and goes to the bathroom to freshen up. I pull my lounge pants and boxer briefs back into place. I still had my shirt on. I wasn't expecting her mouth to take me to new heights.

Once she slides back into bed, I kiss her softly and go to the bathroom myself. On the way back, I unlock the bedroom door and open it before easing under the covers and tugging her into my arms. It takes no time before we're both sound asleep.

I wake to soft whispers. Slowly, I blink my eyes open. The room is darker than before, and there is a new body in my bed.

"Daddy was sleepy," Kennedy says softly. "How are you feeling?" she asks my daughter. I watch as she places the back of her hand against Blakely's forehead to test her fever. "You still feel warm."

"Yeah," Blakely agrees. She's still not her happy, cheerful self, and I hate it. I hate when she's sick like this.

"Are you hungry?" Kennedy asks her.

"Can I have water?" Blakely asks.

"Of course you can, baby girl. Come on. Let's go get you a drink." Kennedy climbs to her feet and lifts Blakely into her arms.

I watch as she snuggles Blakely to her chest and carries her out of the room. I exhale a heavy breath. Kennedy makes it impossible for me not to fall for her. I told her not to worry about her living in a completely different state and that we would figure it out. Only I have no plan. I don't know how we'll figure it out, but I need a plan. Fast. I don't want this to end. I want to see where this goes. I want to watch her as she falls in love with my daughter and my daughter with her. I want to fall asleep with her next to me and wake up the same way.

I'm in deep.

I have no idea how we're going to figure it out. I just know that we have to. My plan was to make her fall for me, but then it backfired. I'm the one who's fallen ass over heels for this woman, and now I have to figure out how to keep her.

I find my way to the living room. Kennedy is holding Blakely on her lap while Blakely is using her cup and straw, which I'm sure has Pedialyte in it.

"There are my girls," I say, entering the room.

"Hi, Daddy. Kenny gave me the drinking medicine."

"Thank you." I make eye contact with Kennedy, and she nods.

"And look at my new blankie. Kenny said it glows in the dark. It's so soft, Daddy."

"I can see that. Do you have room for one more?" I ask them.

"Daddy, you have to sit behind Kenny. That's how it works. The daddy holds their family."

My heart stalls in my chest. I stand still until it starts again, beating a furious hard-rock beat in my chest. I wait for the panic to hit that my daughter is attached to Kennedy. The panic never comes. Instead, I'm even more determined to figure out a way for this to work. I don't want to let her go, and I know that Blakely doesn't either.

The daddy holds their family.

I want us to be a family. It's clear as a bright Georgia sky. I can see it in my mind. I just don't know how to make it my reality. I'll figure it out. I won't lose her. I won't lose this feeling of rightness that washes over me every time I'm close to Kennedy or hear her voice. She's a part of us, and I need to figure out how it stays that way.

I never thought I would consider leaving Willow River. I loved growing up here, and my family is here, but for Kennedy, well, if it comes down to that, I have to think about all options. It would be hell selling the business and starting over, building clientele, but people have done crazier things for love, right?

The rest of the day, we cuddle, watch movies, and eat Kennedy's homemade chicken noodle soup. Even though Blakely isn't feeling well, I can't remember a day that felt more right in a very long time. If ever.

I wonder what she would do if I asked her to stay forever?

Chapter 17

KENNEDY

I'M DRIVING THROUGH TOWN, HAVING just dropped my grandma off at sewing club. She's getting around really well, and she's going stir-crazy inside the house. She told me I was not allowed to come back before eight o'clock tonight. It's one now. That's a hell of a lot of sewing, but it's what they enjoy. Who am I to judge? Besides, I think they do a lot more gossiping than they do sewing.

As I get closer to Declan's shop, I decide to stop and say hello. Maybe I can steal a kiss while I'm there. I should feel guilty for interrupting his workday, but I can hear his voice in my head telling me that if I'm in town and I don't stop to see him, he'd be upset. That's what he said earlier this week. I drove Grandma to her appointment, and she tried to get me to stop, but I said no, that he was working. I told him about it later when we were having dinner at the pizza place with Blakely.

The door is barely closed behind me when I hear an excited

204 | KAYLEE RYAN

yelp, and my legs are being attacked. I brace my hands on the wall next to me and smile down at Blakely. "Hey, sweetie. What are you doing here?"

"Mamaw and Papaw had to go to the doctor's," she tells me.

"It's just for a few hours," Declan says from his seat behind the desk. "I'm pulling desk duty until then."

"And you get to come to work with Daddy." I push Blakely's hair back out of her eyes. "I love your overalls," I tell her. She's wearing pink bibbed overalls that look adorable on her.

"These are my wiener pants," she tells me.

"What?" I ask, barely containing my laughter.

"Blake," Declan groans. "I told you to stop calling them that."

"But, Daddy, they give me a wiener. Kenny, did you know boys have wieners, but girls don't? But I do when I wear my wiener pants." She points down at the crotch of her overalls that are bunched up.

"I think that's just the way the material lays," I explain.

"That's what Mamaw said, but it looks like Daddy when hims wears jeans, but his wiener is real."

"That's enough, young lady," Declan scolds. "No more." He points his index finger at her as he uses his dad look. I can see the sparkle in his eyes, and I know it's killing him not to laugh at his daughter.

I step farther into the small waiting area. "What if I take Blakely with me for the afternoon?" I suggest. Blakely immediately cheers, but before Declan can respond, his phone rings.

"Hey, Palmer," he greets his sister-in-law. "Are you sure?" he asks. His eyes flash to mine and then to his daughter. "Yeah, Blake and Kens are both here with me at the shop. I'll put her on." He hands me the phone. "Palmer wants to talk to you."

I take the phone from him, placing it to my ear. "Hello?"

"Hey, you. What are your plans for tonight?" My eyes find Declan, but he's not giving anything away.

"I don't have any that I'm aware of. I have to pick Grandma up from her sewing club meeting or get-together, whatever you want to call it, later today. What's up?"

"What do you think about a girls' night?" she asks.

"Sure."

"It's not your average girls' night. Ramsey and I have been promising Blakely we'd have another sleepover. This time it's going to be at my place. Ramsey, Jade, and Piper will be there as well."

"Should I invite Alyssa?"

"Oh, shit!"

"What?"

"Why have we never invited her before now? Damn. We've failed. I'll call her. It should come from one of us. I feel terrible."

"It's an easy oversight." I don't say it, but I'm sure it's because Alyssa isn't involved romantically with Sterling. The rest of us are. Like she said, it's an easy oversight, but I'm glad that they're going to include her.

"She's cool as hell too. I feel awful. My place, six o'clock. Tell Declan that I'll pick Blakely up from his parents.'"

"Actually, I'll just bring her with me."

"Even better. We're spending the night," she reminds me.

"I'll have to check in with Grandma and leave to pick her up, but that all sounds good to me."

"Great. I'll see you tonight."

"What do I need to bring?"

206 | KAYLEE RYAN

"Just you and the lady of honor."

"I'll text Alyssa later and see if she wants a ride as well."

"That would be great. Damn, I can't believe we didn't think to include her before now. I'm going to call her, then call Ramsey."

"See you later." I hand Declan back his phone. "I'm sorry I should have made sure her plans were okay with you before I agreed." It hits me that I just made plans for his daughter without asking.

He grins. "She lives for these nights." He nods to where Blakely is sitting at a small table in the corner coloring. "I knew what she wanted when I handed you the phone."

"You're okay with us going?"

"Come here." He stands and reaches out, pulling me into his arms. He couldn't care less who sees us. "You don't need my permission."

"Not for me, but for her."

"I trust you, Kennedy. That little girl is my life, and I trust you with her. I trust you to make choices that are in her best interest."

My eyes well with tears. "T—" I swallow hard. "Thank you."

He pulls me into a hug, his lips pressing to the top of my head. He holds me for what feels like forever and not long enough. Eventually, I pull out of his arms and smile at him, letting him know I've composed myself.

"Thanks for stopping to see me."

"Can I take her with me? We'll go have lunch and just hang out. The manor doesn't have anything going on today, and I dropped Grandma off at the sewing club. I don't have to pick her up until eight tonight. I'll have to leave Palmer's and then go back."

"How about I pick her up? My girls are busy tonight, which leaves me with time on my hands."

"Time to chill. Grab a beer with your brothers. Sleep." I chuckle. "Besides, I don't know if having you alone with Grandma is a good idea."

"Why?"

"She's already trying to convince me we're going to get married one day. I don't need her hounding you as well." I only have a short amount of time with him left. I don't need my grandma and her plans of marrying me off to scare him away. I want every second of his time that I can get before I have to go home.

"I'm not afraid of Maureen." He smirks.

I don't fail to notice how he doesn't comment about Grandma insisting that Declan will be married to me one day. "Use your night wisely," I tell him.

"I will. And I'll also be Maureen's driver. I'll make sure she's home and settled and still be able to meet my brothers for a beer. You just enjoy your girl time." He kisses the corner of my mouth before calling out to Blakely, "Hey, squirt. Do you want to have a girls' night tonight at Aunt Palmer's?"

"This day?" she asks.

"This evening, yes," he answers.

"Yes!" She throws her tiny fist in the air. "Can Kenny come?"

"I'll be there, sweet girl. In fact, I thought you and I could go together." I'll admit I'm looking forward to hanging out with her, and the other ladies, of course.

"This is the best day ever."

Declan chuckles. His arms are still around my waist, so he pulls me close and presses a kiss to my temple. "Take the Tahoe. I'll keep your car."

"We can just move the car seat."

"Why? It's easier to just leave it. Leave your keys. How long since you had an oil change?" he asks.

"I don't remember. It's on the little sticker they put on my window."

He just shakes his head and softly smiles. "Take care of my girl. I'll take care of Maureen, and your car."

"Dec—" I start, but he stops me.

"I'll take care of it."

"I feel like you're getting the short end of the stick with this deal. She's relentless."

"I can handle it," he assures me. "Blake, do you want to spend the day with Kennedy?"

She looks up and then down at her crotch. "I'm wearing wiener pants."

I can't help it. This time I lose the battle with my laughter. "How about we go to your place so that you can change? You'll need to pack for tonight anyway." I turn to look at Declan. "Anything specific that she needs?"

"No. She's an easy kid unless she's wearing wiener pants," he says, rolling his eyes playfully.

"Okay."

Blakely stands, and Declan points back at the table. With all her sass, she goes back to the table and packs the coloring book and crayons into a pink backpack, and drags them to where we stand.

"Thank you." Declan releases me, takes the bag, sets it under the desk, and lifts her into his arms. "You be a good girl for Kennedy today and tonight. Mind your manners," he tells her.

"I will, Daddy." She gives him a loud smacking kiss that he returns with vigor. Finally, he sets her on her feet. "Kennedy is the boss."

"She an adult," Blakely says.

"That's right." Declan nods.

It's so much fun to watch the two of them. "Do you need us to bring you lunch?" I ask him.

"No, thanks. Mom brought lunch when she dropped Blake off."

"You better let her know she doesn't have to pick her up," I remind him.

He nods. "I will. You two have fun."

"Bye, Daddy. I love you."

"Bye, baby girl. I love you too." He waves to her.

She's already pulling on my arm, trying to drag me toward the door. "Just a second," I tell her before turning back to Declan. "I'll take care of her," I assure him.

"I know you will." He leans in and kisses me softly. "Have fun, baby."

My belly twirls with lust and so many other emotions where Declan is concerned. With his daughter's hand clasped tightly in mine, we head outside to Declan's Tahoe.

"I'm here!" Blakely calls out as we walk into Brooks and Palmer's house. Everyone laughs, and my little companion eats up the attention. "I brought Kenny," she tells the room.

"Come on in. The pizza was just delivered," Palmer tells us.

I get busy making Blakely a plate with a slice of cheese pizza and pouring her a glass of milk in her new cup with a straw that I bought her during our trip to Target earlier today. "Here's a napkin," I tell her, sitting her at the table. "I'll be right back." I then go back through the line to make myself a plate.

"You're good with her." I look up to see Ramsey watching me.

"She's such a good kid," I tell her.

"It's different, though. It's... more. That's the best way that I can describe it."

"I'm not doing anything more than what the rest of you have done for her."

"Haven't you? She watches you." She nods to where, sure enough, Blakely is eating and watching me. She waves and smiles before taking another big bite of her pizza. "The two of you have a connection."

"I've been spending a lot of time with them."

She nods. "I worry about that too," she says softly.

"Yeah, you're not the only one. They're hard to resist. Declan can be very convincing."

She laughs. "Oh, I know. My fiancé is the same way. I'm not just worried about them, Kennedy. I'm also worried about you. It's easy to see how much you care about both of them."

"I do." There is no point in denying it. I tried to fight it, but it was a waste of energy.

"How long until you go home?"

A knot forms and twists in my stomach. "Grandma has a couple more weeks in her cast. We'll go from there." I look at her, worried she's going to tell me to stop spending time with them. I know that I should, that hearts are going to break, but I can't help it where they're concerned.

"I'm not going to warn you off," she says, and my shoulders instantly relax. "I will, however, tell you to think about your future. What do you want it to look like? Where do you see yourself in five years? Ten? Are they a part of that? If so, there are some hard choices that need to be made."

"Declan tells me not to worry about it. That it will all work out."

She nods. "They're my cousins, but I think of them as brothers. They're all honorable and trustworthy, and when they love, they'll love you with everything inside them. For the right woman, he'd uproot his family."

"I don't want that. I mean, I don't want him to leave Willow River. He has his business, and he needs the support for Blakely."

"I agree with you. That's why I'm telling you this. You need to decide what you want and talk to him about it. Declan isn't a man who will just let you walk away."

Hot tears well behind my eyes. "This is such a mess. I don't see a way out."

"Don't you?" Ramsey tilts her head to the side. "Sometimes it's the fear that keeps us from seeing clearly. When you're too close to a situation, it's hard for you to see the forest for the trees." She places her hand over mine. "I can see the forest, Kennedy. You fit here with them. With all of us." With that, she takes her bottle of water and joins everyone else at the table. I grab a couple of slices of cheese pizza, so that I'll match Blakely, a bottle of water for myself, and move toward the dining room as well. I'm not going to drink tonight. Not when I promised Declan I would take care of his little girl. I don't expect anything to happen, but if something does, I'll be alert.

"Tell them, Kenny," Blakely says, laughing. "Daddy wears makeup." She's giggling so hard her little body shakes.

"I've never seen your daddy wear makeup," I tell her.

"Uh-huh. 'Member hims puts on armpit makeup."

This time it's me who chuckles. "Silly, that's deodorant."

"Daddy says I'm not old enough to wear makeup just armpit

makeup." The table erupts in laughter, and my little sidekick eats it up.

After dinner, Blakely says it's time for hair and makeup since her daddy only lets her on girls' nights. We spread out in the kitchen, with Blakely being our sole focus. Alyssa is curling her hair, and Jade is doing her makeup. Piper, Ramsey, and Palmer are drilling her about what ideas she has for her photo shoot. I guess this is their thing with her, and it's easy to see how much they all love her, and she them.

My phone rings, and it's Declan. "Hey, you."

"Are you surviving?" he asks.

"She's perfect, Declan. I'm the one who should be asking you that."

He laughs, and the sound fills my heart. "I'll be fine. Orrin and Brooks are riding with me while Sterling and Deacon man the grill."

"Oh no. Declan, that's a terrible idea. There will be witnesses," I hiss, stepping out of the room but still staying where I can see Blakely. I don't know why. These women are her family.

"It's fine, babe. We can handle Maureen."

"You underestimate her, Dec."

"You worry too much. Is Blake close?"

"She is. Hold on." I walk back into the kitchen. "Blakely, Daddy's on the phone."

"I can't talk right now," she says, holding up her hand.

I laugh and place the call on speakerphone. "Dec, you're on speaker. Miss Blakely is afraid to mess up her hair and makeup."

"Blake, are you being good?"

"I'm always good," she fires back.

"Your aunts and Kennedy are in charge," he reminds her.

"I know, Daddy."

"I love you."

"Love you too."

I take the call off speakerphone. "She's having so much fun," I tell him.

"What about you? Are you having fun?"

"I am. Your family is amazing, Dec. Everyone is welcoming and they dote on her."

"Told you she eats that shit up."

"Her photo shoot is next."

"That girl is not the least bit shy."

"No, she's not. I should get back in there. Text me once Grandma is dropped off, and I'm sorry in advance for anything she throws at you. Tell your brothers I'm sorry too. At least they're both taken."

"So am I." He lets those three words hang between us. "You ladies have fun," he tells me.

I open my mouth but quickly close it. I almost told him I love him. It seems like the natural thing to do with Declan, especially when I've handed him my heart on a silver platter. He might not know it, but it's the truth. However, I can never tell him. That will only make matters worse when I move back home. This was only supposed to be temporary, but nothing about the ache in my chest at the thought of losing Declan and Blakely feels temporary.

It's tangible.

A constant ache.

What have I gotten myself into?

Chapter 18

DECLAN

"THIS IS IT," I TELL my brothers as we pull into the driveway of a small house in the center of town. "I'll try to be quick," I tell them.

"I'll move to the back," Brooks says.

I was expecting them to give me shit for agreeing to do this, but it was the exact opposite. They offered to ride with me. I don't know if they understand the importance of this moment. The way Kennedy and I have switched roles, her watching over my heart while I make sure her grandmother is delivered home safely. We're becoming one, and I couldn't be happier about it.

I make my way up the sidewalk, step onto the porch, and knock on the door. Miss Hattie answers. She's a widow and never had any kids. She's lived in Willow River all her life. Everyone knows Miss Hattie.

When she pulls open the door, she places her hand across her chest. "Why, Declan Kincaid, what can I do for you?" There is a glint of mischief in her eyes.

"Evening, Miss Hattie. I'm here for Maureen. I'm her ride home."

"I thought her granddaughter was coming to get her?"

"Yeah, what happened to Kennedy?" Maureen says as she rolls up behind Hattie, one knee propped up on her scooter.

I wink at Maureen. "You knew I was coming to get you." She blushes just a little, so I decide to take things up a notch. "I even brought two of my brothers with me."

"Three of them?" Miss Hattie turns to look at Maureen. "Maybe we should move the party to your place."

I toss my head back in laughter. "We couldn't handle the ladies of the sewing club," I tell them.

"Damn right, besides, this one is taken." Maureen points at me.

"Yes, ma'am." I have no plans to dissuade her from insinuating that Kennedy should be a permanent figure in my life. We have the same goals. We both want to keep her here. I just wish I knew how to do that.

"Well, help me with my coat," Maureen says, nodding toward the coatrack next to the door.

I do as she asks and help her into her coat before staying right by her side, helping her to Kennedy's car. "What's she driving?" she asks as I open the passenger door for her.

"She's got my Tahoe. She took Blakely with her today, and it has the car seat."

"Good man," Maureen says as she maneuvers into the passenger seat. "Boys," she greets my brothers.

It's comical because even the twins can't be classified as boys.

My brothers reply with polite hellos, and I can hear the amusement in their voices. Maureen chats our heads off all the way back to her place. From telling me how adorable my daughter is to telling Brooks how she's helping Mom make a blanket for his new baby. Thankfully that wasn't a surprise.

"Did you fellas know that your brother is going to marry my Kennedy?" she asks.

"No," Brooks says slowly. "We didn't know that."

"A new development," Orrin comments.

"Oh, he hasn't asked her yet. I just know things," Maureen tells us. "I can sense it."

I eye my brothers in the rearview mirror, and they look equal parts amused and horrified. "We probably ought to slow that train down a little, Maureen. We've got to get her to stay here first."

"I can't do it all, Declan. I need you to do your part." She huffs out an exasperated breath, and I have to bite down on my cheek to keep my laughter at bay.

It's not long before I'm pulling into her driveway. Once I'm out of the car, I rush to her side to help her out and into the house. "Can I do anything for you while I'm here?" I ask as she wheels herself to the chair in the living room.

"Just take care of my granddaughter."

"Yes, ma'am."

"He never loved her, Declan. Lyle never loved her like a man should love his wife. She needs a man to show her what that's like."

"She's already found him," I tell her.

She nods. "Good. When's the wedding?"

My head falls back in laughter. "Let us work through the

logistics of her not living in Willow River, and then we can talk wedding bells." I find that the idea of forever with Kennedy doesn't scare me.

"Fine." She sighs. "I'll start working on that."

"You do that," I tell her. "Have a good night."

"You too." She smiles, and I know that whatever she's just thought of is causing that smile. I can see it in her eyes that she's already concocting a plan. Whatever it is, I hope it works.

"We were just debating if we should knock on the door and rescue you," Brooks tells me as soon I settle back in Kennedy's car.

"Nah, she's harmless." Instead of heading back to Orrin's place, we stop in to say hi to our parents, who are huddled up on the couch. The TV is off and the house is quiet. They do this a lot, and I always thought that it was weird. However, now that I have Kennedy in my life, I get it. Just sitting in silence with her is better than anything else.

I've got it bad.

"This is a nice surprise," Mom says, sitting up a little straighter on the couch.

"We had to drop Maureen off at her place," I tell them.

"Oh, Brooks, Orrin, I have something for Jade and Palmer. I already gave one to Ramsey." She digs herself out from beneath the covers, and they follow her to the kitchen.

"What's on your mind, son?" Dad asks.

"How do you do that?" I ask.

He chuckles. "Years of practice. You can't tell me you don't know when something is amiss with Blake."

I nod. "Yeah," I agree.

"So you want to talk about it?"

Our parents never pressured us growing up, and they don't do it now that we're adults to talk. However, just them asking always led to us spewing whatever's on our minds. We know we can do so without judgment, and they've always helped guide us in the right direction.

"Kennedy."

Dad smiles. "We like her."

"So do we," I reply, talking about Blake and me.

"Maureen is convinced Kens and I are going to get married one day." I smile at the thought.

"And what do you say?"

"I can see it," I tell him honestly. "She's great with Blake, and they have a fondness for one another. She's beautiful and kind and funny, and I love spending time with her."

"I'm not seeing the problem here, Declan."

"She doesn't live here, Dad. She still plans to go home to Florida."

"Then you have to change her mind."

"How do I do that? How do I make her see that she's it for me? I feel it here." I place my hand over my heart. "Everything is different with her."

"Show her your heart, Declan. I know you keep things bottled inside since Cassie. Losing her was tragic, but it wasn't your fault. Give Kennedy your heart, and she'll stay forever."

"And if she doesn't?"

"You have to have faith, Dec."

"I can't leave Willow River. My business is here. You and Mom, my brothers, nieces and nephews of the future. Blake needs to be surrounded by family." What I don't say is that even though I say that I can't leave, I've considered it. Leaving everything we know, and everyone we love to be with her.

"Would she not be doing the same?" he asks.

"Yeah, but there is so much more here for her than in Florida. A Kincaid support system, her grandma, and Blake and me."

"Show her your heart, Declan. You know our motto." He smiles.

"Work hard. Love harder."

"Love her hard. Work at loving her and showing her what life in Willow River would look like."

"I'm running out of time."

He smiles. "Then you better lay it all out for her."

"Yeah," I agree. "Looks like that's my only choice." I know he's right. I need to show her, and I feel like I have been. Although, I've been trying to go slow with her too. However, I don't have time for that now. She's going to be leaving in a few weeks, and I don't want to watch her drive away from me. Dad's right. I need to show her my heart.

"Thanks, Mom," Orrin says as they step back into the living room.

"Palmer's going to love this," Brooks adds.

"What is it?"

"A cookbook. I added some of my recipes that you boys loved growing up. A little taste of home."

"Do I not get one?" I ask her.

"Your wife will."

"He's wifed up, Momma," Brooks tells her. "Maureen says he's going to marry Kennedy."

Mom laughs and shakes her head. "She told me all about it. It's not up to her."

"What if I want her to be right?" I say, shocking my brothers.

"Then I'd say I have one of those"—she points at the cookbook that Orrin is holding—"with her name on it."

"Hey, beautiful, are you okay? The baby?" Brooks says, answering his ringing phone. He smiles. "Yeah, I can do that. Anything else?" He listens intently. "Got it. We'll be by soon. Love you." He ends the call sliding the phone back into his pocket.

"Everything all right?" Dad asks.

"Yeah, everything is fine. Apparently, she thought we had ice cream, but she ate it." My brother's smile is huge. "I can't keep it in the house. Anyway, they promised Blakely an ice cream sundae, so we need to run to the store and drop off some supplies."

"Why don't we just call the others and tell them to meet us there? They can pack up the burgers, and we can eat at your place?"

"Crash girls' night?" I ask them.

"Yep," Orrin and Brooks reply in unison.

"Let's do it."

Mom and Dad's laughter follows us out of the house.

When we pull into the driveway, it looks as if every single light in the house is on. Deacon, Sterling, and Rushton are already here from the looks of the trucks in the driveway. Orrin and I, with our arms loaded with bags of junk food, follow Brooks through the front door and into the house. Laughter rings out, and we follow it to the living room.

Maverick and Merrick are dancing with Alyssa being silly, while the rest of them are cheering and hooting at their ridiculous moves. My eyes find Sterling's. He's smiling and laughing with the rest of them, but there is something else in his gaze as he watches our little brothers dance and act like a fool with his best friend. It's easy to see it's all in good fun, but the look in his eyes tells me that while it's funny, he's not exactly fond of them touching her. I don't know how I didn't see it before now. I mean, I did, but not like this.

He's jealous.

"Daddy!" Blakely sees me, but she doesn't come running like she normally would. Instead, she remains on Kennedy's lap motioning for me to come to them. I hand Rushton the bags in my hands and move to sit next to them. I hold my arms out for Blakely, but she just leans over to hug me and stays in her spot with Kennedy.

"Love you, squirt," I tell her.

"Love you too, Daddy," she replies, her eyes still dancing with laughter as she watches her uncles make silly dance moves. Those two are always the life of the party.

I lean in and press my lips to Kennedy's. "Hey, baby."

"Declan," she softly scolds me.

"What? Can I not kiss you hello?" I won't force her, but I also won't stop just because she thinks we shouldn't be kissing in front of them. I kiss her in front of my daughter all the time. I won't hide how I feel about her from my family.

"They're all watching us," she says softly.

"Good. Let them see what you mean to me." Her eyes widen, and I know I owe Dad a drink for the advice. Does she really not know what she means to me? Have I not told her that she's revived my heart?

After losing Cassie, I felt guilty. So much guilt over letting her leave upset that night. Even if she hadn't been upset, it wouldn't have changed the outcome, though. Boyd was drinking and driving. That was his choice to make. He took both of their lives. I still closed my heart. No new members were allowed. My family, and my daughter, others need not apply.

Until Kennedy. The woman who leaped the walls I had erected and scaled them with absolute efficiency.

Love harder.

Show her your heart.

Give her your heart.

My dad has yet to give any of us a bad piece of advice. I'm going all in. "I missed you." Hell, I've been all in. I guess I just never told her. It's time to change that.

"It's been a couple of hours." I can hear it in her tone of voice. She thinks I'm just feeding her a line. If she knew how many times a day I thought about her, she'd know I'm telling her the truth.

"Don't do that. Don't disregard how I feel. He didn't appreciate what he had, but I promise you I won't make that same mistake." I put my arm around her, and she leans into me. This is where she belongs. In my arms. I watch as she runs her fingers through Blakely's now expertly curled hair. This feels right. Just like every other moment with her, when she's with us, everything clicks into place. It's as if Blakely and I have been waiting on her to come into our lives.

"Blakely!" Brooks calls out. "I have something for you in the kitchen."

My daughter gasps, jumps off Kennedy's lap, and rushes to the kitchen. I should be offended that it took ice cream to get her to leave Kennedy, but I'm not. I love how close they are. We need her in our lives, and I know that receiving love from Blakely lets her see that. At least, I hope that it does.

The twins plop down next to me on the couch, and there is

only room for one of them. I lift Kennedy onto my lap, and Merrick grins, moving to my other side.

"Thanks for holding her for me, Dec," Merrick says. He reaches for Kennedy, but I smack his hand away.

"Hands off." It's a playful smack, but he knows I mean business.

"So testy," Merrick replies.

"Where are Archer and Ryder?" I ask Maverick. I'm ignoring his twin for trying to take my girl.

"Ryder met a girl at Sage," he tells me.

"What's Sage?" Kennedy asks.

"It's a nightclub in Harris. It's twenty-one and over, which is why we're here," Merrick explains.

"You know we're good company," Ramsey tells him.

"Damn right we are," Deacon agrees with her. She's sitting on his lap, and I'm pretty sure she could tell him the sky had bright green polka dots, and he'd agree with her. He loves her unconditionally.

"Is he dating her?" Sterling asks.

"He wants to be," Maverick tells us.

"I think they were going to meet up with her and her friend tonight."

"Damn," Rushton says. "We're dropping like flies."

"Nah, just three of us," Merrick reminds him. "There are still six Kincaid brothers who are single and ready to mingle."

"Five. Might as well count Ryder out. We all know that none of us put in the effort unless it means something," Rushton tells him.

"This means something," I whisper in Kennedy's ear. She

turns to look at me over her shoulder, and I tuck her hair behind her ear, holding her stare. I will her to believe me. I don't know how I'm going to convince her to stay. My only plan is to do what Dad said and show her what she means to me. That starts tonight and each day moving forward that I have with her.

"Last call for ice cream," Brooks calls out.

"It's yummy!" Blakely adds.

The room quickly clears out, leaving Kennedy and me alone.

"How, Declan? How do I feel so strongly for you in such a short amount of time?"

"It's been weeks," I remind her.

"Weeks. Love—" She freezes.

I watch her as she swallows hard.

"Kens—," I try, but she talks over me. My heart feels as though it might pound right out of my chest.

"What I mean is these feelings, the connection, the chemistry... I care for you. And I care for Blakely, and it's all happened so fast."

"Does it feel right?"

"More than anything else ever has."

Fuck me. She feels this too. "That's all that matters, baby. You and me, and Blakely. She's a part of this too."

"I know she is, and that makes it worse. I don't want to hurt her."

"You won't."

"When I leave..." She swallows hard a second time. "When I leave, it will break her heart."

"Mine too," I tell her.

"I don't want that."

"Then stay." The words are out of my mouth before I can stop them. I didn't mean to bring it up tonight, but now that they're out there, I don't want to take them back.

She doesn't get the chance to answer me or even comment before the room fills once again with my family. The twins crank up the radio and take turns dancing with all the ladies. Everyone is laughing and having a good time. The ladies don't seem to mind that we crashed girls' night. Not even Blakely since her uncles lather her with attention.

This is our future. This is the future I'm going to fight for. More nights like this.

Chapter 19

KENNEDY

I CAN'T KEEP THE SMILE off my face as Blakely bounces on the balls of her feet in excitement. She's standing at the front of the room with Brooks and Palmer, and they're about to pull the confetti cannon to reveal the gender of their baby. Blakely asked if she could help, and as if they knew she would, they bought her one of her own, only smaller.

"They already know, right?" Archer asks.

"They do," I confirm. "She had a doctor's appointment earlier this week." She's been sending messages to the group chat all week with the ladies and me planning for this event. There wasn't anything scheduled at the manor, so Grandma readily agreed to hold the gender reveal party here.

"I don't get it?" Maverick speaks up. "What's the big deal with engagement parties and gender reveals? Can they not just tell us?"

"It's a big deal," Orrin speaks up. He's sitting in the chair next to us, with Jade on his lap. "Why not celebrate it? Besides, we're all here. Might as well make an event of it."

"You didn't do that with Blakely," Maverick says, looking at Declan.

"That was... a different situation," Declan tells him.

"So what you're telling me is that for all of you that are wifed up, every time we have a new Kincaid baby, this is what to expect?" Maverick asks.

He's trying to sound irritated and doing a poor job of it. It's the smile on his face that gives him away.

"What we're saying is until it's you and your baby, you don't have a say," Orrin tells him.

"You know what?" Maverick drains the Solo cup of punch he was drinking. "You fuckers, just wait. When it is my turn, I'm going to go all out. I'm going to be a pain in your ass with all the celebrating." He looks smug as he sits back in his seat.

"What else is new?" Sterling asks. Maverick punches him lightly in the arm, which only makes him laugh.

Declan gives my hand a gentle squeeze. I glance over to find him watching me with a soft smile playing on his lips. He brings our joined hands to his lips and kisses the back of my hand.

"So let's go down the list," Merrick says, plopping down into the seat next to his twin. "Deacon and Ramsey are getting married in June, Orrin and Jade are engaged but haven't set a date, Brooks and Palmer are married, and adding a new baby Kincaid to the clan pretty damn close to Ramsey's wedding, and then we have the two of you." He points at Declan and me. "What have the two of you got to throw at us?"

"Like we would tell you." Declan laughs, as do Orrin, Sterling, and Archer, who are sitting at our table with us.

Merrick points at Sterling. "And you—" he starts, but Sterling holds up his hand to stop him.

"We are not having this conversation again. Tink and I are just friends."

"Come on, bro. You're not blind. Alyssa is hot as fuck," Merrick tells him. He glances across the room where Alyssa stands, talking to Piper.

"Enough." Sterling's voice leaves no room for negotiation on the matter.

"Can we have everyone's attention?" Brooks asks from the front of the room. He waits for the room to quiet down before he continues. "Thank you all for being here today. Palmer and I are blessed to have so many great people in our lives and the lives of our baby."

"And me." Blakely pipes up. The room erupts in soft laughter.

"And our niece, Blakely, of course." Brooks smiles down at her, and you can see the love he has for her.

"Anyway, thank you for being here. Now let's find out if we're adding a little girl or another rowdy Kincaid boy to the mix."

"A girl!" Carol Kincaid shouts once again, and the room fills with laughter. After raising nine boys, I expect she would wish for a granddaughter or two to spoil.

"If not, I'll be sure to think girl next time," Brooks tells her. Palmer's face heats as she shakes her head at her husband.

The room is filled with all of Declan's family, as well as Palmer's. Her brother is marrying Declan's cousin. Everyone is intertwined. Both sets of parents are here as well. My grandma sits at a table with both of them. She's been a social butterfly and thrilled that Palmer extended the invitation to her.

So easily, I've fallen into a routine here in Willow River. Not just routine, but the relationships I've formed here are most unexpected. Not just my relationship with Declan, but with his

230 | KAYLEE RYAN

daughter and his family and extended family. I feel as if I've lived in Willow River all my life.

"Ready, Blake?" Brooks asks.

"Ready!" she cheers.

"Ready, beautiful?" he asks Palmer.

From where I'm sitting, I can see the tears already welling in her eyes, but her smile is radiant. Brooks smiles back at her, and they count down from three.

Two.

One.

Brooks, Palmer, and Blakely all pull their cannons, and pink confetti fills the room. Blakely squeals as Brooks lifts his wife into his arms and spins her around. She's barely back on her feet before he's crushing her mouth with his.

A ball of emotion wells in my throat while tears prick my eyes. I'm happy for them, thrilled, but I'm also a little jealous. Not of the love they share, although it does seem to be one for the storybooks, but of the baby they've created. The life that Palmer will get to feel grow inside her. Something I'll never be able to do. My heart is equal amounts heavy and full as I watch them celebrate the life that they created.

"You good?" Declan asks. His lips are next to my ear.

I turn, and he's close, so close that all I have to do is lean in just a fraction of an inch to press my lips to his, so that's exactly what I do. If there was ever a time for a kiss from Declan, now is it. His kisses make everything better.

"I'm okay," I say, pulling away. "Happy and sad at the same time." I've never not been honest with him, and I'm not going to start holding back now. If we manage to make the distance between us work, something I've been thinking about nonstop since he asked me to stay last weekend, our communication is going to have to be impeccable.

"You're going to be an amazing mother." His words grip my heart like a vise. There is no hesitation or doubt in his words. Is he talking about Blakely? She's a very special little girl, and it would be an honor for her to call me mom, but I don't know if that's what he means or if he's just telling me that it will happen for me.

I know that I can adopt or even obtain a surrogate or be a foster parent all on my own, and I'm willing to do that, but I also crave what I see between Brooks and Palmer. I might not be able to carry a baby, but I can love one. I can love one with my whole heart, but I want a partner to do it with me.

Is Declan telling me he's willing to adopt? To foster? To toss around the possibility of a surrogate?

"I can see the wheels in your head spinning, baby. I remember every word of every conversation. I know that it's unlikely for you." He nods toward Brooks and Palmer. "I also know that there are a lot of babies and kids out there who need a family."

"W-What are you saying?"

"I'm saying that Blake can be a big sister anytime you're ready. We'll discuss our options, the risks, and anything else that we need to discuss, and then we'll make it happen."

"Declan." I whisper his name.

He stands, lacing his fingers through mine, and pulling me out of the banquet room and down the hall to my grandmother's office. We slip inside unnoticed as he closes the door and locks it. He advances until my back hits the wall. His lips mold with mine as his hard body presses against me.

He kisses me like it might be the last time he ever has the chance, and my heart aches just from the thought of never having him like this again. So open, carefree, and loving. I've never been with a man who's so open and romantic. He's always touching me. Not always sexual, although any touch from him lights my body on fire. His touch is just to assure me he's there, or maybe it's to assure himself. Either way, I've quickly become addicted. I should never have started this with him. I'm breaking more hearts than my own.

"Stay with me tonight."

"Are you sure?"

"Positive."

"Okay."

"That was easier than I thought it would be," he says, kissing the tip of my nose. "We better get back out there before they send out the search party. The last thing I want is to embarrass you in front of my family."

"We should talk," I say. "About what you said."

"We will. Not here. I want to make sure I give you my undivided attention when we have that conversation."

Without another word, he pulls open the door, and we step out hand in hand. He weaves us into the crowd as if we'd always been there. We wait patiently for our turn to congratulate Brooks and Palmer before returning to our seats.

"Daddy!" Blakely comes rushing toward us. Declan scoots his chair back from the table and catches her as she launches herself at him. "I'm gonna have a baby girl cousin," she tells him.

"I heard. You're going to have to teach her everything you know."

She nods. "Uncle Brooks says she won't be my sister." Her nose scrunches up.

"No, sweetie," Ramsey says gently. "We talked about this, remember?"

"I know." Blakely sighs. "Daddy needs a wife for me to get a brother or sister." She sounds completely defeated.

"Thanks, Rams," Declan says, his voice thick.

I love the dynamics of this family. They're all there to jump in when needed. They say it takes a village to raise a child, and

Declan has that. Blakely is a very lucky little girl to have so many people who love and care about her.

My heart breaks for her and what she's missing. She longs for the conventional family, and with every fiber of my being I wish that I could give that to her.

"Remember when we talked about love and patience?" Ramsey asks her.

"You tolded me that Daddy needed to fall in love to have a wife and a baby."

"That's right." Ramsey smiles at her. "And that love takes time. You have to find someone special."

Blakely rests her head on her dad's shoulder, and we all assume the conversation is over. My heart squeezes in my chest for this little girl and her daddy and all that they've lost. She's trying to understand why she doesn't have a mommy here on earth with her and why everyone else seems to be getting married and having babies, but not her daddy. It's heartbreaking to witness. Declan holds on to her. He kisses the top of her head over and over while running his hands up and down her back, trying to soothe her and possibly himself as well.

We've talked a lot about Cassie and my ex-husband, Lyle. I know the guilt he feels for letting Cassie leave that night. Her passing wasn't his fault or even hers, but the guilt for his little girl still weighs heavy on him.

Deacon, Ramsey, Sterling, and Alyssa are all sitting at our table with us. They're talking about Ryder and his mystery girl. Declan is lost in his thoughts, and I can't tear my eyes away from Declan and his daughter to pay attention to the conversation.

That's when Blakely lifts her head, her eyes finding mine. "Kenny?"

"Yeah, sweetie?" I lean up in my chair to be closer to her.

"You're special," she tells me.

I didn't know it was possible for your heart to feel as if it's swelling like an overinflated balloon, but at this moment, I know it's more than possible. "You're pretty special too." I reach out and tuck her hair behind her ear.

"Daddy, you like kissing Kenny. Can she be your special person so we can have a wife and a baby brother or sister?" she asks.

"Baby girl." Declan's voice cracks. He hugs her tight as I sit frozen in my seat. The table around us is quiet as six adults try to navigate an explanation of adult relationships to this little girl.

"Can I hold her?" I ask Declan. My voice is soft and raspy from the emotions flowing through me.

He nods, swallowing hard. "You want to sit with Kenny?" he asks her.

Her reply is to reach her arms out to me. I pull onto my lap and hug her as tightly as I can without crushing her. I don't bother to lower my voice, knowing that everyone at this table, especially Declan, is going to hang on my every word. I don't know what I'm going to say until I open my mouth and words begin to flow.

"Blakely, you are so incredibly special," I tell her. "You're bright, beautiful, and such a joy to be around." I pause to take a breath and will my tears at bay. "I care about you and your daddy very much. I would be honored to be the special person in your life and your daddy's. But, sweetheart, I don't live here." I might as well start this process. It's going to hurt all of us regardless of when I end up leaving Willow River. "I live in a different state. That's where my mommy and daddy live."

"But Maureen is your mamaw, and she lives here. And me and my daddy. We live here, and I gots lots of aunts and uncles that I'll share with you."

"Oh, Blake." My voice cracks. "I know that you're little and don't understand, but sometimes things are just not that easy."

"I'd be real good," she tells me, further twisting the knife into my chest.

"You're such a good girl," I tell her. "My going home has nothing to do with you. That's my home. That's where I live."

"We have a big house," she tells me. "Daddy can share his room 'cause that's what mommies do, or I'll share mine."

The innocence of a child. "You're so good at sharing," I tell her.

My eyes find Declan's. I'm pleading with him to help me help her understand. However, it's not Declan that comes to my rescue. It's Sterling.

"Blakely, I need cake."

"Cake?" She sits up on my lap. "I like cake."

Sterling smiles softly. "Yeah? You want to help me grab a slice for Tink and me?"

"Yes!" She's off my lap in a flash and racing around the table, taking Sterling's hand. His eyes find mine and I mouth, "Thank you." He looks at Declan and nods before turning and walking away.

"What have we done?" I ask, staring after them.

"Nothing," Ramsey assures me. "She's a little girl who doesn't understand what this is." She points between Declan and me. "She's resilient. No matter what happens, she's going to be okay. She has a huge support system to make sure of it."

"We're all here for you," Alyssa says, wiping a tear from her eye. "Whatever you need."

"We shouldn't have let this happen," I tell Declan. "We're hurting her."

"And what? Do you think that this doesn't hurt me? Do you think I like knowing that my daughter wants you to stay just as badly as I do? I let her get close to you. This is on me."

"We both knew that I was only here for a limited amount of time," I remind him. A lone tear slides over my cheek. "I was selfish. I wanted time with both of you."

Declan turns to face me. He studies me, the anguish in his eyes matching my own. "Stay."

My mouth drops open. My eyes dart around the table. Ramsey and Alyssa both have small smiles on their faces while Deacon watches Declan closely.

"We said we would talk about this later." I really don't want to have this conversation in front of his family. They've heard and seen enough already.

"Let's go then." Declan pushes back from the table and offers me his hand.

"Blakely."

As if she knew we were talking about her, she comes racing over and grips Declan's legs. "Daddy, Papaw said I can spend the night and make a fort!" All sadness from earlier is washed away.

"We're heading out," Raymond says, joining us. "You mind if we take her for the night?"

"You sure? She's there all week."

"Am I sure? Yes. She's my princess. The house is too quiet these days. Besides, I've been promising to have a fort camp out with her for a while now."

"Please, Daddy? I'll be real good."

"Of course you can." Declan lifts her in the air, making her laugh. As he lowers her, he kisses her cheek.

"Kenny kiss too," Blakely tells him. She leans over, and I kiss her cheek. When she's back on her feet, she takes Raymond's hand, and they walk away.

"Ready?" Declan offers me his hand, and I take it. He leads

me to Brooks and Palmer so we can say our goodbyes and then head out to his truck.

I'm not ready for this to be my last night with him, but we have to stop. We can't keep doing this to Blakely or to ourselves. The entire drive to his place I fight my battle with tears. I need to stay strong. It's not lost on me that walking away from Declan and Blakely hurts a million times worse than my marriage ending.

Chapter 20

DECLAN

THE DRIVE TO MY PLACE is quiet. I hold Kennedy's hand tightly in mine, resting them on my lap. I've asked her to stay twice now, and she's yet to answer me either way. I see the worry and the hesitancy in her eyes. I wish I knew what to do or say to take that away. I wish she could see inside my mind and my heart to know that I want her.

We want her.

My baby girl loves her just as much as I do. She ripped my heart to shreds earlier. I wasn't able to find the words to help her because, in my mind, I was begging Kennedy to stay with us too.

I understand she's freshly out of a divorce. I get that she's scared, I do, but so I am. I'm afraid she's going to drive away from us. I'm afraid that both my daughter and I have fallen in love with her, and she doesn't love us back. There are so many worries and fears, but I still want her.

Pulling the Tahoe into the garage, I release her hand to climb out. She meets me at the door and takes my hand once again, allowing me to lead her into my house. I toss my keys on the kitchen island and turn to face her. She looks on the verge of tears, and I can't stand it. I open my arms for her, and she steps into my embrace.

"How do you do that?" she asks, tilting her head back to look at me.

"Do what?"

"Make it all go away just by wrapping your arms around me? Make me feel safe from such a simple gesture?"

"Because this is where you belong." I hold her just a little tighter. "We need to talk, Kens." She stiffens for a moment before letting her shoulders fall.

"Can we just... pretend? For a little while, can we pretend that there are no hard choices to make?"

I want to tell her no. That we need to talk about this, but she already knows that. "Tell me what you want." Anything but letting her walk away, I'll do whatever it takes to give it to her.

"You, Declan. I want you."

I feel as though her words have a double meaning, but when she kisses the underside of my chin, I know which one she's going to be open about. "I'm right here, baby."

Stepping out of my arms, she lifts the hem of my shirt, and without being told, I raise my arms in the air, ducking my head so she can pull it off me. She lets my shirt fall to the floor as she runs her hands over my bare abs and chest.

She hooks her arms around my neck, and I bend to lift her. On instinct, she wraps her legs around my waist. She takes control, placing her palms on either side of my face and kisses me with everything inside her. Her tongue demands entrance, and I give it to her, allowing her the freedom to explore my mouth on her terms. I hit the light and walk blindly down the hall to my bedroom. When my knees hit the mattress, I stop and break out of the kiss.

"Before we do this, I need you to know that I want you to stay. I know you don't want to talk about it right now, but we have to. We're running out of time, and I need for you to know that I want you here. In my home, in my bed, in my life, and in my daughter's life. I want that with you, Kens. I know it's been a whirlwind the last couple of months. I know that you're just out of a marriage and that the last thing you wanted was to jump right into something else, but, baby, we're here. We've both already jumped. I just need you to paddle with me. I need you to hold steady against the waves."

She takes a calming breath. "I never expected you or the feelings that I have for you."

"I'm falling in love with you." It's only partly the full truth. I've already fallen, but she's scared enough. I don't know how she's going to take my confession. I turn so that I'm sitting on the bed, with her straddling me. Her legs are still wrapped around my waist.

"Oh, Declan," she says, her voice thick with emotion. "I love you. That's what scares me. I knew my ex for years, we were friends before dating, and we failed. We made a choice to move on, but with you... if I were to lose you, I don't know that I could come back from that."

"It's because we're different. We're solid. I don't need years of time to know that. I can feel it here." I place her hand over my heart. "I have more than just me and my heart to think about. I'm not saying this lightly. I'm not just tossing around words of love because I can. I want you to stay."

"I thought we weren't talking right now?" she asks.

With my hands on her hips, I rock her over my cock. "Tell me you know this means something to me."

"It means something to me too," she says softly.

Good enough. For now.

It's my turn to strip the sweater she's wearing from her body. The room is dark, just the small glow from the moon shining through the windows, but that's not going to work for me. I need to see her.

I tap her thigh. "Stand and strip, baby." She scrambles off my lap, and by the time I have the bedside lamp on, she's standing before me in nothing but a matching bra and panties, if you can call the small fabric covering her pussy panties.

"I love the way you look at me," she says softly.

"How do I look at you?" My voice is gravelly.

"Like I'm beautiful. I feel sexy with your eyes on me. It's more than that, though," she rambles. Her voice is soft, almost hesitant, but that doesn't stop her from telling me exactly how my look makes her feel.

"I feel wanted, Declan. I've never felt more wanted, more cherished than I do than when I'm with you."

My hands move to the waistband of my jeans and I release the button. I shove them and my boxer briefs to the floor in one quick motion before standing and striding toward her. The dim glow of the lamp is enough to memorize every inch of her. Not that I haven't already, but tonight is different from all the times before. She knows that I'm in love with her, and she's letting me inside her.

This is definitely a night I'll always remember.

"Good. That's what I want you to feel when you're with me and even when you're not. I want you to know without a shadow of a doubt that your place in this life is with me. However, you did forget something." My hands slide around her, allowing me the freedom to trace my fingertips over her spine before releasing the clasp of her bra. I take my time sliding the straps over her shoulders before letting them fall to the floor.

"W-What did I forget?" she asks, as my lips trail softly over her collarbone and up her neck until I reach her ear.

"Love, baby. You forgot, love. I want you to feel loved every second of every day. I want you to feel my love no matter where you are." There's a real possibility with her refusing to talk about staying that she might be driving away from me, and no matter where she is, I know deep in my soul that I'll always love her. I need her to know that.

"I feel it," she replies softly. Her nails dig into my back, and my hard cock presses against her belly.

"Now," I say, kissing the corner of her mouth. "Let me show you."

Without having to ask her, she removes her panties and crawls onto the bed. Her hair is fanned out over the pillow. She's a vision. My heart thumps against my chest as I think about the possibility of losing her. I'm trying to show her my heart. Fuck me, I've handed it to her to do as she wishes. I just hope that it's enough.

Reaching into the bedside table, I grab the unopened box of condoms. I threw the old unopened box away. They were expired. I guess there's another confession I need to release tonight. "I should warn you," I tell her. Her hooded eyes watch me intently. "This is going to be fast."

"Are you going to explain that?" she asks. She knows me well enough that there is a story behind my declaration.

"I haven't been with anyone since Cassie. Not since the night we conceived Blakely. It was a drunken mistake with my best friend. That night gave me my daughter, and I will never regret her. However, I promised to focus on her. Then we lost Cassie, and I was doing it on my own. Thank God for my brothers and my parents."

"You've dated. You told me about them."

"Yeah, but none of them were someone I could see spending my life with. Sex leads to babies, and babies lead to a lifetime with that person. While Cassie was my best friend, I got lucky there, but I wasn't willing to risk it with some random woman."

"Well." Her body grows stiff. "You don't have to worry about that with me." She looks to my hands, where I still hold the unopened box of condoms. "We don't even need those. It's not possible for me, remember?"

"Fuck." Tossing the condoms down on the bed, I move to lie next to her. My hand rests gently against her cheek to pull her eyes to mine. "That's not what I meant, and you damn well know it. I was giving you a piece of me, Kennedy. A piece I've refused to give to anyone else since the moment I drunkenly slept with my best friend almost six years ago."

"I get it."

"No, baby, I don't think that you do. I was trying to tell you that I'm more than likely going to come within a handful of minutes of sliding inside you if I last that long. It's been too long, and I want this with you. Only with you. And these—" I reach behind me and grab the box of condoms. "—will protect you. I'll always protect you, Kennedy. When we're ready to talk about another baby, we can toss them and try our luck. They told you it was highly unlikely, but we'll try."

"I don't think we'll have to worry about that," she says sadly.

"There are lots of ways to grow our family, Kens. Until then, we should practice." I bounce my eyebrows, and she giggles. "There it is. There's that beautiful smile I've been missing. Now, lie back and let me make a fool of myself." She smiles and shakes her head. "Let's get the embarrassing out of the way so I can spend the rest of the night making love to you."

The time for talking is gone as I hover over her and press my lips to hers. I take my time, tasting her before my lips move to her breasts. I give each soft globe and pebbled peak the same attention before moving farther south. I kiss just above her pussy when I feel her hands tugging at my hair.

"Next time," she says, already breathless.

"Patience, baby."

"Now, Declan. I need you now."

I ignore her and slide one long digit inside her, causing her back to arch off the bed and a "Fuck," to fall from her lips. "You're teasing me," she accuses.

"No, baby. I'm enjoying you. There's a difference. I know you're going to get cheated. I know that it's not going to take much once your pussy is milking my cock. It's been too damn long. I need you to get off before that happens."

"You said you were going to make love to me all night. There will be other chances."

"That's a guarantee, Kens. But it's going to happen now too." My mouth covers her clit, as I apply light pressure with my tongue. She moans like a fucking porn star and my cock throbs against the mattress.

I add another finger and pump into her, making a come-here motion. "Declan," she moans, and I smile. I increase the pressure of my tongue, matching the rhythm of my fingers, and when her body stiffens, her pussy grips my fingers, and her hands grasp my hair so tight I'm worried she might rip it from my scalp. I know she's there. She calls out my name and a bunch of gibberish that I can't quite understand slips past her lips, but it doesn't really matter. I don't stop until every last tremor has worked its way through her body.

"Damn," she mutters, and I chuckle, kissing my way back up her body. When I'm close, she pulls me into a kiss, her tongue lapping against mine. She moans at the contact, and if I wasn't already in love with her, this kiss, her tasting herself on my tongue, would have pushed me over the edge of never looking back where Kennedy is concerned. However, it's too late. I've already reached the point of no return. She's got my heart in her hands.

I start to move back, but she locks her legs around me, holding me close. "Stay."

I smile down at her. "That's my plea, baby," I tease. I kiss her hard before pulling out of her hold and reaching for the box of condoms. I open it in record time and have a small foil pack in my mouth, tearing it open and sliding it over the steel rod between my legs.

I'm knocked off balance when she pushes me to the side and straddles my lap. "My turn," she tells me.

Placing my hands on her thighs, I nod, letting her know she's in control. She's told me enough about her previous relationship to know that there wasn't much adventure. While I hate thinking about her with him, he is her past, just like Cassie is mine.

"This is your show, Kens."

"Will you help me?" Her long lashes rest against her cheeks as she stares down at me.

I grip my cock as she rises up on her knees and slowly falls onto me as I guide my cock inside her. "Fuck," I hiss.

"I wasn't sure it was going to fit," she says. Her words cause my cock to twitch inside her and a moan to fall from her lips.

"Tell me what you need, Kens."

"I don't know. I just need... a minute," she says, her eyes closed tightly.

I want to give her what she needs, but it's taking everything I have not to maintain my control. I start to tell her that very thing when her hips begin to rock. It takes her a few times before she has a rhythm going. She lifts, then lowers herself, grinds her hips, and repeats the process over and over again, driving me fucking insane with desire for her.

"Kennedy—"

"I'm close." Her hands cup her breasts and play with her nipples.

I can't take it. I sit up, place my hands on her hips, and lift her off my cock before slamming her back down again. Over and over, we repeat this process. Her head is tilted back, her hair falling over her back, and her tits are right in my face. I suck one into my mouth but lose the connection as I lift her and slam her back down again.

"Declan!" she roars, her orgasm tearing through her.

Her pussy strangles my cock, and all too soon, I'm shouting her name, keeping her thighs gripped tightly as I spill into the condom. My arms wrap around her as I hold her tightly. I never want to let her go.

We're both breathing heavily, and we're covered in sweat, but neither of us seems to care as we hold on to one another, as if our very lives depend on the connection. In a way, it feels as if it does.

Finally, I pull back and look into her eyes. "I love you."

Tears fill her eyes. "I love you too."

We lie in each other's arms while our breathing regulates back to normal. My hold on her is tight. I need her to know that I'm never going to let her go.

"Let's get cleaned up." I need her in my arms, but I need to take care of the condom. It's time we talk about what comes next for us. I know what I want our future to look like. I need to see where her head is at with all of this.

I let her go first while I remove the condom and toss it in the trash can next to the bed. When she exits the bathroom, I kiss her quickly before disappearing behind the door to clean up. When I get back to my room, she's asleep. At least, that's what she wants me to think. I'll let her have it tonight. Tomorrow, we talk and plan for our future. I just hope that we have a future to plan. I pull her into my arms, and within minutes I'm falling fast asleep.

When I wake up hours later, she's gone. I find a note on the kitchen counter that said she needed to get home to Maureen. It's an excuse, and we both know it.

Looks like I get to track her down today. We have things we need to say.

Chapter 21

KENNEDY

I T'S WEDNESDAY AFTERNOON, AND I'M running on fumes. I skipped out on Declan Saturday night, leaving him with a note saying that I needed to get home to Grandma. It took everything I had to crawl out of his bed, but I made myself do it. Luckily, I'd parked at his place, and we rode to the gender reveal together. Carol and Raymond brought my grandma with them since Declan, Blakely, and I went early to ensure everything was set up by the staff as it should have been.

Sunday, he called and wanted me to come to family dinner, but I declined. Grandma wasn't feeling well, and the guilt of how much I've been leaving her was already heavy on my shoulders. He walked over with Blakely to bring us dinner. They stayed for a while to visit, but we didn't have the chance to talk.

Monday, there was a busted pipe at the manor that I had to deal with most of the day. By the time I made it home, it was after seven, and I still had a manuscript that I needed to wrap up edits on and send back to the author to make my deadline.

Tuesday, I was dealing with cleanup at the manor, and that afternoon, Grandma had a specialist appointment an hour away with a dermatologist. She had a suspicious mole on her arm, and she'd been waiting to get in for months. Of course, she told them it was to establish care and not that she was having an issue. I made sure to scold her for that, and she blew me off, stating she was just being extra cautious, but I still went back with her and made sure she was honest with the doctor. Thankfully, he, too, thought it was fine, but they did a biopsy to be sure. We went to dinner after and got stuck in traffic, a water main break on the way home. It was after eight, and I was beat. Declan was disappointed, but he understood.

Now it's Wednesday, and I finally have a minute to breathe. I sent my author's manuscript back and didn't have another until Monday. The manor is repaired, and everything is cleaned up, thanks to the staff. Grandma is doing well. She has an appointment in two weeks to have her cast removed and X-rays on her leg.

As I'm closing my laptop to pack up and head home for the day, my cell phone rings. Expecting to see Declan's name, I'm surprised to see Palmer's. "Hey," I greet her.

"Hi, what are you doing right now?" she asks.

"Just leaving the manor for the day."

"Can you come to my place?"

"Sure, is everything okay?"

"Yes. Piper requested an impromptu girls' night, and I volunteered our place. Well, Brooks volunteered. He's heading over to hang out with Declan and Blakely."

"I haven't spoken to him." I don't tell her that I've had little time to do so in the past several days or the relief I've felt even though I've missed him. He asked me to stay, and I don't know what I'm going to do.

"That's what he said. Anyway, just bring yourself. I'm ordering pizza. Everyone will be here at six."

I glance down at my watch and see it's a little after four. "Okay, I'll be there. If you think of something I can bring, just let me know."

"Will do. Thanks." We end the call, and I finish packing up before locking up the manor and heading to my car. Once inside, I start the engine and decide to call Declan to check in.

"Hey, Kens," he says. He sounds like he's laughing.

"Hey. You sound happy."

"My daughter." He laughs.

"What did she do?"

"Brooks is here. We're just having a chill night while you ladies get together. Which, by the way, I'm going to miss you again. Do you think you can swing by so I can at least hug and kiss my girl? It's been since Sunday since I've had my hands on you."

"I'll see what I can do." His request makes me smile. I do that a lot around the two of them. "So Blakely?" I prompt.

"So Brooks and I are just hanging out. We told the other guys if they wanted to stop by that we would be here. Anyway, Brooks comes in wearing sweats, a hoodie, and slides. Blakely comes walking into the kitchen and notices. She says, 'Uncle Brooks, I like your sandals.' Nothing to it, right? Well then, she speaks up and says that 'Papaw wears strap-ons.' Brooks and I lost it. Thankfully we were the only two here at the time. Dad has sandals that he has to strap onto his feet. Some kind of hiking sandals. That's what she meant, and we knew that because we know our dad, but damn, in the wrong company, that could have been bad for Dad." He chuckles.

"That's great." I laugh. "He's lucky the twins weren't there to hear that."

"Oh, they're going to hear about it. This is too good for us to keep to ourselves."

"You're terrible."

"You love it," he fires back.

"I do."

"I miss you, Kens."

"I know. I miss you too. This week has been crazy. I'm heading home from the manor now. I'll stop and say hi on the way to Palmer's."

"Be safe, baby."

"Will do." I end the call and head toward Grandma's. When I get there, she's dressed and ready to go to the sewing club. Carol is going tonight and driving her to and from, which leaves me off the hook. "Have fun and be good." I point at her as Carol laughs.

"I'll keep her in line," she assures me. "You do the same. I hear that all the ladies are getting together tonight. You all be safe."

"As far as I know, Piper requested it, and we're just hanging out and having dinner."

"I hope everything is okay with Heath."

"Me too." I don't know why Piper requested a girls' night, but I do know that with this group, when someone needs help or even just a chill night, you rally around them, and I'm thrilled to have been included.

I'm barely out of my car when Declan comes running down the front steps to greet me. He lifts me into his arms and smashes his lips to mine. I allow myself to get lost in him and his kiss, something that's easy to do where Declan is concerned.

"Do you have time to come in and say hi to Blake and Brooks?" he asks, placing me carefully back on my feet.

"Yeah. I don't have to be there until six." I have just about thirty minutes I can spend with them before I need to leave.

"Come on." He laces his fingers through mine and leads me into the house. "Blake!" he calls out. "We have company."

"I know, Daddy. Uncle Brooks is here."

Declan and I both chuckle. "I guess I'll take all of Kennedy's hugs."

"Kenny!" she shrieks, and the pitter-patter of little feet hitting the hardwood floor echo throughout the house. I bend down and brace myself for impact as she launches herself at me. However, I didn't brace good enough because we both fall back laughing as we tumble to the floor.

"Easy, Blake," Declan tells her.

"Sorry, Kenny, I's just so happy to see you. Did you come to play?"

"Sorry, sweetie. I have a meeting," I say carefully. If she gets wind of "girls' day," she's going to be crushed she can't be there. I catch Declan's eyes, and he nods, pretending to wipe the sweat from the back of his forehead, making me smile.

"Let her up, squirt, so we can talk for a few minutes before she has to leave," Declan instructs. Blakely jumps to her feet, and Declan offers me his hand, helping me to mine. He kisses me once more, slow and deep, until Blakely yells for us. He breaks the kiss and smiles down at me. "I don't like going days without doing that."

"It's been three days." I shake my head at him.

"Too damn long, Kens." With his hand on the small of my back, he leads me to the living room, where Blakely and Brooks are coloring.

I spend the next twenty minutes talking to them before I have to go. After a spectacular hug from Blakely, Declan walks me to my car and kisses me goodbye, telling me to let him know that I made it safely and sends me on my way.

"What's in the bag, Pipe?" Palmer asks her sister.

"I was waiting until everyone was here." She nods to me and Alyssa, who were the last to arrive.

The last time we got together, everyone made a big deal about Alyssa being there and apologized for not including her before then. She smiled and shrugged like it was no big deal, but we could all tell that she was happy to be included.

"The bag?" Ramsey prompts Piper.

Piper takes a deep breath and grabs the reusable grocery bag that sits next to her, and stands. She turns it upside down on the coffee table, and six boxes fall out.

"Are those pregnancy tests?" Palmer asks, lifting one to inspect it, and sure enough, it's a pregnancy test.

"Piper!" Palmer screeches. "Are you pregnant?"

"I don't know." She smiles. "I'm late, but I've been too nervous to take a test. That's why I called a girls' night. I want you all to take one with me."

"Um, Pipe's, I'm already positive." Palmer laughs, placing her hands on her small baby bump.

Piper smiles. "I know, but I need you all to do this with me. Please?"

"Why?" Ramsey asks her. "We'll be here with you. Why waste these tests?"

"I just... I just need you all to do it with me. We know Palmer's will be positive, and it might be the only one."

"What kind of result are we hoping for?" Jade asks.

"I don't know."

"Yes, you do." Palmer stares at her sister.

"Fine. Yes, I do. I want it to be positive. I know that we're not married, hell, we're not even engaged, but I love him, and we've talked about it. Sure, this is sooner than what we talked about, but I know Heath will be happy."

"Why not take the test with him?" Alyssa asks.

"I don't want him to be disappointed."

"He loves you," Jade tells her. "He would want to be there for you."

"I know he loves me. Maybe I should do this with him, but you all are who I need right now. My sister." She smiles at Palmer. "My sisters," she amends, letting her eyes fall on each of us.

I feel a lump form in my throat. This group of incredible ladies have accepted me into their lives as one of them.

"I'll do it," Palmer agrees. "I mean, I never got to do the whole pee on a stick thing. Everyone should experience it, right?"

"I'm in," Ramsey says, holding out her hand. "However, not a word about this to Deacon. He's ready to have babies, and even though we're trying, I don't want him to be disappointed."

"Hit me." Jade holds her hand up for a box.

Alyssa glances over at me, and I shrug. "Us too," I tell them. Piper smiles and tosses us both a box.

"So how are we doing this?" Palmer asks. "We are not all peeing on a stick at the same time."

"No. Well, maybe. We have four bathrooms, and there are six of us. So Palmer, you can go last since we know your result." Palmer beams at her sister, once again rubbing her baby belly. In fact, I don't care what order we go in, but I'm going last.

"I'll go." Alyssa stands. "Lead the way, our fearless leader."

Palmer and Piper jump off the couch and move down the hall with us following along behind them armed with our pregnancy tests.

"Just place it upside down on the counter when you're done," Palmer tells her, shutting Alyssa into her master bathroom.

"Why upside down?" Piper asks her.

"Because we're doing this together, and you wanted to find out with us. Sometimes these things are positive, like right away. No spilling your surprise."

"You think I'm pregnant?" Piper asks with tears in her eyes.

Palmer shrugs. "I'm not sure, but I know it would be cool as hell if our babies grew up together." Palmer points at Ramsey. "Then all we have to do is help Deacon talk to this one and there'll be three new babies in the family to grow up together."

"Let us get through the wedding, and then I'm all in," Ramsey tells them.

Palmer grins. "Does Deacon know that?"

"We've discussed it, but nothing concrete," Ramsey tells her.

"Next," Alyssa says a few minutes later. Jade jumps to her feet and takes her turn.

"I actually have to pee, so I'll go next," I tell them, making them laugh. When Jade exits, I enter and do my thing, leaving the test on the counter with the others.

"You're up," I tell Ramsey. She grins and moves into the bathroom to take her test.

"Done. And you better hope the guys don't come home to see a pile of pregnancy tests on the counter."

"Hey, I'm already preggers," Palmer reminds her. "In fact, if this bump isn't enough to prove it, I'll show you my stick." She winks and heads into the bathroom to do her thing. A few minutes later, she reappears. "You're up, sister." They hug as Piper takes a deep breath and disappears into the bathroom.

A few minutes later, she exits the bathroom and grabs her phone. "Five minutes," she says.

"This is going to be the longest five minutes of my life," Ramsey comments.

"Why? You're not pregnant, are you?"

"Not that I know of, but now that I've peed on that damn stick, I want to know for sure." We all laugh at her, shaking our heads.

"So I have to tell you what happened earlier." I tell them the story that Declan told me about Blakely and the strap-ons earlier.

"That girl." Ramsey smiles. "I love her so much."

"We all do," Palmer adds. "Declan's going to have his hands full with that one."

"Nah, she's just a little girl who doesn't know the meaning. She's sweet and has a huge heart. He's going to do just fine."

"Time!" Piper shouts, fumbling with her phone to stop the timer. "How do we do this?"

"Together." Jade stands, and we all do the same, and the six of us move into the master bathroom.

"How are we supposed to know whose is whose?" Alyssa asks.

"I didn't think it mattered since we know who the positives are going to be," Jade replies.

"I put mine over here." Piper points at the lone pregnancy test on the opposite side of the sink.

"Well, turn it over," Palmer tells her.

With a shaky smile, Piper turns the test over, and tears well in her eyes. "Positive," she whispers. She looks up at us. "It's positive."

We all cheer and hug her, giving our congratulations. My heart is heavy, but I'm happy for her. For them.

"Is it bad that I want to keep mine for my baby book? I mean, I have one from the hospital, but I kind of want the stick," Palmer says.

"Not at all," Ramsey assures her. "Just dig it out of the pile."

Palmer moves to do just that, but she stops once they're all flipped over. "Um, ladies, we have a situation." She holds up two positive tests.

"Oh, shit!" Piper laughs. "Whose is it?"

"How the hell would we know?"

"Not mine," Alyssa pipes up. She doesn't give further information.

"I can't have kids," I blurt out.

"What?" They all gasp.

I spend the next ten minutes giving them the CliffsNotes version of my teenage medical scare and the demise of my marriage. "So yeah, not mine." I shrug.

"Ramsey and Jade, that leaves the two of you," Palmer says. They both look equal parts scared and elated.

"Okay. I know how we can fix this. Don't move." She rushes out of the room and down the stairs, and we hear the front door open and close, and then again, before her feet are pounding back up the stairs. She's holding another reusable bag from the grocery store. "I bought extras." She grins. "I wasn't sure one would be enough."

"So, ladies." She hands Ramsey and Jade a new test, then turns to Alyssa and me. "For solidarity and all that." She winks and hands us both another test. "This time, you keep your test in your hands. Wrap it up in TP or something, so we're not tempted to look early. That way, we know whose test is positive." Piper is smiling from ear to ear, and I have to admit her enthusiasm is contagious.

"I'll go," I say, because I'm the only one here that's certain that the test is negative. Alyssa goes next, then Ramsey, and finally Jade.

Piper starts the timer and smiles. Ramsey and Jade both seem nervous, and that's to be expected. Knowing that they might flip over their tests and be positive is life changing.

"I'll give you the number to my ob-gyn. Brooks insisted that's who I see," Palmer tells her sister.

"Thank you. I guess I need to call and make an appointment."

"When are you going to tell him?" Alyssa asks.

"Tonight? I can't do it over the phone, so I guess I'll stop there after I leave here."

"Do you need us to come with you?" Jade asks.

"No. I'll be okay. I needed you for this initial part, but I've got this. Besides, you might be having a very similar conversation."

A slow smile spreads across Jade's face. "Orrin will drag me to the courthouse." She laughs.

"He's been pushing for a wedding date, but I don't want to take away from Ramsey and Deacon's day."

"What?" Ramsey asks. "Girl, just do it. I don't care if it's before or after mine, or hell, the same weekend. Orrin loves you, and I know it's killing him that you've yet to set a date."

"This"—Jade nods to the test in her hand—"might speed up the process."

The buzzer sounds and Piper looks at Ramsey and Jade. "I'll

go," Ramsey says. Taking a deep breath, she turns her test over. "Negative." She gives a sad smile and looks at Jade.

"My hands are shaking," she says as she turns her test. "Negative."

"Oh, shit," Palmer mutters.

I look at Alyssa, and she looks at me. "Mine is negative," she assures us. She flips it over, and sure enough, it's negative.

"Mine is too. Must be a faulty test." I flip mine over, and my heart stops. I stare down at the word *positive*. It's mocking me. "No. This can't be right," I say, my voice thick with emotion. "I need another test." I look up to find all eyes on me, but mine is locked on Piper. "I need water and another test," I tell her.

"I have two more." She holds up the boxes.

"I'll grab some water." Palmer races out of the room.

"Breathe, Kennedy," Alyssa says, reaching out to hold my hand. "Declan is crazy about you. He's going to be happy about this."

"No. It's—It can't be his. We—" My voice cracks as I struggle to breathe. I faintly hear Palmer coming back into the room. Suddenly there are five sets of arms surrounding me. Holding me together. I take a few minutes to calm myself down so I can tell them. "Declan and I—Our first time was Saturday night. No way this could be positive from him." I should feel bad about spilling the beans about our intimacy to them, but right now, I can't seem to find it in me to care.

"Have you been cheating on him?" Ramsey's voice is hard.

"No. No. No. I would never." My voice cracks, and the tears coat my cheeks as I tell them about the night that Lyle brought the divorce decree. "We didn't use protection. I couldn't get pregnant. And we thought we were okay." I look up to find all of them watching me closely. "Declan's going to hate me. I love him so much, and he's going to hate me. He asked me to stay. He's going to take it back." My tears come harder.

I don't know how much time passes when I finally gather my composure. "I'm sorry. I never meant for this to happen. I never meant to hurt him. I-I didn't know, but I can't be mad that I'm going to have a baby. I've always wanted to be a mom, and I never thought it would happen for me."

"You have every right to be happy." This is from Ramsey, the anger in her voice replaced with care. "This is your baby to love. Just do me a favor, tell him. Tell Declan. Be honest with him. Let the card falls where they may. Don't run back to Florida with him never knowing the reason you won't stay."

"What makes you think I would have stayed?"

"How upset you were," Piper adds. "You were devastated that he asked you to stay and will take it back."

"He loves you," Alyssa tells me. "I've spent the most time with the two of you, and it's clear as a bright blue sky. I agree with Ramsey. Tell him. Give him a chance to choose."

"I can't leave Florida and take my child away from his or her father."

"One day at a time, Kennedy," Palmer says. "Tell Declan, and call your ex. See how it plays out."

"I can't bear to see him look at me with hatred."

"He won't," all five of them reply at once.

"My uncle Raymond has all of these little snippets of wisdom that he likes to dole out." Ramsey smiles. "The one he says the most is to work hard and love harder. It's easy to see that you love him. You might have to love him a little harder at first, but it will all work out like it's supposed to."

"I didn't expect to come to Willow River and find all of you, but I am forever grateful for your friendship."

"Group hug!" Piper calls out. They tackle me, and it's through them and their encouraging words that I know what I have to do. I have to tell Lyle and then sit down with Declan and have that talk he's been wanting to have. Only I have a plot twist he wasn't expecting.

Chapter 22

DECLAN

I DIDN'T TALK TO KENNEDY last night before bed like I'm used to. I sent her a text this morning that also went unanswered. I texted Palmer, and she said that she talked to her after she got home last night, and she's spoken to her today. That means she's avoiding me. I know that she's been avoiding me, but this conversation is one we can't ignore. I won't let her leave me without a fight. I know asking her to stay is a big ask, but it's not just me that she'd be staying for. She has her friends, my family, her grandma, as well as Blakely and me.

She belongs here.

It's just after lunch and I can't take it. "Gus!" I call out. "I have to go. Can you lock up if I'm not back?"

"Sure thing, boss. Everything good?" he asks.

"Fine," I assure him. "Just let the machine get the calls. I'll handle them tomorrow."

"Will do."

Grabbing my keys, I rush to the Tahoe and head toward Maureen's. I don't care if her grandmother is there. She can come with me, or we can have this conversation in front of her. I can't handle not knowing if I'm about to lose the love of my life.

The drive to Maureen's is a blur. The Tahoe is barely in park before I'm pushing open the door and running up the steps. I knock on the door three times in quick succession. "Coming!" I hear Kennedy call out.

She pulls open the door. "Declan?" She gasps in surprise.

"What's wrong?" I can tell that she's been crying. Her hair is in a messy knot on top of her head. "Are you sick?"

"No. I'm not sick."

"Tell me, Kens." I step inside the house, kick the door shut, and pull her into my arms. She burrows into me. "Get your things. We'll go to my place."

"Grandma is at sewing club. She'll be there until I go pick her up around five."

That's all I need to know. I lift her in my arms and carry her into the living room, sitting on the couch with her on my lap. I just hold her. Sobs rack her body, and my heart cracks wide open. I don't bother trying to get her to talk to me. Instead, I just hold her as close as I can, rubbing her back, hoping like hell her tears don't mean that she's leaving me.

I don't know how I'll handle that.

When she's finally composed herself, she stands and moves to sit next to me on the couch. I hate the distance, but if that's what she needs to have this conversation, I'll deal.

"Why are you avoiding me?" We both know why, but I ask the question anyway.

"Declan, there's something I need to tell you. I need you to listen and let me get this out."

"Okay."

"The day I found out Grandma broke her leg is the same day that Lyle brought the divorce decree stating our marriage was officially over."

"You told me that."

She nods. "What I didn't tell you was that I slept with him that night. It didn't mean anything. I just thought of it as closure. It had been months since he'd moved out and months before then since we'd been together."

I pull in a deep breath hating the thought of anyone touching her but me. "Babe, we all have a past. Lyle is your ex-husband. I'm your future. At least, I hope that I am."

"Declan," she breathes before she places her hand over her mouth, trying to cover the sob that breaks free.

"I love you."

She smiles through her tears. "I love you too." She takes a deep breath, and her next words rock me on my axis. "Declan, I'm pregnant."

"What?"

"I'm pregnant." She goes on to tell me about last night and the shocking revelation that she's pregnant. "I'm sorry. I never meant for this to happen, but this baby, I love this baby so much." Her hands cover her belly, and I've never seen heartbreak and healing in one person at the same time, but that's exactly what I'm witnessing. She's racked with tears and sorrow, but her eyes, they're happy. They show surprise and elation at the fact she never thought she would be able to get pregnant.

"Congratulations." The word tastes bitter, but I know she wants this. She wants to be a mom. Her dreams are coming true.

"I never meant for this to happen."

"Have you told him?" The asshole let her go. He tossed her aside because of her dream of being a mom, and now he gets to live it with her while my heart shatters into a million pieces.

"Not yet. I was getting ready to call him."

I nod toward her phone on the table. "Call him. I'll stay with you."

"You don't have to do that."

"I know you, Kens. You're worried about what he's going to say, and you need support. I love you. I'm going to be that support." Even if it kills me, I'll do whatever she needs. This is what she's always wanted. I might be losing her in the process, but I'll never feel anything for this woman but love. Even when she's with him, I'll love her.

"I can't ask you to do that."

"You didn't. Call him, Kens."

She nods and retrieves her phone. She surprises me when she puts the call on speaker. "I don't ever want to hide anything from you."

"Kennedy, hi. How's Maureen?" a guy answers.

"Hi, Lyle. She's good. She goes in two weeks for X-rays, and we go from there."

"How have you been?"

"Good. Willow River has proven to be unexpected."

"I can see you loving small-town life." He laughs.

"It definitely has its appeal."

"You met someone?" he guesses.

"I did."

"I'm happy for you, Kennedy."

"Thanks, Lyle. Listen, I have something to tell you, and I don't know how to other than just blurt it out."

"You can tell me anything, Kennedy. You know that."

"I'm pregnant."

"Seriously? Hell yes. Kennedy, this is what you wanted. Damn, when can I meet him?" Lyle asks.

"Lyle, the baby is yours," she says softly, but he hears her.

"What? How is that possible?"

"The divorce decree," she reminds him.

"You're sure?"

"Positive."

"Kennedy... I can't. I don't want this. You know that."

"Well, it's happening, Lyle."

"No. I mean, yes, you don't need my permission to have this baby, but I don't want to be a part of it. I'll support you. I'll give you whatever you need, but I don't want to be a father."

"You should have thought about that before you fucked me without protection," she sneers.

"This wasn't supposed to be able to happen. Were you lying to me all this time?"

My anger boils over. I stand and stalk to where she stands. My hands are fisted at my sides, but I rein it in, seeing that she needs my strength, not my anger. "I love you," I whisper as tears well in her eyes. She stumbles, and I wrap my arms around her.

"I don't want any part of this, Kennedy. My parent—You know how I grew up. I don't want to be a dad. I don't know how to be.

I'll do anything you need, support you financially, but I can't be this kid's father. I'm sorry."

"You're just in shock," she tells him.

"No. I don't want this. I never wanted this, and you knew that. Call me if you need anything, but otherwise, pretend it's not mine." With that, the line goes dead.

Taking the phone from her hands, I toss it on the couch and hold her tighter. She grips my shirt as the tears begin to flow even harder. I'm pissed. What kind of man just tosses his kid away as if he or she is not the greatest gift they will ever receive? Lyle Edwards is a bigger prick than I originally thought. He let Kennedy and their child slip through his fingers. Hell, he released them.

"I'm here, baby. I'm right here," I tell her. My heart is shattered for her and for me. I don't know what to say to make this better.

"I need you to go." She pulls away from me, taking a step back just out of my reach.

"What?"

"You need to go. You have a business to run. Why are you here in the middle of the day?"

"Because you were avoiding me, and I needed to see you."

"Well, you've seen me. Now go."

"No." I know she's upset and heartbroken about her ex, but I won't let her push me away. I have so many feelings roaring through me that I can't concentrate on just one.

"Leave!" she screams.

"Kens, let me be here for you. I want to stay."

"GET OUT!" she yells at the top of her lungs. Her body shakes with the intensity of her sobs. "Please, Declan, just go. I need to be alone. I need—I don't know what I need, but I know that I need you to go."

"I can't leave you here on your own," I tell her.

"I'm a big girl."

"Kens."

"Go, Declan."

I pull my phone out of my pocket and search for the number I'm looking for. "Declan?" Alyssa answers.

"Hey, Alyssa, can you do me a huge favor? I know you're at work, but Kennedy, she needs someone, and she won't let that be me." Even I can hear the sadness in my voice.

"Oh no, is Grandma okay?" she asks.

"Not even a little bit." I pick up on her subtle cue that she needs a family emergency in order to leave work.

"I'm on my way. Tell Grandma I love her."

"Thank you, Alyssa." The call ends, and I shove my phone back into my pocket. "I'll wait in the car until she gets here. I'm leaving because that's what you asked of me. Not because I don't love you. I need you to tell me that you understand that before I walk out that door."

She nods.

"I know you're hurting, and that hits me here." I place my hand over my heart. "I'm here for you, Kens. We'll work this out."

"This isn't on you, Declan. This isn't your problem to figure out. I'm on my own."

I shake my head and take a step toward her.

"Go. Please. Just go."

I move to her, pulling her into a hug, pressing my lips to her temple. "I love you. I'll be right outside until Alyssa gets here." She doesn't respond, but I don't expect her to. She's in shock. I know she didn't expect Lyle to react that way. She was nervous to tell him, but neither of us expected that level of "I don't give a fuck" from him. I know she expected him to be upset but never did either one of us think this would be his reaction.

I sit outside in my Tahoe. I keep my eyes trained on the windows as she walks past every few minutes, pacing the floor. When Alyssa pulls in, I jump out of my car. "Thank you for coming. I'm sorry to call, but she won't let me stay."

"What happened?"

"She told him, and he was a complete dick." I know that Alyssa was there the night she found out.

"Shit," Alyssa mutters.

"I wanted to stay. She screamed for me to leave. It's not good for her or the baby to be that upset. That's why I called you." I pause. "I love her, Alyssa. This is killing me."

"I'll take care of her. I'll text you and let you know how she's doing."

"Thank you. Maureen needs to be picked up at five. I'm happy to do that. I'm not going back to work."

"I'll let you know." She gives my hand a gentle squeeze. I don't leave until I see her disappear inside.

I'm sitting in the living room with an untouched bottle of beer in my hand. I texted my mom to let her know tonight might be a late night, and she said if I needed her to bring Blake to me, that she would be happy to. That's when I allowed myself to grab a beer from the fridge and open it, but I've yet to take a drink. I don't want the beer or the temporary relief it will bring. I just want Kennedy.

There's a knock on my door, but I ignore it. Everyone thinks I'm at work. However, when I hear a key in the door, I turn to watch as Brooks walks inside. "What are you doing here?"

"It's my day off."

"So what? You hang out at my place while I'm at work?"

"Alyssa texted us. I was off, so I volunteered to come and check on you."

"I'm fine. You can go."

"Well, you look like shit," he says, plopping down on the couch.

"Had a shit day."

"So I've heard. Want to fill me in?"

"Nope."

"Too damn bad. Come on, Dec. What's going on?"

"Kennedy's pregnant."

"Really?" His eyes light up.

"It's not mine."

"What?"

"Fuck, fine. I'll tell you. Might as well get comfortable." He smirks, kicking off his shoes and kicking his socked feet up on the coffee table. "You good?" I ask, annoyed.

"Proceed."

So I do. I lay it all out for him. It's not my story to tell, but I know I can trust my brother with her secret. I start at the beginning and don't stop until I get to him showing up at my door.

"Fuck." He runs his hands through his hair. "He really said that to her?"

"Yep. I was on speaker."

"What a piece of shit."

"Agreed."

"So what are you doing here?"

"Did you not hear the part where she screamed at me to leave? I had to call Alyssa to come and sit with her."

"I heard it, but that still doesn't explain why you're here and not there."

"It's not good for her or for the baby to be that upset."

"And you're not the one who upset her, Declan. Her ex-husband carries that badge. Not you."

"She didn't want me there."

Brooks sits up, resting his elbows on his knees, letting his hands hang loose as he locks his gaze on me. "I'm going to ask you a few questions," he tells me. "I want you to answer me honestly. Don't think about your answers. Just sound off with the first thing that comes to your mind. Ready?"

"I am not playing some stupid game with you. There are more important things to think about right now," I tell him.

"Humor me."

"Whatever." I fight the urge to roll my eyes. It's easy to see where he's going with this. He wants to prove that I'm in love with her, but we both already know that. It's not a truth I'll ever deny.

"Five years from now, who do you see next to you?"

"Kennedy."

"When Blake goes to her first prom, who is shopping with her?"

"Kennedy."

"When you go to sleep at night, who is next to you?"

"Kennedy." I huff out a breath. "This is pointless. I'm in love with her. I've admitted that. I love her. She's a part of me."

"A couple more," he says, his eyes boring into mine.

"When she told you she was pregnant, what was your first instinct?"

"To hold her." All I wanted to do was wrap my arms around her. I needed her to know that I was there for her.

"Were you mad at her?"

"No. Of course not. I was confused at first, but after she explained, it all came together."

"One more question."

"Fine."

"I want you to picture Kennedy in the hospital in a few months delivering her baby. Who's with her? Who is standing next to her, holding her hand? Who is telling her how strong she is and how beautiful she is? Who do you see, Declan?"

"Me." My reply is instant. I see me. There isn't a single scenario he could paint that I wouldn't see me with her or vice versa.

"Love harder," he says.

I nod, my throat thick with emotion. I remember the conversation I had with my dad.

"Show her your heart, Declan. I know you keep things bottled inside since Cassie. Losing her was tragic, but it wasn't your fault. Give Kennedy your heart, and she'll stay forever."

"There he is." Brooks smiles. "I can see the determination in your eyes. If you love her, Declan, if you answered all of my questions honestly, and we both know that you did, then you have to fight for her. That piece of shit tossed her aside, and he's doing it again. She needs to know you're all in. Not just with her but with this baby."

"I love her."

"I know you do, brother."

"Thanks for coming over."

"Always, Dec."

We spend the rest of the afternoon just hanging out. He talks about Palmer and the baby, and I offer to help him put the furniture together this weekend. Talking to him has helped me organize my thoughts.

When I told Kennedy that I was in love with her, it was without reservation. Now it's time to show her.

Last night when I texted Kennedy, she texted me back. I all but begged her to let me come and see her or for her to come to me, but she refused. She said that she was tired and needed to rest. I knew she was right, so I told her to sleep well and that I loved her. It took me hours to fall asleep.

It's after nine on Saturday, and I'm already forming a plan of what I'm going to say when I see Kennedy. There's a knock on the door. When I answer, I don't expect to see Sterling and Alyssa on my doorstep. "Come on in. Not that you're not welcome, but what are you doing here?"

"We're here to watch Blake," Sterling tells me.

"And you need to go." Alyssa hands me a piece of paper.

"Go? Where am I going?" I ask her, taking the piece of paper. I peer down and see an address. "Where is this?"

"That's where Kennedy will be at ten."

"What? Is she okay?"

"She's fine," Alyssa assures me. "That's the address of the ob-gyn that Palmer goes to. She referred Kennedy. She's considered high risk with her history, so they worked her in. I was there when she called yesterday."

"Who's going with her?"

"No one. She's convinced she can do this on her own. And I have no doubt she can, but I also know that you don't want her to."

"We took a chance," Sterling says. "If we're wrong, we can go, but—" He doesn't finish his sentence, and he doesn't need to.

"Blake! Uncle Sterling and Aunt Alyssa are here to see you." I look back at my brother and pull him into a hug. I then move to Alyssa. "Thank you for this. I don't know how to tell you how much this means to me. You're right. I want to be there for her. With her. I need to be there."

"You better go get ready. As it is, you're going to be pushing it."

"Thank you." I race to get dressed and haul ass to her appointment.

The office is busy on a Saturday morning. I scan the waiting room, but I don't see her. I make my way to the reception desk. "Hi, I'm looking for my fiancée, Kennedy Edwards. I'm running a little late." The lie of who I am to her falls freely from my lips.

"Oh, she's already in a room. I'll take you back."

"Thank you." She points at the door to her left. The door buzzes, and the lock releases. I step inside and follow her down the hall. She stops outside of an exam room and knocks on the door. "Kennedy, your fiancé is here."

I step into the room. "Hey, Kens."

"Declan," she breathes.

"The doctor will be right in." The receptionist shuts the door.

I make my way to the exam table, where she's sitting in a gown with a white paper blanket thrown over her lap. Moving one of the chairs next to the bed, I reach out and take her hand in mine.

"What are you doing here?"

"You're here."

Tears well in her eyes, and because I can't resist, I stand and kiss her softly. She doesn't have time to question me further before the doctor comes in.

He goes through the exam, and I watch him intently as he does. He takes the time to get to know her as they go through her medical history. I sit and listen, just holding her hand, lending my support.

"Given your history, I'd like to do an ultrasound today. Just to get eyes on the baby. We're going to be a little extra cautious just to ensure you and your baby are getting the best care we can provide."

"Thank you," Kennedy and I say at the same time.

The doctor smiles. "Hold tight," he tells us. "I'll send the tech in."

He closes the door, and her watery eyes find mine. "Declan, why are you here?"

"I already told you. You're here. Where else would I be?"

"Where's Blakely?"

"She's hanging out with Sterling and Alyssa at home."

"Alyssa."

"Don't be mad at her. She knew I'd want to be here, and she knew that you needed me, whether you want to admit that or not."

"I can do this, Declan."

"I know you can." I bring our joined hands to my lips and kiss her knuckles just as another knock sounds at the door.

"Hi, I'm Jasmine. I'll be doing your ultrasound today. We're going to try the traditional way. From the date of your last period, we're calculating you to be around eight weeks. The ultrasound will tell us for certain, and you get to see your baby." She smiles kindly, moves to the machine sitting in the corner, and gets everything set up.

My heart hammers in my chest. This isn't the first time I've been here, but it makes it no less incredible. I give Kennedy's hand a soft squeeze. I wouldn't want to be here with anyone but her.

Chapter 23

KENNEDY

D ECLAN SQUEEZES MY HAND, AND I'm glad he's here. I'm nervous that they're going to find something wrong with my baby. This was never supposed to happen for me. It's been a total of a couple of days that I've known, but I love this baby with all that I am.

"Ready to see your baby?" Jasmine asks.

"Yes," Declan and I say at the same time.

My head whips to the side to look at him.

"I love you." His voice is strong and clear.

My lips tremble as I fight my tears. He stands and kisses me. It's just a soft peck on the lips, but it calms me, soothes me in a way that only he can.

"This might be cold," Jasmine says, and she peels back the

blanket and pulls up my gown to add gel to my belly. "The warmer has been acting up," she tells me.

"It's warm."

"Good. All right, let's do this." She keeps the screen toward her as she pushes the wand all over my belly. She taps on the keyboard a few times, moves the wand some more, and repeats the process. I'm just about to ask her if everything is okay when she turns the screen toward us. "Your turn." She grins. "This"—she points at a small blob on the screen—"is your baby. Measuring right at eight weeks. That puts your due date at or around September twentieth."

"Hear that?" Jasmine asks. I nod, as does Declan. "That's your baby's heartbeat."

Tears pool in my eyes, as I listen to the sound. "Healthy?" I manage to ask. Thankfully she understands my meaning.

"Yes. Everything looks absolutely perfect."

I feel Declan squeeze my hand. When I turn to look at him, he's watching me. "Mine." He mouths the word, and my heart soars. Is this moment really happening? Am I dreaming?

"Everything looks good?" Declan asks, turning his attention back to the screen.

"Yes. The baby is measuring great, and everything is as to be expected at this stage in the pregnancy. Congratulations," she tells us. She prints us a long strip of images and hands me a wad of paper towels to clean up. "You can get dressed. Just stop at the desk and make your next appointment for four weeks. They'll have your prescription for your prenatal vitamins. If you need us before, then don't hesitate to call us."

With that, Jasmine hands Declan the printed images and walks out the door. I watch as he stares down at them. When he lifts his head, there are tears swimming in his eyes. He opens his mouth, but I hold up my hand to stop him.

"Not here. Please."

"Okay." He sets the strip on the counter and helps me get dressed. I don't bother telling him I can manage. I soak up this time with him. He grabs the strip of images and folds them carefully before handing me my purse. He puts his palm on the small of my back and leads me to the receptionist's desk to make my next appointment and retrieve my prescription. I notice that he adds the date of my appointment to his phone. I don't comment to either one of them that I might not be here then. I have a lot to figure out.

Declan walks me to his Tahoe instead of my car. "What are you doing?"

"Please, just get in the car, Kens."

I do as he asks, assuming he wants to take me to lunch. He slides behind the wheel and drives two blocks to the Holiday Inn. "What are we doing?"

"We need to talk. I assume you don't want to have this conversation with Maureen listening in, and my house is occupied. I'm going to get us a room. We're going to get settled and discuss this. Discuss us."

"Declan—"

"Please, Kennedy. Do this for me."

"Okay," I concede. This has to happen, and he's right. This is probably the best place for privacy without having Sterling and Alyssa take Blakely out of the house, and that's her home. She shouldn't have to leave. This is a better choice.

In the room, he tosses his keys on the small table. He guides me to the bed, and I sit on the edge. I expect him to sit next to me, but he surprises me when he falls to his knees in front of me. He moves between my legs and wraps his arms around me. On instinct, I run my hands through his hair. We sit like that for what feels like hours when in reality, only a few minutes have passed.

When he pulls back, his eyes find mine. "I'm in love with you." He pauses and places his hand over my belly. "All of you."

I can't stop the sob that fills the room.

"I want to be the man you lean on during your pregnancy. You once told me you wanted a partner to do this with, and that's who I want to be. I want to be your partner. I want to be there for every appointment and when you bring this little one into the world. I want to witness every milestone, and when you're ready, we'll try again, or adopt, or foster, or whatever we have to do to keep growing our family."

My tears are flowing so hard I don't bother trying to wipe them away. Declan tries with his thumbs, but they keep coating my cheeks. "I want this baby to make Blakely a big sister and me a daddy again. I want you to stay forever."

My tears fall harder.

He stands and sits. "Come here, Kens."

Not needing to be told twice, I move to straddle his hips and bury my face in his neck.

"I've got you, baby. I'm right here, and I'm not going anywhere. I know asking you to stay is a lot. I know you'd be leaving your best friend and your parents, but we have a huge support system here. I have my business, and you'd be here for Maureen. This baby will have so many aunts, uncles, and cousins that he or she will never be lonely and will be loved. So much love, Kens."

"You really want that?" I ask. "Knowing this baby—" I can't make myself say the words.

"I want you to be Blakely's mom. Does it matter to you that she's not yours?"

"Of course not. I love her."

"And I love this baby. He or she is a part of you, Kennedy. How could I not love a piece of you?"

"What about your family?"

He smiles. "They love you too."

"I mean the baby."

"Is mine." He gauges my reaction. "I can see your wheels turning. We can tell them or not. I don't care. This baby is mine in every single way that matters."

"I don't want to lie to the baby. I just... I want to be honest."

He nods. "When the time is right. When he or she is old enough to understand, we'll do it together."

"I'm sorry, Declan. I wish this baby were yours."

"Hey." He tilts my chin up to look at him. "This is my baby. Do you hear me? It might not be my DNA, but my heart, it's already got a piece carved out for this little one. It will be my name on the birth certificate. It will be me who rocks him or her to sleep. It will be me who he or she calls daddy. It will be me who loves this baby just as much as I love Blakely."

"I love you. I love you so much." My heart feels as if it could burst from the love that I have for this man.

"I love you too. Now, tell me, baby? Are you going to stay forever?"

"Yes." I don't even think about my answer. My life used to be in Tallahassee, now it's in Willow River. I know that with a clarity I didn't expect. My answer is without question or reservation. I want to stay forever with Declan, Blakely, and this baby.

He kisses me. It's tender, showing me that it's not just words. He means everything he says. "One more thing."

"Yes, I agree we should not let this perfectly good hotel room go to waste." I smile through my tears. Tears of happiness, not sorrow.

"Okay, two more things." He smirks.

"Well, let's hurry with the first, so we can get to the second."

"I couldn't agree more." He taps my thigh, and I take the hint and stand. He does as well but quickly drops to his knees. "I don't have a ring, but we're going to take care of that today. Right after we take advantage of this perfectly good hotel room. However, I can't wait for another second to ask you. Kennedy Edwards, will you marry me? Will you stay with me forever? Will you let me love you until we're old and gray?"

I don't even have to think about my answer. "Yes." It's too soon. I'm fresh off a divorce, but this time it's different. It's not the logical next step. It's passion and love and everything in between. I know that Declan is in my future. I know that the life he painted for us is one I can't wait to live with him. I can't wait to stand next to him as we make it all come true. Society standards be damned. I love this man, he loves me, and this is our life.

"Fuck yes." He stands and lifts me into the air, spinning me around. Then he proceeds to strip me naked and make love to me. We make use of the hotel room twice before he demands that we go pick out an engagement ring.

"I want you to pick it out," I tell him as we check out of the hotel. The lady behind the counter gives us a knowing look, but neither one of us can find it in us to care. We're both on cloud nine. Nothing is going to break this spell that we're under. This is who we are. This is how we love. Endlesslessly and without reservation.

"What do you want to do?" Declan asks once we're back on the road.

"I want to go see Blakely." I hesitate. "I need to call my parents, and Morgan, and... your family."

"We're going to go to my place. We'll hold off on telling Blake. You can decide how you want to announce it. I know the ladies already know. I assume some of my brothers do as well. I know Sterling and Brooks know."

"I guess I need to pack up my place in Florida and put it on the market. I'll have to find storage and talk to Grandma about staying with her a little longer."

"Whoa, now, hold up. You're staying with me. In my bed. Every single night. You agreed to be my wife. There are no take backs, Kens."

"I just thought until we told everyone, you'd want to go slow."

"Fuck slow. I want you with me. I want to be there for the cravings and the nesting. I want to watch your body change and grow, and I want to make love to you every single night. I can't do that if you're not living with me."

"We're really doing this?"

"It's done. You said yes." He grins and leans over the console to kiss me. "Now, let's go see our little girl."

My heart is so full that it could burst. When I came to Willow River, it was to take care of my grandma. I never expected to fall in love and form such close friendships. I hate that my grandma broke her leg, but that fall brought me here. To the man who healed my heart and loved me with everything that he is.

"I love her," I tell him as we turn on his road. "I promise you there will not be a day that goes by that that little girl won't know how much I love her. Thank you for trusting me with her heart and yours."

He pulls into the garage and turns to face me. He reaches out and places his hand over my belly. "I love you."

"I love you too."

"Welcome home, Kens." He smiles, and it's one I'll never forget. Pure happiness and love radiate from him. I follow him into the house, and immediately Blakely comes running.

"Kenny! I missed you whole bunches."

Dropping to my knees, I pull her into a hug. "I missed you too."

My daughter.

It's not my DNA running through her veins, but I'll be the one to fix her scraped knees, teach her to cook, and help her pick out her wedding dress. She'll never wonder what the love of a mother feels like. She'll have all of mine.

I stand and go to Alyssa and pull her into a hug. "Thank you for everything."

"You're welcome. All good?" she asks.

"Perfect," I tell her.

She smiles. "Told you it would work out."

"You were right," I tell her. I could never have imagined that this is how things would turn out, but I'd be lying if I said I wasn't hopeful that Declan would still want me. *Want us,* I think as I place my hands on my belly.

"Who's hungry?" Declan asks.

"Me!" Blakely jumps, raising her hand in the air. "Can we have pizza?"

"Babe? How does that sound to you?"

"Sounds perfect."

"Kenny likes cheese like me," Blakely tells her dad.

His eyes find mine, and he winks.

We spend the afternoon chatting with Sterling and Alyssa. When we finally get Blakely to bed, we form a plan to tell our families. We decided that inviting my parents to Willow River was the easiest. They just got back from an Alaskan cruise. When I call Morgan and ask her if she can come, she tells me she's pregnant and has been sick, and doesn't want to travel. It's soon as Iris is just four months old, but she's thrilled, and I'm thrilled for her. I spill the beans catching her up on all that's happened since the last time we talked. I apologize for not calling her much while I've been gone. She said we have our own families, and no matter where life takes us, we'll always be best friends.

We managed to gather everyone at Declan's place two weeks later. We stand in front of our family and friends as he asks me to marry him again. This time with a ring. Then we let Blakely tell them that she's going to be a big sister. Everyone congratulates us, and never in my life have I felt more content and loved.

Willow River is my home, and I intend to stay forever.

Epilogue

DECLAN

THIS IS THE DAY WE'VE all been waiting for. Blakely, most of all. She's been dying to know if she's going to have a little brother or little sister. So much so that she decided that her birthday cake is going to be either pink or blue, depending on the gender of the baby. It's going to be a challenge not to fold and tell her before her party next week. Kennedy and I will be the only ones that know until then. I was hesitant at first revealing the gender at Blakely's birthday party but that's what she wanted, and who I am to say no to her with such a simple request?

She turns five next weekend, and it's hard for me to believe. My little girl is growing up way too fast, but I know she's going to be the best big sister. She follows Kennedy around everywhere she goes.

Kennedy works from home, so my parents have been freed up to do some traveling. They still call and ask for Blakely, and when they're not gone, she still stays with them three days a week, but Kennedy insisted that she get at least two days with our daughter. She knows that if her workload gets too heavy, my parents, Ramsey, or my brothers will step in to help us out.

"Ready?" Jasmine asks.

"Ready," my wife and I say at the same time.

Did I forget to mention that bit of news? Kennedy and I planned a small wedding at Willow Manor. It was the third week of March, just three short weeks after I proposed in front of our families, and we told them about the baby.

Orrin put his foot down and married Jade four weeks later at the manor. Neither one of them wanted to wait for a second longer, and well, when you have an in with the owner of the manor, and your mother-in-law is Carol Kincaid, shit gets done.

My mother is beside herself. Two new grandbabies to spoil. She's not pressuring Orrin, but I know, hell, we all know she'd be over the moon if he were to announce that they were expecting. In time. I know they're both ready, hence the rush to get married. They wanted to start their forever.

"Congratulations! It's a boy," Jasmine tells us.

"A boy." My voice cracks.

"A boy," Kennedy repeats, tears in her eyes.

"I love you and our boy." I bend to kiss her lips.

"I love you and our girl," she replies.

I'm sure Jasmine thinks we've lost our damn minds, but that's okay. This is our life, and we're living it. We're loving it, and we're happy. We work hard, and we love harder.

That's what matters.

Epilogue

KENNEDY

OUR LITTLE GIRL TURNS FIVE today. She made me a mommy first, and I love that she's my shadow. She's been bouncing off the walls all week. She's excited to cut into her birthday cake and reveal the gender of her baby brother or sister.

We've had to go to great lengths to keep her from the cake. So much so that I asked Ramsey and Deacon to pick it up from the bakery for me yesterday and keep it at their place until they arrive for the party today.

I've given my brothers-in-law, Maverick and Merrick, strict cake-watching duties. Under no circumstance are they to let Blakely near the cake until it's time to cut it. They're taking their duties seriously. They've set up two chairs in front of the cake table. Their thick corded arms crossed over their chests as they glare at Blakely.

"But you're my favorites," my daughter tells them.

I can see that they're ready to crack. "Blake," I warn her. Maverick and Merrick shrug, admitting they were ready to cave. She bats those long eyelashes that she gets from her daddy and his brothers and her papaw, and we're all toast. Even me.

"But, Mommy, I really want to know." She's been calling me a mommy for months now, and every single time my heart melts. I couldn't love her more if I'd given birth to her.

"I know, baby girl, but we talked about this. This is your birthday party. We don't want to take away from that. You need to play and eat and open presents."

"But the baby is my present. I asked Santa to bring us a wife, and he gave us you. It was late, but he did, and now the baby. That's what I asked for. Please, Mommy?"

"She's right," Declan tells me. He wraps his arms around me from behind, resting them on my baby bump.

"It was the sweetest thing," Palmer says from where she's sitting with her feet propped up. She's only a few weeks from delivering their baby.

"Are you sure, Blake?" I ask her.

"Yes!" She jumps in the air. "I need to know. It's killing me," she says with the flair and dramatics that only my five-year-old can muster.

"All right. Daddy?" I look over my shoulder at Declan.

"It's really hard for me not to spill the beans. The sooner it's out, the better. I've been avoiding my friends all week and all day." My husband laughs.

"You do the honors," I tell him.

"Mommy, don't you know we have to do it together? We're a family, remember?" Blakely asks.

"Come here you." She rushes toward me, and I hug her tight. "I love you."

"I love you too, Mommy."

Maverick and Merrick move their barricade in front of the cake, and together on the count of three, we assist Blakely in cutting into her birthday cake.

"A boy!" she screeches. "A baby brother!"

Declan lifts her in his arms and wipes her tears. "Did you not want a baby brother?" he asks her.

"I'm so happy, Daddy. We have a wife, a mommy, and a baby brother." The three of us stay huddled together until Blakely is ready to eat her cake.

"Wait, Blake," I call out for her. I make eye contact with my mom. She and my dad flew down and are looking at houses in Willow River this weekend. They want to be closer to their grandchildren.

"Blake, we have to sing 'Happy Birthday.' How about we use this cake?" My mom grabs the cake that was sitting on a chair beneath the table next to her.

"What is it?"

"Come look," Mom tells her.

"A princess cake!" she cheers. "Thank you, Mamaw." She hugs my mom, who kisses the top of her head.

We sing "Happy Birthday" to the birthday girl, and everyone seems to understand that this is her day. They quietly congratulate Declan and me as they grab their cake, but today isn't about us. It's about our daughter. It's about a little girl wishing for a family, and dreams coming true.

It's about showing those you love your heart and letting them know that you want to stay forever.

DECLAN

G LANCING AT THE CLOCK ON the wall, I see it's just after six. I should have left over an hour ago, but I can't seem to stay focused long enough to get through the rest of these messages and parts orders. I really do need to consider hiring someone to do all of this. I know it takes away from the bottom line, but the shop's doing well, and it would free me up to do other things and put me at home at a decent hour.

Ramsey called earlier and asked if she could take Blakely to dinner. I guess Deacon is working late on a case, and she thought it would be the perfect opportunity to spend some girl time with my daughter. I'm so damn lucky to have the family support that I do. Yes, was a single father, but I couldn't imagine raising her without them. I sometimes feel as though I lean on them more than I should.

Anyway, the guilt of working late is missing tonight, but that doesn't mean I want to be here any longer. I love my business. I love what I do, but I also love getting time away. My mind instantly goes to Kennedy. I haven't talked to her today, outside of a few text messages. Maybe I can wrap this up, and we can have a quick dinner before Ramsey brings Blakely home.

A knocking on the door pulls me out of my thoughts. Glancing up, I smile when I see the woman I was just thinking about standing with a bag of takeout in her hands and a smile on her face.

Jumping from my chair, I rush to open the door for her. "This is a nice surprise," I say, leaning in to kiss her hello.

"I just left the manor. I had to do a showing for a potential wedding in the fall. I was driving by and saw the lights on." She holds up the bag of takeout. "I thought that you might be hungry." She sits the bag on the reception desk, pulls the sweater she's wearing off, and places it on the filing cabinet.

My mouth waters as I take in her skimpy purple tank top. She takes my breath away. "I'm hungry," I tell her, pulling her into my arms. My mouth covers hers, and she doesn't hesitate to open it for me.

"Our dinner is going to get cold," she says unconvincingly as she grips my white tank top.

"Fine." I kiss her once more before releasing her. She looks a little dazed as she smiles up at me before taking the bag to the other side of the desk and begins to take items out one by one.

Dragging a stool over, I take a seat and pull her onto my lap. I wrap my arms around her from behind. "I like this shirt, but aren't you cold?" I ask her.

"It was a warm day, and I had my cardigan on over it the whole time. What about you?"

"I had bibs on most of the day. Got hot, so I stripped down."

"Hmm, I wish I would have been here to see that."

"I strip for you every night," I tease her, nipping at her neck. She settles against me, her back to my front, and all is right in my world. Slowly, I glide my hand up under her shirt. "How are you feeling?"

"Good."

"Next week, by this time, you'll be my wife."

"You still have time to back out."

"Never. I want you. I want our baby and the family that we're building."

"I don't know what I did to have you and Blakely and your entire family come into my life, but I thank God every single day for all of you."

"This is where you belong. Not just here in my arms, but in Willow River."

She turns to face me and rests her hands against my cheeks. "I belong where you are. That's where I want to be. You asked me to stay forever, remember?"

"Oh, trust me, baby. I remember." I wrap my arms around her, pulling her close. "Thank you for dinner."

"We haven't even eaten yet."

"Damn, you're right. I should fix that." With my hands on the backs of her thighs, I stand, lifting her into my arms.

"Declan!" She half laughs and half yells.

"You said I needed to eat my dinner," I remind her.

"Then why are you carrying me down the hallway?"

I kick open the door to my small office and then kick it closed before stalking to my desk and placing her on top of it. "You're my dinner."

"Is that right?" She leans back, balancing her weight on her arms.

Moving, I stand between her legs and make quick work of the button on her jeans. "Lift," I instruct. She does as I ask, allowing me to remove them.

"Won't be wearing these much longer," she comments.

I place my hand over her belly. "I can't wait, Kens. To see your body change and grow. Tell me we can do it again."

"What?"

"More babies. I don't want this one to be our last."

"We're going to need a bigger house." She laughs.

"We can add on or move, and I don't care. Just tell me this isn't it for us."

"What if I can't a second time?" she asks, and I can hear the worry in her voice.

"We'll find a way," I assure her.

"You are everything, Declan. I love you so much."

"I love you too." I know she hears my words, but I want to show her. Stripping my tank over my head, I drop it to the floor before discarding my jeans and dropping to my knees.

"Declan."

"Kens?" I peer up at her.

"I feel exposed."

"You are. To me. Only to me."

"What if someone comes in?"

"The doors are locked, and the staff is gone for the night. They won't be coming back."

"Your brothers?"

"Trust me?"

"With my life."

"Good. Lie back, and just feel." She does as I ask, and I don't waste any time burying my face between her thighs. She squirms, and I smile as I slide one finger inside her.

"Dec," she breathes, and the sound goes straight to my cock.

"I've got you, Kens."

"Just—I need you inside me."

"We'll get there. I have dinner first."

She huffs out a laugh. "I brought us real dinner, and I want to get to it. I'm starving. I haven't eaten since breakfast."

I stop, wiping my mouth on the back of my arm, and I stand. "You can't do that, Kens." I place my hand over her barely there bump.

"I know. Time got away from me."

"Up you go." I reach for her hand, but she's already shaking her head.

"I need you."

"You need to eat."

"I will, just—make the ache go away."

"This will be quick."

"I'm more than ready and on board with quick." Her belly growls, and I go to step back, but she's faster, locking her legs tight around my waist. "Quick and dirty, Declan."

"Promise me you won't go all day without eating again."

"I had a late breakfast, but I promise." She smiles, and my heart literally stalls in my chest. I can't say no to her.

"Come here." She sits up, bringing us eye to eye. "I love you."

Her eyes soften. "Love you too."

"Quick and dirty."

"Please."

"Hold on to me." She does as I say, placing her hands on my shoulders. I line myself up at her entrance and push inside. Her wet hot heat surrounds my cock, and we both groan at the feel of being connected. Leaning my forehead against hers, I let the realization wash over me that this woman is mine forever. I'll forever be able to feel her from the inside.

Only Kennedy.

"Are you trying to torture me?" she asks as her pussy squeezes my cock.

"Just relishing you, baby."

"Next time."

"Next time," I agree with a soft laugh. Pulling out, I thrust back in. Over and over again, I move into her with hard strokes. Her head is tilted back, her hair falls down her back, and her nails dig into my bare shoulders.

"There," she commands.

Sliding my hand between us, I gently press my thumb over her clit, and begin to massage. It's not ten seconds later, and she's screaming out my name and coming all over my cock. I spill inside her, and both of us are spent from the intensity of our orgasms.

I want nothing more than to hold her close, but we need to get cleaned up and dressed so that I can feed her. "Up you go." I tap her thigh as I step back, my cock falling free of her body. I don't look down because I know if I see the evidence of what we just did, my future wife and our baby aren't going to get fed anytime soon. Instead, I kiss her softly and move to the small bathroom inside my office to grab her some paper towels to clean up.

We quickly get dressed and move back to the main reception area of the shop to enjoy cold cheeseburgers and fries, but we do it with smiles on our faces.

"Worth it," I mumble, popping another fry in my mouth.

Kennedy grins. "So worth it."

Thank YOU

for taking the time to read ***Stay Forever***.

Want more from the Kincaid Brothers?
Look for Sterling's story, ***Stay Tonight***
releasing January 10, 2023.
Grap your copy here:
kayleeryan.com/books/stay-tonight/

Never miss a new release:
Newsletter Sign-up

Be the first to hear about free content, new releases, cover
reveals, sales, and more. kayleeryan.com/subscribe/

Discover more about Kaylee's books here:
kayleeryan.com/all-books/

Did you know that Orrin Kincaid has his own story?
Grab ***Stay Always*** for free here:
kayleeryan.com/books/stay-always/

Start the Riggins Brothers Series for FREE.
Download ***Play by Play*** now
kayleeryan.com/books/play-by-play/

More from KAYLEE RYAN

With You Series:

Anywhere with You | More with You | Everything with You

Soul Serenade Series:

Emphatic | Assured | Definite | Insistent

Southern Heart Series:

Southern Pleasure | Southern Desire
Southern Attraction | Southern Devotion

Unexpected Arrivals Series

Unexpected Reality | Unexpected Fight | Unexpected Fall
Unexpected Bond | Unexpected Odds

Riggins Brothers Series:

Play by Play | Layer by Layer | Piece by Piece | Kiss by Kiss
Touch by Touch | Beat by Beat

Entangled Hearts Duet:

Agony | Bliss

Cocky Hero Club:

Lucky Bastard

Mason Creek Series:

Perfect Embrace

More from KAYLEE RYAN

Standalone Titles:

Tempting Tatum | Unwrapping Tatum | Levitate
Just Say When | I Just Want You | Reminding Avery

Hey, Whiskey | Pull You Through | Remedy
The Difference | Trust the Push | Forever After All
Misconception | Never with Me

Out of Reach Series:

Beyond the Bases | Beyond the Game
Beyond the Play | Beyond the Team

Kincaid Brothers Series:

Stay Always | Stay Over | Stay Forever | Stay Tonight

Co-written with Lacey Black:

Fair Lakes Series:

It's Not Over | Just Getting Started | Can't Fight It

Standalone Titles:

Boy Trouble | Home to You | Beneath the Fallen Stars
Tell Me A Story

Co-writing as Rebel Shaw with Lacey Black:

Royal | Crying Shame

Acknowledgments

To my readers:

Thank you for continuing to show your support with reading each and every release. I cannot tell you what that means to me. Thank you for taking the journey with me.

To my family:

I love you. You hold me up and support me every day. I can't imagine my life without you as my support system. Thank you for believing in me, and being there to celebrate my success.

Wander Aguiar:

Thank you for another cover worthy image.

Tami Integrity Formatting:

Thank you for making The Stay Forever beautiful. You're amazing and I cannot thank you enough for all that you do.

The Book Cover Boutique:

You nailed this series. I rambled about what I wanted, and you came up with something even better. Thank you!

My beta team:

Jamie, Stacy, Lauren, Erica, and Franci I would be lost without you. You read my words as much as I do, and I can't tell you what your input and all the time you give means to me. Countless messages and bouncing idea, you ladies keep me sane with the characters are being anything but. Thank you from the bottom of my heart for taking this wild ride with me.

My ARC team:

An amazing group of readers who shout about my books from teh rooftops, and I couldn't be more gratfeul for every single one of you. Thank you for being a part of the team, and a critical part of every single release.

Give Me Books:

With every release, your team works diligently to get my book in the hands of bloggers. I cannot tell you how thankful I am for your services.

Grey's Promotions:

Thank you for your support with this release.

Deaton Author Services, Editing 4 Indies, & Jo Thompson:

Thank you for giving this book a fresh set of eyes. I appreacite each of you helping me make this book the best that it can be.

Becky Johnson:

I could not do this without you. Thank you for pushing me and making me work for it.

Marisa Corvisiero:

Thank you for all that you do. I know I'm not the easiest client. I'm blessed to have you on this journey with me.

Chasidy Renee:

How did I survive without you? Thank you for making my life so much easier.

Lacey Black:

There isn't much I can say that I have not already, exceot for I love ya, girl. You're frienship means the world to me. Thank you for being you.

Bloggers:

Thank you, doesn't seem like enough. You don't get paid to do what you do. It's from the kindness of your heart and your love of reading that fuels you. Without you, without your pages, your voice, your reviews, spreading the word it would be so much harder if not impossible to get my words in reader's hands. I can't tell you how much your never-ending support means to me. Thank you for being you, thank you for all that you do.

To my Kaylee's Crew Members:

You are my people. I love chatting with you. I'm honored to have you on this journey with me. Thank you for reading, sharing, commenting, suggesting, the teasers, the messages all of it. Thank you from the bottom of my heart for all that you do. Your support is everything!

Much love,

Kaylee Ryan
AUTHOR

www.ingramcontent.com/pod-product-compliance
Lightning Source LLC
Chambersburg PA
CBHW070847260626
47170CB00007B/2535